DREADFUL

JANA DELEON

Now you see me...

Six years ago, five friends went to New Orleans for Mardi Gras. Four of them returned. One simply disappeared. Jenny Taylor has never gotten over the disappearance of her twin sister, Caitlyn, but now things are even worse. Caitlyn calls to Jenny in her dreams, begging her sister to find her. But Jenny's memory of the entire night is completely gone.

Shaye Archer knows better than anyone what it's like to have gaping holes in your past, and how horrific dreams can cripple you. But this case presents problems on every level. An adult woman disappearing from the French Quarter during Mardi Gras is hard enough to get answers for, but when it happened years before, the difficulty level increases exponentially. But Shaye's empathy for Jenny prevents her from saying no, even though she doesn't expect to find anything.

Then a witness is murdered, and Jenny's memory starts to return. What did she see in the alley that night? And how many more are in danger because of it?

1

Mardi Gras Night, February 9, 2016
Ponchatoula, Louisiana

THE MOON PEERED out from behind the dark clouds that *covered almost every inch of the vast night sky. But deep within the swamp, even the tiniest sliver was like a beacon in the pitch black. The path she walked was barely discernable in daylight, which made it practically impossible now.*

But she knew the way.

The sounds of the night insects filled the air as she walked, her steps barely registering as she trod on the soft moss and weeds. Somewhere in the distance, an owl screeched, ominous and piercing.

Not much farther now.

She heard the frogs before she reached the water, their

rhythmic croaking like a round-robin song in a kindergarten classroom. She smiled, remembering her own childhood, sitting on the blue tape that formed a circle on the old tile floor of her classroom, but as she walked into the clearing at the edge of the bayou, the smile faded.

It was time.

She stepped up to the edge of the water and opened her hand to stare at the locket she'd been clutching, its chain wrapped around her fingers. It was an ornate silver heart—an heirloom —with a picture of two young girls inside. One of them was her. The other...

Was waiting.

She lifted her arms and started to sing, a lullaby that their mother had sung to them when they were young. The heart began to warm in her hand, and she opened her hand enough to let the chain slip down, allowing the pendant to hang, suspended in front of her. Her singing grew stronger as her voice went up an octave, and the pendant emitted a faint yellow glow, growing brighter with every note.

Then it began to pulse.

First so faint she could barely see it, then stronger and stronger, until she could see it flex with every beat of her own heart. The wind swirled around her, lifting her hair and causing it to twist around her face. The water in front of her stirred, and the glow from the pendant shot out to its rippled surface like a beacon. The ripples grew in size and intensity until a circle of waves crashed against themselves, as if trapped inside an invisible wall.

The winds picked up her tune, providing accompaniment, and from the center of the waves, she emerged. Rising above the water in a gown of white, her long blond hair swirling around her with the same intensity as the angry waves. Her head was lowered, as if studying the water beneath her, but then she lifted it up and locked red eyes on the woman on the bank.

Find me.

Her haunting voice carried across the water, and the woman on the bank began to cry.

"*I don't know how,*" *she said.*

Find me. I'm all alone.

The woman on the bank sank to the ground, begging the apparition to tell her how.

Alone. Alone. Alone.

The voice faded along with the apparition.

"*No!*" *The woman on the bank sprang up and rushed toward the disappearing apparition, but the second her feet touched the water, a bright light flashed from the pendant, blinding her. She threw her hands up in front of her face and screamed.*

JENNY TAYLOR BOLTED upright in her bed, her own screams echoing in the empty bedroom. Frantic, she scanned the room, but the swamp she expected to see was gone, replaced by four light green walls illuminated by the static-filled screen of the television on top of her dresser. She grabbed the remote and turned the set off, then fell back onto her pillow.

Sweat rolled off her forehead and down the side of her face, and it wasn't long before the tears that had been threatening to fall followed the same path. As she lay staring into the darkness, she knew with certainty that it was time. The dream was too intense. Too frequent.

It was time to find Caitlyn.

2

Monday, February 15, 2016
French Quarter, New Orleans

SHAYE ARCHER PULLED the steaming latte from the fancy coffee maker Corrine had given her for Christmas, giving silent thanks for her mother's stellar taste in kitchen appliances. Shaye would have never purchased one for herself, mainly because she didn't know it existed and wouldn't have known where to start looking for one. According to Corrine, many options were available but only this one was worth the price. Shaye had no idea what the machine had cost, but she agreed with Corrine on the strength of the output alone.

She reached into the refrigerator and pulled out Reddi-whip, then dressed up the top of the latte before heading into her office. A stack of administrative work awaited her, and she couldn't put it off any longer. The last couple months had been relatively quiet workwise. She'd had plenty to do, but it was all insurance work. The bland, safe kind that made Corrine really happy but left Shaye restless and a little bored.

Shaking her head, she slipped into her office chair. It was a catch-22. She wanted something more interesting to do but at the same time, didn't want people going through the agony that always came with more interesting things. She checked her phone for the tenth time, hoping for a message from a new client, then sighed at the stack of folders, all needing invoices. Tonight, she was having dinner with her mother and Eleonore Blanchet, her mother's best friend and Shaye's therapist. The two women had been inseparable for decades and had been unrelenting in helping Shaye work through her horrible past.

Unfortunately, it never completely went away.

Things were definitely better now. In fact, when Shaye considered how far she'd come, just in the past year, she was amazed. She'd finished her internship as a PI with the agency she'd worked with during and after college, opened her own shop, and she'd had instant success helping the police take down some of the worst criminals the city had seen in years. More importantly, she'd solved the mystery of her own missing past and seen the man who'd abused her die. But memories that had been long buried continued to surface periodically, and she had to remind herself not to lapse back to the past hurts and anger every time a new memory emerged.

With every new revelation came another round of processing and documenting, because despite everything she knew, there were still gaps she hoped to fill. Often sad, horrific gaps, but they were hers and she wanted them whole. Before her memory had started returning, she'd always believed that not knowing was worse. Now that she had remembered the majority of her past, she was certain of it. No matter how difficult a memory was, it couldn't be dealt with until it was present. Lurking back in her subconscious, all it did was let fear and distrust fester, which could easily cloud the future.

So every day, Shaye made a conscious decision to live forward and not behind. To cherish what she had today, in spite of what it took for her to be here. And every day, it had gotten easier, to the point that her morning routine had become no more than giving it all a passing thought before starting her day.

A big part of her transformation was her relationship with Detective Jackson Lamotte, who'd been with her when she'd discovered the truth and hadn't left her side ever since. His unique ability to discern when she needed space and when she needed to talk, or when she just needed a distraction or to be left alone in her thoughts had endeared him to her, and the trust she'd previously held for only a few people now extended to him. With that trust came giving herself permission to step into the unknown world of a romantic relationship. Shaye would be the first to admit that if she thought too hard about it, the fear was still there, just not as acute. And ultimately, a little fear was worth what she had gained. Jackson was one of a kind, and Shaye was finding it hard to imagine her life without him in it.

She blew out a breath and picked up the first set of documents she needed to record and invoice and accessed the accounting software on her laptop. Sitting here mulling over her life wasn't going to get those reports done, and Shaye could easily spend years considering her life and its many nuances. An afternoon was child's play.

She'd completed two of the eight reports she needed to send out when there was a knock at her door. She frowned and checked her phone, but there were no text messages from any of the sum total of four people who might drop by without an appointment. Her current workload was insurance cases only and all handled over the phone, so no reason for anyone to pay her a personal visit on that account.

She started to get up but then took a couple seconds to access her front security camera. After all, there was no point in having security if she wasn't going to use it. The camera was outside under an eave of her apartment and offered a clear view of anyone standing on the sidewalk in the vicinity of her front door. Two women and a man stood outside, probably mid- to late twenties, and all of them looked slightly uncomfortable.

Might as well see what this was about.

She didn't get much in the way of door-to-door soliciting, and these people looked too young and casually dressed to fit in with the religious crowd that came by from time to time to pitch the local churches. It wasn't election time, so she had no fear of having to listen to a bunch of political ranting. Worst case, it was a charity pitch. That was something she could deal with and didn't really mind, especially when it interrupted paperwork.

She opened the front door and the young woman with long blond hair started a bit, then looked over at the other woman. The other woman had shoulder-length mahogany-colored hair and piercing green eyes. She glanced at the blonde woman and then the young man before giving Shaye an awkward smile.

"We're sorry to bother you," she said. "We don't have an appointment, but we'd like to talk to you about a job... Jenny would like to talk to you." She inclined her head toward the blonde woman. "If you're busy, we can make an appointment...or if you're booked then that's okay too."

Her discomfort was so obvious that Shaye felt sorry for her. The blonde woman had spent the whole time staring at the sidewalk, and it was clear that the woman speaking was somewhat uncertain about even being there.

"That's okay," Shaye said. "Please come inside and we can talk."

The three stepped inside the front room that served as her office and Shaye pulled a chair from the back corner of the room so that there were three of them in front of her desk. They all glanced around, then slowly took seats, the blonde woman in the middle.

"Would any of you like something to drink?" Shaye asked. "Water, tea, soda? Or I could put on a pot of coffee?"

The blonde woman and the man shook their heads and the brown-haired woman said, "No. Thank you. We just came from lunch."

"Great," Shaye said and took a seat behind her desk. "So you already know that I'm Shaye Archer. What are your names?"

"I'm Marisa Sampson," the brown-haired woman said. "And this is my friend Jenny Taylor and my husband, Rick."

"It's nice to meet you," Shaye said. "Do you live in New Orleans?"

Marisa shook her head. "We drove in from Ponchatoula. We hoped you'd meet with us. We should have called, though."

"That's all right," Shaye said. Ponchatoula was a typical small town about an hour from New Orleans. She'd been there once when Corrine had roped her into going antique shopping with her. She remembered it as quaint and somewhat sleepy, with an abundance of older people, but most of them were probably from out of town and were drawn there for the antique shops just like Corrine.

"So how can I help you?" Shaye asked.

Sometimes, she tried small talk, but with Marisa answering for everyone and spending more time apologizing than explaining, she figured it might be easier to get right to the point of their visit.

"I want you to find my sister," Jenny blurted out.

Shaye focused on the clearly upset woman. "Your sister is missing?"

Jenny nodded. "My twin sister, Caitlyn."

"Did she go missing in New Orleans?" Shaye asked.

"Yes," Jenny said.

"Have you reported her disappearance to the police?" Shaye asked.

"The police can't find her," Jenny said, her voice increasing in pitch and speed. "They're not even trying anymore. She doesn't matter." Jenny covered her face with her hands and started to sob.

Marisa put her arm around Jenny and mumbled some comforting words to her, then gave Shaye an apologetic look. "Caitlyn disappeared six years ago. I'm sure the police did everything they could at the time, but..."

Marisa didn't have to finish her sentence. If Jenny's sister had been missing for six years, the case had gone cold long ago. The police would have worked the clues at the time, but as the weeks and months passed, the fewer items they'd had to go on until they'd exhausted everything and were forced to shelve the case in favor of more recent crimes that they had a better chance of solving. On the negative side, that meant Shaye didn't have much to go on either, and the trail was now six years old. On the plus side, she might not step on as many toes down at the police department looking into something that happened on the previous police chief's watch.

"Tell me what you know," Shaye said and pulled out a recorder. "Do you mind?"

Marisa and the silent Rick both shook their heads. Jenny leaned against Marisa and still had her eyes closed.

"We were all in New Orleans for Mardi Gras," Marisa said. "Me, Rick, Jenny, Caitlyn, and our friend Sam. Jenny, Caitlyn, and I were hometown friends, and then we all went to college together at LSU. We met Rick there. It was our senior year, and since we were all finally twenty-one, we decided to go to Mardi Gras. We'd never done it before. Not in New Orleans, I mean."

Shaye nodded. Most cities around Louisiana held some sort of Mardi Gras celebration but none of them compared to the party in NOLA.

"Where were you when Caitlyn went missing?" Shaye asked.

"At a bar in the French Quarter," Marisa said. "We'd been walking the Quarter, partying at different places all night. The last was a place called the French Revival."

"I know it," Shaye said. She'd never actually been inside, but since she wasn't much of a social drinker and didn't enjoy crowded, noisy places, that wasn't much of a surprise.

"Anyway, we were drinking and dancing and there was karaoke. Sam cut out before that. He wasn't much of a party guy, and I think it was all a little overwhelming for him. Caitlyn got up to sing and afterward, she said she was going to the bathroom. Jenny went shortly after. Some time passed and they never came back to the table, so I went to look for them.

"They weren't in the bathroom, and when I asked one of the waitstaff, she said she saw someone go out the back door into the alley where people went to smoke," Marisa continued. "Neither of them smoked, but I figured maybe they went outside to get some air. I only found Jenny, and she was starting to panic."

"Was someone bothering her?" Shaye asked.

Marisa shook her head. "She said she couldn't find Caitlyn. I checked the alley and then we went back inside, but Rick hadn't seen Caitlyn either. He searched every inch of the bar and even went around the entire block asking people if they'd seen her, but no one knew anything."

"And you never saw her again?" Shaye asked.

"No. It's like she simply vanished," Marisa said. "How does that happen?"

"Easier than you would think," Shaye said. "Did Caitlyn have a cell phone?"

"Yes. I called immediately, but it went straight to voice mail. We left messages and sent texts, but never got an answer. At least, not that night."

Shaye had been jotting some notes on a pad, but now she looked up at Marissa. "What do you mean 'not that night'?"

"The next morning, I got a text from Caitlyn that read 'You be you. I'll be me. Tell Jenny I love her.'"

"Did the police trace the phone?"

"They said the text was sent from somewhere in the French Quarter, but they couldn't narrow it down more than that, and by the time they got the cell phone service to track it, the phone was turned off."

"Do you think it came from Caitlyn?" Shaye asked.

Marisa shrugged. "I don't know. It sounded like something Caitlyn would say, but if it was her, why didn't she ever come back? Caitlyn was always the extrovert of our group, and it wouldn't have been completely unusual for her to jet off on her own—she's done it before—but never for more than overnight. And she would never have left Jenny and her parents hanging like this. She was adventurous, maybe even a little wild, but she wouldn't have been that cruel."

"Was there any other indication that Caitlyn was still around New Orleans the next morning—credit card usage, for example?"

Marisa nodded. "Two hundred dollars was withdrawn from her account the next morning, about an hour after I got the text. The camera on the ATM was spray-painted over, though, so the police couldn't get video."

"But nothing else after that?"

"Nothing else ever again. That was the last sign of her. We called Jenny and Caitlyn's parents, and they came right away. We all stayed in New Orleans for a week, walking the streets and showing everyone we could think of a picture of Caitlyn, but we never got a response."

"I'm sorry," Shaye said. "I can't imagine how hard that must have been."

And a nearly impossible task. With over a million people flocking to the French Quarter for Mardi Gras every year, the chances of someone remembering a specific young, pretty blonde girl were probably less than zero.

"It was really hard on all of us," Marisa said, "but it was the worst on Jenny." Marisa glanced at Jenny, clearly worried. "You see, Jenny can't remember any of it."

"What do you mean?" Shaye asked.

"It's like the entire night is scrubbed from her memory. She doesn't even remember going into that bar. Doesn't remember being in the alley, looking for Caitlyn, or even going back to our hotel. It's like someone took an eraser to the place in her mind where that memory should be. The doctors said it was so traumatic that she blocked it."

Shaye studied Jenny, who'd finally opened her eyes and lifted her head. The woman seemed worse than distraught. She seemed partially checked out of reality. Shaye understood that better than anyone, as she'd spent a lot of time in that emotional limbo. And she had intimate knowledge of what missing pieces of memory could do to a person's mental state.

"Jenny, do you have any idea why your sister would leave?" Shaye asked.

Jenny shook her head and sniffed. "She wouldn't have. The police said...they said she probably ran off, but they're wrong. I know my sister. She wouldn't have just left like that. Maybe overnight, but not forever. Something happened to her. I'm sure of it."

Shaye didn't want to agree with her out loud but she thought that was exactly what happened. Young women didn't often disappear by choice. Not permanently. Shaye was no stranger to just how easy it was for someone to be picked up off the streets and trafficked or simply killed. And with all the swamps surrounding the city, bodies didn't always turn up.

"I tried to get past it," Jenny said. "You know, move on, like my friends and the doctors said I should do. But then the dreams started. She's calling to me. Begging me to find her because she doesn't want to be alone. She doesn't want to be alone!"

Jenny started sobbing again and Marisa looked at Rick, who simply shook his head, clearly not knowing what to do either.

"I know this is all a very cursory explanation of the situation, but will you look into it?" Marisa asked.

"I can," Shaye said, "but I have to be honest with you about my potential for success."

"We don't expect miracles," Marisa said. "We're just asking you to cover everything and see if you come up with something that the police missed. If you don't, then we'll all accept that."

It was clear to Shaye that Marisa was attempting to

provide Jenny some closure, one way or another. Shaye's assessment of Marisa was that she was worried and upset about Jenny and wanted to help but wasn't unreasonable about what she thought Shaye could do.

"Okay," Shaye agreed. "I'll take the case." She pulled a client agreement from her drawer and slid it across the desk. "This is my standard agreement. For this type of work, I usually collect a retainer of a thousand dollars. Is that all right?"

"That's fine," Marisa said, and pulled a checkbook from a large handbag. She handed Shaye the check, then pulled a file from the handbag and slid it across the desk. "That's a copy of the police file. It's everything they have. I got it this morning. My and Jenny's contact information is on a sheet inside."

"You got the police file?" Shaye said. "That's great."

"I figured they wouldn't say no to Jenny and I was afraid...I followed your story on the news and I know there's some friction between you and the police department. And well, I just didn't want any problems, so I thought I'd help out."

"I really appreciate it. Even if I could have gotten the file, this is faster and easier."

"I need to go," Jenny said. "I need to go home."

Marisa jumped up from her chair. "Come on. I'll take you to the car and we'll go home." She looked at Shaye. "I only covered the basics, so I know you'll probably need to go over everything in more detail and have more questions once you review the file. Just give me a call when you are ready to talk more. I'm sorry, but we have to go."

Jenny jumped up and practically ran out of the apartment without so much as a backward glance, Marisa hurrying behind her. Rick waited until they were gone, then turned to Shaye.

"I'm sure you've figured it out already," he said, "but Jenny's a real mess. Anxiety, depression...the doctors haven't made much headway. Fact of the matter is she's even worse now than she was then. I mean, she was never tough, you know, but at least before this happened, she could handle regular life things okay."

"I'm sorry," Shaye said. "It must be hard to see that."

Rick nodded. "It's hard and sometimes I get angry. It's all a waste, you know? Knowing something won't change what is. Jenny stopped living when Caitlyn disappeared, and that's stupid. And selfishly, I wish she'd move on because she keeps everyone around her trapped in the past. I know I shouldn't feel that way, but I'd just like one week without Marisa rushing to Jenny's house to talk her off the ledge. We've never gotten to be normal. I can't even get Marisa to move out of that Podunk town because she won't leave Jenny."

Shaye could hear the man's frustration, and she understood why he felt that way. Jenny was holding them all emotionally hostage, even though she probably wasn't trying to. Shaye knew she'd done the same thing to Corrine when she'd first come to live with her. Her adoptive mother had changed almost every aspect of her life to care for Shaye those first few years, and even though she never once saw Corrine frustrated, Shaye knew that at times she had to be. No matter how much you cared about someone, carrying them still tired you out.

"I'll see what I can find," Shaye said. "And I'll be thorough. If I can't find anything, then I'll do my best to get Jenny to accept that. I'll even ask my own therapist to talk to her."

A tiny sliver of hope flickered in his eyes as he nodded. "Thank you."

He left the apartment, and Shaye went to the door and locked it behind him. She looked out the window as he climbed into the driver's seat of an SUV and pulled away. Marisa was sitting in the passenger seat but was turned around, looking at the pale woman in the back seat.

Shaye went back to her desk and opened the police file. The entire situation was sad, and she knew her chances of helping improve it were slight. The best she could hope for was answers, but even that was a long shot. Because no matter how much she'd like to believe it, she didn't think there was any chance Caitlyn was still alive.

If she was, she was likely in a living hell.

3

MARISA HELPED JENNY INTO HER HOUSE AND PUT HER to bed. Jenny's mother was sitting on the back porch but didn't even move out of her rocking chair when the women entered the house. That didn't surprise Marisa at all. Virginia Taylor preferred to sit in that rocker and let her life waste away. As far as Marisa was concerned, it only contributed to Jenny's emotional problems, but all of Marisa's attempts to get Virginia to counseling had been met with complete silence. To Marisa, the Taylor house resembled a tomb, only the dead were still breathing.

Rick was already frowning when Marisa climbed back into the SUV and she knew it wouldn't be a second before he started in.

"This was a complete waste of time and money," he said. "Why do you humor her? She needs to be in a home or a facility or something."

"The money came from my inheritance from my grandmother," Marisa reminded him. "It's not like I asked you to pay it."

"Like I would even have that kind of money. You keep us trapped here in this shit town, where there's only shit jobs that are totally beneath our education. I'm an attorney, for Christ's sake, and I make 40k a year. Mark Cooper—remember him? Graduated with a lower GPA than me? He's already an associate at a firm in New Orleans and is pulling down a quarter mil."

Marisa held in a sigh because it would only make him angrier. And an angry Rick was not someone she wanted to go home with. It's not as though she didn't understand his frustration, but on this one issue, she'd dug in her heels. Rick assumed it was because she wouldn't leave Jenny unless or until the young woman regained her shaky sanity, but if Marisa was being honest, Jenny was an excuse. Certainly Marisa felt responsibility to help her childhood friend, but Jenny's condition wouldn't have prevented her from leaving Ponchatoula if she'd really wanted to.

What prevented Marisa from leaving Ponchatoula was Rick.

The truth was her marriage had been in trouble from day one. Marisa just hadn't figured out how much trouble until later down the line. Rick had been extremely vocal about hating being trapped in Ponchatoula, until she'd had their daughter—the result of an accidental pregnancy that Marisa had been actively trying to prevent.

Not that she regretted having Maya. The two-year-old was her biggest joy, but Marisa had never intended to bring a child into her iffy marital situation. Rick had backed off his complaints for a while but in the past year, he'd started up again full force. His temper was a problem, and it was a problem that seemed to be growing with every day that passed with him still living in Ponchatoula.

But Marisa's parents lived there, and they cared for Maya for free while Marisa and Rick were at work. Rick argued that the increase in salaries they'd see from moving to a big city would more than outweigh the cost of day care, but Marisa had countered with the quality of care difference and her obligation to Jenny. Rick had a lot of faults, but the one thing Marisa was certain about was that he adored their daughter. It was impossible to argue that complete strangers, watching over a roomful of other people's children, would provide the same level of care as two doting grandparents.

"You can always commute to New Orleans," she said. The drive in today hadn't been all that bad, although it would probably be worse during peak work traffic times.

"You'd like that, wouldn't you? Lawyers at big firms work eighty to one hundred hours a week. Then add two to three hours of commute time and you'd never see me."

She would like that, but no way would she admit it.

"It was just a suggestion," she said. "The drive today wasn't that bad, so I thought..."

"Maybe I'll do just that—get a job in New Orleans

and make some real money. Then I can afford to buy a house instead of renting a shack like we live in now, and I'll just move you, Maya, and your parents to the city where we can all have a higher quality of life."

"You should look into it," Marisa said. He was just blowing smoke. He'd threatened to do something similar for years, but it never materialized. And Marisa knew exactly why. To other people, Rick made it sound as if he wouldn't like spending so much time away from Marisa and Maya, but the truth was he was afraid to let Marisa out of his sight for that long. He'd always been afraid that if he wasn't around, exerting his control over her, she'd get ideas. Ideas that included a divorce.

Marisa was the first to admit that she considered it every day, but the situation was complicated now that she had Maya. No way was Marisa going to risk losing her daughter, and she was absolutely certain Rick would do everything possible to ensure that she did. And being an attorney, he knew all the tricks to make sure it happened. The bottom line was Rick wanted Marisa as his wife and if she tried to leave, he'd make her pay with the one thing she cared about the most.

So she stayed put and prayed a lot and wished she had made different choices. Of course, looking at her life from the advantage of today's viewpoint, that was easy to say. But if she could turn back time, chances were she'd make the same choices all over again. At one time, she'd loved Rick, and she believed he'd loved her. Real love. Not whatever this controlling thing was that he felt for her now. But after Caitlyn disappeared, everything had started to deteriorate. If they hadn't been about to graduate and their summer wedding hadn't already been planned, Marisa wondered if she would have gone through with it.

But none of those questions mattered. This was her life and her situation, and she would manage it as she always had, day by day.

———

SHAYE HURRIED into her mom's kitchen, fifteen minutes after the time she'd said she would be there. Eleonore was sitting at the island, a glass of iced tea in front of her, and Corrine was pulling a tray of enchiladas out of the oven.

"Sorry I'm late," Shaye said. She gave Eleonore a quick hug, then went around the island to kiss her mother on the cheek. "Mexican night? Yum."

Eleonore nodded. "That's what I said. And she went all out—cheese and beef enchiladas, black bean dip and queso, and a little salad garnish for anyone who might feel guilty about the healthy side of things."

"No guilt here," Shaye said. "I did ten miles on the treadmill this morning."

"Ten?" Corrine's eyes widened. "I'm only doing three. Ten is just showing off."

"Maybe," Shaye said, "but between you and Jackson, I've been eating twice the calories I used to. So it's either cut out the good food or increase my time at the gym."

"You've made the obvious and logical choice," Eleonore said. "If I cared about things like being fit, I would do the same. Fortunately, a trim body is not something I ever desired."

"You look great," Corrine said.

Shaye nodded. The psychiatrist might avoid the gym and flock to great food, but she was still in good shape. She complained about her doctor, who insisted she needed to lose twenty pounds, but didn't appear to be concerned with his assessment.

"It's all the walking you do," Shaye said. Eleonore scheduled her clients thirty minutes apart so that she could take a twenty-minute walk in between each session. She listened to the previous session notes for the next client on the schedule while she walked to help prepare her. She could have done the same thing sitting at her desk, but she claimed walking made her more acute mentally and unleashed a creative side of thought that came in handy in her sessions. It made sense to Shaye. She'd come up with some creative investigative ideas while on the treadmill.

"These just need a couple minutes to cool," Corrine said. "Do you guys want to eat in the dining room?"

"Formal dining and Mexican do not go together," Shaye said. "Just slide the dip across the island and let's do this bar style."

"Agreed," Eleonore said. "No use hauling it all over

the house. It tastes just as good sitting here and then that way, I don't have to get off this stool. I'm fairly comfortable."

"You're fairly lazy," Corrine said. "The breakfast nook is just right over there."

Eleonore shook her head. "That nook is for breakfast, hence the name. Kitchen islands are for Mexican and beer."

"You don't drink," Corrine said.

"Shaye does, and she looks like she could use a beer about now."

Shaye grinned and went to the refrigerator. "You read my mind, because I can't think of anything that goes better with enchiladas than beer."

"Margaritas?" Corrine suggested.

"Now she's getting fancy again," Eleonore said. "Break out the paper plates and let's get this rolling."

Corrine put down a bowl of bean dip and stared at Eleonore in dismay. "I do not own paper plates."

"You should get some," Shaye said. "After all, they're recyclable and think about all the water you save not using the dishwasher."

"How about I use the everyday china and write a check to the Sierra Club?" Corrine asked.

Eleonore motioned to her to pass the food. "At this point, no one cares. Serve it up on the Christmas china if you'd like. Just pass it over."

Corrine laughed and started scooping queso into individual serving cups and pushed them across the island before cutting into the enchiladas. "So what held you up?" Corrine asked. "Were you delayed by a handsome detective?"

Shaye felt a light blush creep up her neck. No matter how many times Corrine did it, her mother's teasing still embarrassed her. Just a little. And not in a bad way. More in an I-can't-believe-I'm-actually-dating-a-great-guy way.

"No," Shaye said. "The handsome detective is on a kidnapping case that has him working some long hours."

Corrine sobered. "Did he get that home invasion kidnapping?"

Shaye nodded. The night before, a couple had been the victims of a home invasion. They'd both been beaten. The husband had lost consciousness, but his injuries weren't life-threatening. The wife had been struck with a crowbar and was in the hospital on life support. Their thirteen-year-old daughter had been taken. Finding the girl quickly was paramount, and Jackson and Detective Grayson had been working almost nonstop ever since they'd gotten the call.

"I think he's slept a couple hours in the last twenty-four," Shaye said.

No one said anything because they knew the score. In this type of case, time was of the essence. Every second that passed decreased the odds of finding the girl alive or at all. And they were too aware of what happened to children in those circumstances.

"The grandfather has money, right?" Eleonore asked. "We'll just hope a ransom call is coming soon."

Shaye nodded. It was the best possible scenario in a situation without any good ones. If the girl had been taken for ransom, there was at least a chance that she could come out of it alive and without extensive physical harm. The emotional damage was a whole different animal.

"Nothing yet," Shaye said, "but they're still hopeful."

"As always," Corrine said, "if there's anything I can do..."

"Not right now," Shaye said. "Unfortunately, there's nothing anyone can do, but maybe after..."

Corrine had recently sold off all of her father's businesses and started her own charitable organization, intent on helping as many children as possible. When the real estate renovations were complete, it would include housing for street kids and those in the foster care system awaiting placement as well as a mental health facility devoted to dealing solely with children who had been the victims of a crime.

Right now, things were in the building mode, but Corrine had rented some temporary office space and had two counselors already working with victims. Eleonore had helped her choose the staff and create the overall style and methods the facility would adopt as standard. When she was in momentary fantasy mode, Shaye hoped the facility had no clients and the counselors played *Angry Birds* all day. But then she bounced back to reality and knew the need would always be there. She was beyond grateful that Corrine had the means and the experience to fill a gap for so many kids who fell through the cracks because their family lacked the knowledge or finances to get them the help they needed.

"You working on anything new?" Eleonore asked, changing the subject.

"There's always another insurance case to work," Shaye said. "But as a matter of fact, I picked up a new case this afternoon. I got caught up reading the police file, and that's why I was late."

Corrine paused at the words "police file." "What kind of case?" she asked.

"A cold case," Shaye said. "Missing person from six years ago."

"I presume the police exhausted all resources a long time ago," Eleonore said.

Shaye nodded. "It's a tough one. Twenty-one-year-old girl disappears from a bar in the French Quarter during Mardi Gras."

"Those are not good odds," Eleonore agreed. "I presume the family is pursuing this?"

"The missing girl's twin sister—identical twin—and two of her friends. The photos I saw of the twins were uncanny. Like a mirror image except for apparently different personalities."

"Was she there where her sister disappeared?" Corrine asked.

"Yes, so were the two friends who came with her to my office, husband and wife now. It was a group of five college friends who were attending LSU. They decided to take a road trip to New Orleans for Mardi Gras since they were all legal adults that year. The missing sister went to the restroom, and the twin followed a bit later. When neither came back to the table, the girl friend went looking for them and found the one sister in the alley in a panic because she couldn't find her sister. A statement given by a waitress said she saw one sister go out the back door and told my client when she asked."

"No cell phone?" Eleonore asked. "I thought college kids had cell phones medically attached."

"She had one, but all calls went to voice mail and no texts were answered." Shaye told them about the cryptic text sent the next day and the use of the ATM.

Corrine frowned. "What are the chances she actually sent that text?"

"Given that she's still missing—extremely low, in my opinion," Shaye said. "The usual reason for such a move is to buy time, but this situation is atypical."

"What do you mean?" Eleonore asked.

"If you wanted to buy time, you would send the text that night, before people panic and go to the police. Gives you time to get off the streets or out of the city before an alert goes up."

Eleonore nodded. "I see. And the text came after they'd reported the girl missing."

"Exactly."

"So then what was the point?" Corrine asked. "Why send one at all?"

"I don't know," Shaye said. "But my best guess is that

whoever took her figured she'd be reported missing and since they had the opportunity, they'd use it to get the police to back off. Maybe they didn't think about it right after the abduction. Or maybe they figured the police would be so busy they wouldn't launch an investigation right away. You know the prevailing attitude about teens who disappear. Well, this woman was an adult who probably spent some time living life on the less-than-cautious side."

"So you think someone took her and believed the police would back-burner the case if they thought she'd jetted off with a man by choice or simply checked out of her life?" Corrine asked. "That's...I don't know..."

"Abhorrent?" Shaye suggested.

"Evil springs to mind," Corrine said.

"And clever," Eleonore said. "That's always a bad combination. So did the police back-burner the case?"

"Not really. They called the hospitals the night before, but when she didn't turn up by the next morning, the sister and friends went down to the police station. Of course, they refused to file a report until that afternoon and sent them packing. On the surface, it sounds bad, but I get why. A lot of people get drunk and wander off, then wake up the next day and return to their party. Anyway, the police went down the usual checklist for a missing persons case—checked the dumpsters and the alley—but the street cleaners had already come. So even if there was any evidence the night before, it was gone by the time they checked."

Shaye sighed. "An adult disappearing during Mardi Gras is a hard sell for police attention with all the other things that happen that night. Especially when other things have more evidence and can be solved."

"Any chance you can talk to the officer who handled the case?" Eleonore asked.

"He's retired, which is a plus in my favor," Shaye said. "I tracked him down and left him a message. We'll see if he calls."

"So how do you approach something like this?" Corrine asked.

"Two ways," Shaye said. "First, I trace all their steps that night and talk to as many people as I can find who were in the bar. Sometimes people remember things later on that they didn't right after an event happens. And sometimes things they didn't think were important, therefore didn't tell the police, are relevant."

"So you retrace the friends' steps as well as the detectives'," Eleonore said. "That makes sense. What's the second part?"

"I talk to people who knew the missing woman and see what the odds were that she chose to disappear. It's always a possibility. Slim, perhaps, but people do it."

"If someone wanted to vanish," Eleonore said, "Mardi Gras in New Orleans provides the perfect backdrop."

"It does," Shaye said. "There's one other avenue to check, but it's weak. The group ran into the missing woman's ex-boyfriend in a different bar earlier that night, and they quarreled before the group left. The police questioned him, but he alibied out."

"None of it sounds very promising," Corrine said.

"No," Shaye agreed. "The likelihood of success is really low. I told them that. To be honest, I probably should have told them I'd read the police reports before making a decision."

"Why didn't you?" Corrine asked.

"The twin sister was so distraught. One of the friends did all the talking. When she finally got composed enough to speak she said she kept dreaming that her sister was calling to her because she was alone. And there's another thing—my client can't remember anything about that night. Her doctors said it's memory loss due to traumatic circumstances. Sound familiar?"

"I wonder if she saw something happen," Eleonore said.

"I wonder that myself. I couldn't help but think that her dreams might mean her memory will start returning, but of course, I have no way of knowing that."

"That poor girl," Corrine said. "Maybe if you don't find anything, she'll be able to let it all go. Maybe someone else covering all the ground again will be enough."

Shaye nodded. That was her biggest hope. But she had serious doubts. She'd seen that look on Jenny's face before. So many layers of disbelief, fear, and pain.

She'd seen it in her own mirror.

4

When Shaye left Corrine's house, it was about nine o'clock. About time for the bars to start hopping, but since it was Monday, she figured it wouldn't be impossible to have a conversation with the bartenders. Or at least see if anyone who was working there that night six years ago would be willing to meet her somewhere to talk when they were off.

The French Revival was typical of New Orleans bars —located in a historic brick building, with large doors on the front that were usually open to the street. Tonight was a little chilly, so the doors were closed, and the street offered several prime parking spaces, verifying what Shaye had thought. The bar wasn't overly busy.

The inside was a mix of industrial and historical with Mardi Gras decor hanging from the ceiling and on the walls. A bar stretched across the left side of the room and tables were placed to the right. A platform was at the back of the bar and a DJ was queuing up songs. Two tables were occupied with groups of four and a couple sat at one end of the bar. Shaye said a silent thanks that the music wasn't blaring as she made her way over to the bar on the opposite end from the couple.

The bartender was tall and muscular and probably in his mid- to late thirties. His head was shaved, and he had that erect walk of former military.

"Evening," he greeted her as he approached.

"You look familiar," she said. "Have you worked here long?"

"Eight years now. If you've been in before, I was probably here. Don't get many days off. What can I get you?"

She pulled a twenty-dollar bill from her purse and slid it across the counter. "Five minutes of your time."

He glanced at the money, then studied her for a couple seconds, shrugged, and put the money in his pocket. "What the hell. Can't get in too much trouble in five minutes, right?"

"The jail is probably full of people who thought the same thing."

He grinned. "I guess I'll take my chances. The clock just started ticking."

Shaye pulled a picture of Caitlyn from her purse. "Do you recognize her?"

He took the photo and studied it, frowned, then shook his head. "No. I mean, she sorta looks familiar, but not in a way I can place."

36

"She disappeared from this bar six years ago during Mardi Gras."

"That's it." He nodded. "That's why she looked familiar. The police came around several times, talking to me and the other staff. Even talked to some of the regulars."

Shaye nodded. She'd read all the statements taken from the employees and the handful of regulars the police had talked to, but nothing illuminating had come out of the interviews.

"You don't recall her being in here that night?" Shaye asked.

"Nah. It's like I told the cops. A night like Mardi Gras is beyond crazy, and most people were wearing masks off and on anyway. I mean, she's a pretty girl, but there's a lot of pretty girls down here for the celebration. Between working the bar and having to help the bouncers escort the overly rowdy outside, it's always crazy."

"I understand. Is there anything about that night that you can remember—about her disappearance, I mean?"

He cocked his head to the side and stared at her. "You a relative or something?"

"No. Private investigator. The missing woman's sister hired me."

He frowned. "It's got to be hard for her, right? Not having an answer."

"It's probably one of the worst things that can happen to a person."

"I wish I could help, but all I know about it was what the other bartender told me—that some woman had gone to the ladies, then went out the back door and her friends couldn't find her. The sister was upset, and I remember one of the waitresses asked me for a shot of whiskey to try to calm her down. That was the last I heard about it until the next day when the police came by."

"So you never talked to any of their party, that you're aware of?"

"If I did, it was only to serve them a drink. The drama happened at the back of the bar over near the hallway. I hate to say it, but after pouring that whiskey shot, I didn't think no more about it. People get drunk and wander off down the street all the time, and it's not uncommon for a woman to leave with a man she just met. I know it's probably stupid, especially during Mardi Gras, but it is what it is."

"I'd like to talk to the waitress who asked for the whiskey shot."

"That was Alyssa."

Shaye nodded. That was the name in the police file. "Does she still work here?"

"Yeah, she's right over there—table near the stage." He gestured to the back of the bar.

"And your name is?"

"Cody Reynolds."

She stuck her hand across the counter. "It's nice to meet you, Cody. My name is Shaye."

He released her hand and stared at her for a second.

"Wait. You're that woman from television. The one who busted that human trafficker guy."

"That's me."

"That was one seriously fucked-up situation. All those people. Man. Lucky you were looking into it because the police sure hadn't caught on. Makes you wonder how many people like that guy are just walking around, no one having a clue."

"Probably more than you think, which is far too many."

"Well, good luck with this. If it had been any other night, I might have noticed something."

"Here's my card. If you think of anything, give me a call. And thanks for talking to me."

He nodded and headed back to the other side of the bar. Shaye watched as Alyssa set some drinks on a four-top, then headed her direction as she took a seat two tables away from the foursome. The waitress was young, probably in her twenties

"You moving over from the bar?" Alyssa asked. "Waiting on someone?"

"Yes and no." She pulled another twenty out and put it on the girl's tray along with her card. "I'd like to ask you some questions, if you can take a minute."

The girl looked over at the other waitress and waved, then pointed to the table she'd just served before sitting down across from Shaye. "You're that woman—the society PI."

"Um, well mostly PI. Very little society."

Alyssa smiled. "My parents live in one of those neighborhoods in Atlanta. I spent my childhood avoiding those kinds of people. My parents are still embarrassed that I work at a bar. Doesn't matter that I go to school during the day and am paying my own way."

"They wouldn't help with school?"

"Sure. If I went to the school they picked and studied the major they wanted."

"Ah. Well, good for you."

"What did you want to ask me about?"

Shaye took the picture out and handed it to Alyssa. "Do you remember this woman?"

Alyssa took one look at the photo and nodded. "Sure. That's the woman who went missing...must be five years ago, at least."

"Did you see her in the bar that night?"

"Not that I remember. But a lot of people were wearing masks and there's never a shortage of blondes on the holiday. I just remember her sister freaking out."

"What was she saying?"

"Not much. She just kept saying her sister's name, 'Caitlyn,' over and over again."

"The bartender said you got her a shot of whiskey, but I figured if she was partying, she was already drunk."

Alyssa shrugged. "Maybe. But she seemed more in shock to me than anything. When I was a kid, our next-door neighbor saw a woman get hit by a car, and she looked the same way—that same sorta blank expression. I remember my mom got her a shot of whiskey, so I did the same. I didn't really know what else to do."

"Of course not. It's not the kind of thing you think you'll be dealing with when you come to work."

"Yes and no. I was new then and that was my first, but it happens way more often than you'd think. A couple times a month, at least. Not that they go missing forever. I just mean a woman leaving with some guy she met or just going home without telling someone. The friends always panic at first, but we never hear anything about it again, so we assume all is well. I mean, the cops would be here if it wasn't, right?"

Shaye held in a sigh. She'd like to hope that women were smarter, especially with all the things that could happen, but she knew that a low amount of life experience and alcohol were often a recipe for bad decision-making.

"I'm glad that most turn out okay," Shaye said. "And I'm sure the police would investigate if that wasn't the case. So can you walk me through exactly what happened right before, during, and after your interaction with the group?"

"Sure. I was working this section in the back near the hallway. I saw the sister and another woman come out from the hallway, and the other woman borrowed an empty chair from the table nearest them and pulled it over to the wall and had the sister sit. I figured she was drunk so I didn't think anything of it. When I passed that way to deliver drinks, I heard the other woman reassuring the sister that Caitlyn had probably just gone for a walk and would be right back. But the sister seemed so distressed that I stopped to ask what was wrong."

"And the other woman told you Caitlyn was missing?"

"Yeah, she said that apparently Caitlyn had gone out the back door into the alley and now they couldn't find her. She showed me a picture of the two sisters and pointed out Caitlyn, asking if I'd seen her."

"And did she seem worried?"

"She was definitely upset, but then they were barely legal and not from here, and one of their girlfriends had done a dip from a bar during Mardi Gras. I would have freaked out too."

"Of course. So what did you do then?"

"I asked if they wanted to call the police, and the other woman said no, that sometimes their friend did this and if they got the police involved, she might run into problems with her parents and at school. Then the sister starting doing that name repeating thing, and I went off to get her the shot."

"Did you see a young man with them?"

"Not then, but he was there when I checked on them a bit later. He was telling the other woman that Caitlyn wasn't in the alley. He said he'd walked around the block, but it was so packed there was little chance of finding her. He suggested the other woman take the sister back to the hotel and keep calling Caitlyn's cell while he stayed in the area and looked some more."

"So they left?"

"Yeah, the other woman gave me some money for the whiskey, which I tried not to take but she insisted, then all three of them left the bar."

"And you never saw Caitlyn?"

"No. Honestly, I didn't even think about it again until the next day when the cops showed up. It made me sick to think what might have happened. Made me reassess the way I did things, too, especially when I was out with friends. The older I get, the more I watch the news and am glad I made those changes years ago." She paused. "I'm sorry. I guess I don't have to tell you about the bad things people do."

"No. But you're smart to be more careful. It won't stop someone fixated on you, but you can prevent the opportunist from taking advantage."

"But then he just moves on to the next person, right? The one who isn't as careful."

Shaye didn't answer. She didn't have to. They both knew the score. She rose from her chair. "I've taken up enough of your time, but I appreciate you talking to me. I'd like to talk to another waitress named Carly. Does she still work here?"

Alyssa shook her head. "Got married and moved on to the domestic life a couple years ago. She was local when she left—well, Gretna, so close enough."

"I don't suppose you know her married name?"

"Boudreaux. Husband's name is Brad."

"Thanks. If you think of anything else, give me a call."

"Sure. And good luck. I hope you find something.

Her sister needs to know, even though it's probably not the answer she wants."

Shaye nodded and headed out of the bar. She climbed into her SUV and pulled away, mulling over her conversations with Cody and Alyssa. Nothing they'd said had gone beyond what she already knew from the police reports. But expecting a revelation six years later was asking for a miracle. Tomorrow, she'd look up Carly and talk to her, even though it probably wouldn't accomplish any more than tonight had. It was redundant but necessary.

Once she'd verified everything from external sources, then she'd take a drive to Ponchatoula and have more in-depth conversations with Marisa, Rick, and Jenny, hopefully independently of one another. The entire time they'd been in her office, Shaye had felt an undercurrent. She'd known from the start that Rick wasn't happy about being there, and he'd explained his position after the two women had left.

But there was something else bothering her. Something she couldn't quite put her finger on. She was certain someone was lying...or maybe not necessarily lying but deliberately hiding something. The reality was most people were hiding something. The question was did it matter to this case?

That was something Shaye needed to figure out.

JACKSON LAMOTTE WAS MORE EXHAUSTED than he could remember being in months. He and Detective Grayson had been working almost round the clock on the kidnapping case, checking every possible angle and hoping for a break. So far, their hopes had landed on deaf ears. Jackson set his coffee cup down and pulled up the reports he'd written on his computer screen. Somewhere there had to be a clue. Something they'd missed. The one thing that would lead them to locating thirteen-year-old Brianna LeBlanc.

"Let's get out of here." Grayson's voice sounded behind him, and he turned around to see the senior detective looking down at him, his entire body sagging. "We've been at this too long and need to sleep. We're not doing anybody any good at this point."

Jackson knew he was right. It had taken him reading the list of files on the screen three times before he'd clicked on the right one, but he still hated to leave. It felt like giving up, even though he knew getting some rest was the smartest thing he could do. He blew out a breath and grabbed his keys out of the drawer. Grayson clapped him on the back.

"We'll get them," Grayson said.

Of course, Grayson couldn't make that kind of promise, but he'd said it for his own benefit as much as for Jackson's.

"We always do, right?" Jackson said.

That part was mostly true. Jackson and Grayson's success rate was the highest in the department. It was something Jackson was extremely proud of, but with that success came the responsibility for handling the most difficult cases. And this was definitely one of them. Any time the clock was ticking on a human life, the sense of urgency was completely different from a straightforward homicide. When the victim was a child, it was even worse.

They headed out to the parking lot, silently shuffling to their cars. "I'll be here at seven," Grayson said.

Jackson nodded and climbed into his truck. It was 11:00 p.m. and it felt as if he'd been up for a week. He checked his cell phone and saw a message from Shaye, asking him to call if he got off at a reasonable hour. Eleven p.m. on a Monday wasn't exactly reasonable, and even though Shaye was sort of a night owl, he wasn't about to risk waking her up with a call. Instead he sent a text.

Sorry. Just getting off. Will talk tomorrow.

Before he started the truck, he got a reply.

I'm sorry. I know you're wiped out. Let me know if there's anything I can do.

He smiled. He hadn't been looking for a relationship when he met Shaye. A couple times in the past, he'd taken a stab at them, but nothing had even gotten serious. Mostly, they'd gotten contentious when women realized exactly what his job entailed and that he wasn't going to change it for anyone. Falling for Shaye had been like falling off a cliff. He'd never seen it coming and yet one day, he'd simply realized that he wanted a relationship with her. Something real. Something lasting.

She was perfect for him. Intelligent and direct but warm and kind. She was also the bravest person he'd ever met. And because of what she'd been through and the person she'd become, she not only understood his work better than most people, she wholeheartedly supported the way he approached it. Probably because she approached her work in the same manner, something that gave him a lot of pause and often considerable stress, but he wasn't about to be hypocritical about it. They were both doing what they needed to do and what they were best at. And no one could argue that they weren't helping people.

Can I come by?

He sent the text and waited for an answer.

Of course.

Simple. Direct. And yet in those two words, Shaye had conveyed so many things. That he was welcome in her home anytime. That it was a question he didn't really have to ask. And that level of trust and caring meant the world to him, because he knew exactly what it cost her to give it. The emotional risks she'd taken by letting him into her life.

He directed his truck toward her apartment. The streets were quiet, and the drive didn't take long. Despite the fact that most people were probably home for the night, he managed to find a parking space a couple buildings down from Shaye's apartment, then headed up the sidewalk and knocked on her door. She must have been watching the security cameras, because the door swung open before he even lowered his hand.

She motioned him in, then pulled him in for a hug and a kiss after locking the door. "You look exhausted," she said. "Are you hungry?"

"I'm not sure."

She gave him a sympathetic look. "When was the last time you ate?"

He thought back to his day, trying to remember the last meal he'd had, but it was all a blur. "I'm not sure about that either."

"Step into my kitchen. I have leftover enchiladas."

"I will be your eternal slave."

She laughed. "You better save that for my mother. She's the cook, remember? I'm just the freeloader who scams leftovers off of her once a week."

"How about I appreciate you both and take the two of you to a nice dinner sometime in the future when I'm sleeping like a normal human being again?"

"Deal." She motioned to him to sit at the counter and pulled the enchiladas from the refrigerator. "It will only take a minute to nuke these. Beer?"

"Better not. I've still got to drive home and lack of sleep will make that hard enough."

She pulled a beer from the refrigerator and put it in front of him. "I have a guest room with a perfectly good bed. And you have spare clothes and a toothbrush here. Drink the beer, have some dinner, and get some sleep."

He'd slept at her house before, but usually on the couch, figuring it made her feel better to know he was another level of protection between her bedroom and the front door. But he was careful about pushing certain issues, and this level of intimacy was one of them. Their relationship was definitely progressing, and Jackson felt they were growing closer every day, but he also knew it would probably take Shaye a long time to be ready for certain things. And he was perfectly okay with that. The last thing he wanted to do was pressure her, even unintentionally.

But the thought of walking twenty feet and falling into bed was tempting. So tempting that he didn't even try to force himself onto the other path. Instead, he opened the beer and took a drink. "I will gladly take you up on that offer."

She reached across the island and squeezed his hand. "This is a tough one. Even if I didn't know anything about what you do, I can see it in your expression and in the way you're slumping. I've been where you are too many times before, just for different reasons. You need to sleep more than anything, and the one thing that always helped me sleep was knowing that Corrine was somewhere in the house with me. It's comforting."

He smiled at her and squeezed her hand. "That's a lot of girlie sentiment coming from you."

She smiled, probably because she knew he wanted her to. "Everyone needs a shoulder. Even if they're not leaning on it."

"Have I told you today what an incredible woman you are? Or how lucky I am to have you in my life?"

She leaned over the island and kissed him on the lips. "Then we're the two luckiest people alive, because I feel the same way."

"You think I'm an incredible woman?"

She laughed. "I think you're a questionable comedian."

The microwaved beeped and she pulled the steaming plate of food out and placed it in front of him. "Dig into that," she said. "I'm going to put some clean linens on the bed."

The smell of the food had his stomach clenching and he realized he was starving. He dug into the enchiladas, shoving a huge bite in his mouth, then closed his eyes in momentary appreciation. Corrine Archer was also an incredible woman, but she was an exceptional cook. Even her leftovers tasted like a five-star restaurant. He took another sip of beer, listening to the sound of Shaye's bare feet on the hardwood floors and the creak of the linen closet as she pulled sheets out.

She was right. He could have gone home to his nice apartment and comfortable bed, but it wouldn't have changed the fact that it was empty. Just knowing she was in the other room would make a difference. Hopefully, that difference would give him the edge he needed tomorrow.

AT 1:00 A.M., Cody Reynolds stepped inside his apartment and closed the door. The bar hadn't been busy that night, so he'd made the decision to close at midnight. The owner left that up to the employee scheduled to handle close and so far, it had worked out well. No one wanted to lose money, so it was in the best interest of the closers to keep the place open if the tips were still flowing.

By the time he'd finished processing the last of the credit cards for the regulars, put away the things that had to be refrigerated, and done the host of other things that needed to be handled before he could lock up and leave, it had been twelve forty-five before he'd hopped on his motorcycle and headed home.

Now he paced his apartment, restless. He clenched his cell phone in his hand, wondering if he should make the call he'd wanted to make all night or if he should wait until the next morning. Finally, anxiety won out and he dialed. He probably wouldn't get an answer anyway. He usually didn't.

He was surprised when the call was answered on the second ring.

"Hey, I know you probably can't talk," Cody said, "but I had to let you know a PI showed up at the bar tonight asking questions about Caitlyn."

There was no response, but he could hear breathing, so he continued.

"I told her what I told the cops, but I got to tell you, I don't feel right about this. The PI was that Archer woman. The one from television. She could be a huge problem."

His phone signaled an incoming text, and he realized it was coming from the same number he'd called.

Tomorrow 7 a.m. Metairie Cemetery. Same place.

"Okay then," Cody said. "Tomorrow. But no jerking me around. That Archer woman is serious business. I'm thinking maybe we made a mistake."

The call dropped, and Cody tossed the phone on the couch, then blew out a breath. For six years things had been quiet, and that was just the way he wanted it. The police had given up a long time ago, and he'd figured that was the last he'd ever hear about the missing woman. But now, the sister had hired a private investigator and not just any PI, but Shaye Archer.

Cody knew who Shaye Archer was. Hell, everyone in New Orleans knew about her. About her past and her recent exploits...taking down criminals who had avoided the police. She had unlimited resources and a chip on her shoulder the size of the Atlantic. She wasn't going to let this go any more than she did any of the other so-called impossible cases she'd taken on.

And that worried him. Because he'd thought they were in the clear.

Even though she wasn't there, he should have known Caitlyn would ruin everything.

It was what she'd always done best.

5

SHAYE AWAKENED EARLY. Part of it was wanting to get started on the new case, but mostly, she knew it was because Jackson was sleeping in the next room. His head had started to bob before he'd even finished dinner, and she wondered if he'd taken the time to pull off more than his shoes before collapsing in bed. She wished she could do more for him, but a good meal and a soft bed were the requirements at the time. What he needed today was to find Brianna LeBlanc, and unfortunately, she had nothing to offer him in that regard except hope and an open-door policy for listening.

He'd said he would set his cell phone to wake him up, but he'd also mentioned being at work at seven and hoping he wouldn't wake her. It was just past 6:00 a.m., and a short drive to the police station from her apartment. If he wasn't up in thirty minutes, she'd poke her head in and get him moving.

She headed to the kitchen and put coffee on to brew, then did a quick check of her refrigerator to see what she had in the way of breakfast food. She was somewhat surprised to discover a carton of eggs that were still good and a new half gallon of milk. There were four croissants left in the box she'd picked up from the bakery two days ago, and she always had cereal and Pop-Tarts. If he wanted his sugar in a more natural delivery form, she had pineapple and two mangoes. It wasn't gourmet, but at least she could offer standard breakfast fare.

She reached for the television remote on the counter and turned on the TV to the morning news. The kidnapping case was the top news story, and she watched as a frustrated-looking Grayson gave some clipped comments to a reporter. Grayson, like Jackson, hated media attention. Some cops lived for the public accolades that came along with being the best at their job, but those two men didn't fall remotely into that category. They did the work because they made a difference. They weren't looking for anything more.

The creak of the guest room door let her know that Jackson was up and moving around, and a couple seconds later, she heard the shower fire up. She'd held off on a shower herself, not wanting to wake him. Besides, the luxury of being self-employed was not having to punch a time clock. She had plenty of time to shower and work on the invoices a bit more before heading out to try to get an interview with Carly Boudreaux.

The general social consensus was that it was rude to show up without calling, and if it were a social occasion, Shaye would have conformed to that rule, because that's how Corrine raised her. But this wasn't a pleasant chat with an old friend, and the one thing Shaye had learned quickly about investigating was that if you didn't have an appointment, people didn't have time to get a lie prepared. People also had a much harder time disguising a lie in person. It was far easier over the phone.

She'd looked up Carly's address the night before and planned to head that way midmorning, arriving sometime around ten. That way, Carly should be up and moving around, but maybe not yet gone out on errands. If she wasn't there, Shaye would hang around the area for a while and check back until she made contact. She had a stack of invoices and her laptop ready to go with her. If she was going to be stuck sitting in her SUV, she might as well get some work done.

She pulled the pineapple and milk out of the refrigerator and grabbed a container of protein powder from the pantry. Breakfast had never been a big meal for her and definitely not this early, but if she didn't have something, she'd be starving in an hour and would eat the rest of the croissants. No way was she interested in putting in the time on the treadmill it would take to run all of them off.

She'd polished off half her shake when Jackson came

into the kitchen wearing blue jeans and a T-shirt, barefoot, and rubbing his damp head with a towel.

"I apologize for not completing my grooming before venturing out," he said. "But I got a whiff of coffee and I couldn't contain myself."

"I understand. It's the one call that can never be ignored."

He poured a cup and took a drink, closing his eyes. A couple seconds later, he opened them and shuffled over to the island to take a seat on the stool next to her.

"How did you sleep?" she asked.

"Well, I don't remember getting into bed and the only things that made it off of me were my shoes and my belt. I'm not sure if I slept or fell into a coma."

"Either works. You needed the rest. I'm sure you'll be better today because of it."

"Between that and the shower, I feel like a whole new human being. Thanks for pushing me to stay here. You're right. I slept better than I would have at home."

"Sometimes, I know what I'm talking about."

"I'd say always, but I'm probably biased. So what are you up to today? More paperwork? Someone scamming on a slip-and-fall?"

She rolled her eyes. "Probably plenty of people are doing that. There seems to be no shortage of people trying to get out of real work. And the admin side of things is a never-ending battle of procrastination for me, as you well know because you hear me complain all the time. But I've actually got a new case to work on. A real one, although I'm not sure how much value I can add to what's already been done."

"Why do you say that?"

"Cold case. Six years ago, a young woman went missing from a bar during Mardi Gras."

He shook his head. "That's tough. I assume the family is pursuing?"

"Her twin sister and two of the friends who were also with the missing girl in the bar that night."

"Twin sister? Wow. I've always heard that twins had some special bond."

Shaye nodded. "I've done some reading on them, and the research is fascinating. How twins separated at birth and who know nothing of the other's existence end up in the same career and marrying the same kind of women. They have the same hobbies and often the same style in hair and clothes."

"Is there anything I can do? I can talk to Records and try to pave the way for you to get the police file."

"Actually, one of the friends was wise enough to have the sister request it. She thought, given my rather public past with the department, that I might run into trouble, and she wanted me to have everything I needed."

"Nice. Well, let me know if there's anything I can do."

"You have bigger fish to fry than a case that probably ended long ago."

He nodded but didn't say anything. He didn't have to. They both knew the likelihood of Shaye's missing woman being found alive was practically nil, where

Jackson still had a chance to rescue the girl he was looking for.

"If there's anything I can do," Shaye said, "you let me know. I'm sure I don't have to remind you that I'm not bound by the same rules and red tape as you. And if it comes down to resources—especially the financial kind Corrine can help with—let me know."

"I appreciate it. We're really hoping for a ransom call, but the longer we go without one, the more I worry that the kidnapping was an afterthought and not the reason for this crime."

"The news has only said home invasion, but I know you only give out what you want them to know. What do you think happened?"

"I can't say for sure. The job looks professional because the alarm system was deactivated and the locks were picked. But no family members can find anything in the house that was taken except the wife's wedding ring and the girl."

"Personal?"

"The father was a manager at one of his father's companies, so we're looking into that angle, talking to vendors, employees, and customers. But if it was personal, then either he offended someone who was already a pro at breaking and entering or the offended party hired someone who was." He shook his head. "Maybe I'm reading too much into it. Maybe the intent all along was to take the girl and get money out of the grandfather."

"They could have done that without beating the parents though."

"Yeah, but the fact that they did beat the parents sent a message to the grandfather. Assuming this is a kidnapping for ransom. I figure we'll know today. I can't imagine them taking longer than this to make their move, especially if this was their plan all along."

"And if taking the child was an opportunistic move?"

"The smart play would still be to make contact sooner rather than later. Waiting gives us time to close in."

"That's the smart play from a cop's perspective, but most criminals think they're much smarter than you."

"That's true enough. I guess we'll just have to wait and see. In the meantime, Grayson and I will be going over everything again today. Witness statements, the house, what little evidence the forensic team recovered, the father's work connections, the mother's friends, poking into the family..."

"Sounds like a long day."

"Even longer if that call doesn't come."

She gave his arm a squeeze. "It will come."

Maybe all of them hoping would make the phone ring.

CODY REYNOLDS WALKED through the tombstones in Metairie Cemetery, headed for the meeting place he hadn't used in years after calling a number the night before that he hadn't called in years. It was a bit of a hike to the location, but you had a better shot at privacy that way. These days, with security cameras on every corner, it didn't pay to meet people in the city unless it was on the up-and-up. And this definitely wasn't.

He reached the crypt where they'd met before and took a seat on part of a crumbling wall nearby. He was a little early, but traffic was always iffy and he wasn't sure he'd remember exactly where the crypt was, so he'd built in some extra time for both.

The person he was meeting wasn't there yet, but Cody had no doubt they'd be there soon. He ran one hand through his hair and blew out a breath. He should have never gotten involved. But once again, Caitlyn had gotten the better of him. There was something about her that brought out his worst side. He'd always known it but had never been able to just walk away.

Now the chickens had come home to roost.

The police had been one thing, but given their work-load around Mardi Gras, and with little to go on, Cody had bet on them giving up before discovering anything relevant. And it had been a good gamble. But now he wondered if he'd made the wrong decision. If he should have stepped back in the bar that night and just forgotten he'd ever known Caitlyn Taylor.

Right now, sitting on a cold, hard piece of cement in a damned creepy cemetery, it seemed like a no-brainer. But then, no one had ever accused him of being smart. He heard footsteps behind him and started to turn, but before he moved even an inch, he felt something strike the back of his head.

Pain exploded in his skull, and he screamed as he fell, the second blow catching him as he slumped onto the ground. His vision blurred, and the entire cemetery upended, then began to spin. He saw a shadow above him and blinked, trying to clear his blurry vision.

That's when the final blow came down right on his forehead.

And everything went black.

6

CAITLYN TAYLOR PACED THE LENGTH OF THE BEDROOM, a path worn in the old wood indicating her repeated passage. She looked out the one tiny window and into the woods, feeling like a bird in a cage. "Bedroom" was just what she called the place, but the reality was, it was her prison. Calling it a bedroom made her feel better, as if it were a place she chose to be.

But she knew if she twisted the doorknob, she'd find it locked from the outside. The same with the window. It didn't have a lock, but it was one of those octagon-shaped decorative windows. The kind that didn't open. And even if she could somehow work it out of the wall, it would be a tight fit to get out and a drop down of two stories. She'd spent some time scraping at the caulk around it with a nail file until she got caught. Now the only thing in the room was a hairbrush, a bed, and some clothes. A tiny bath was attached to the room, leaving no viable excuse for her to leave. Not as far as her captor was concerned. Food was randomly delivered when she was asleep, and that was enough to keep her functioning.

She knew the food was laced with drugs. Too many times, she'd eaten, then passed out without even realizing she was sleeping. Other times, she didn't even remember eating but there was an empty plate in the room. When she woke, things were different. Toiletries had been replaced, and sometimes she was wearing different clothes. A couple times, several inches had been cut off her hair.

She had no idea how long she'd been in the room. At first, she'd tried to keep track, but the blackouts made it impossible. The last time she looked, she'd scratched fifteen lines in the floor under the bed, but she couldn't remember if they represented days or weeks or maybe even months. When she tried to think hard about it, everything was fuzzy.

It was the drugs. But she had to eat, and often she was starving before the food arrived.

Sometimes she tried to figure out how she got here, but that was fuzzy too. She remembered Mardi Gras masks, and sometimes she got a flash of a stage where people were singing. Then she saw another mask, and after that everything went blank. Then she woke up here.

And she'd been here ever since.

SHAYE PULLED UP TO THE CURB IN FRONT OF CARLY Boudreaux's house. It was a nice middle-class neighborhood where most everyone seemed to care about their homes and their lawns. Every neighborhood had the usual holdouts who favored weeds and peeling paint, but Carly wasn't one of those. Fresh blue trim framed a neat house with white siding and pretty azalea bushes. A good-sized magnolia tree stood in the middle of the lawn, providing some shade for the front of the house.

A newish Camry was parked in the drive and as she walked toward the house, Shaye saw a baby car seat in the back, a good sign Carly was at home. Also a sign she should knock lightly on the door rather than ringing a doorbell. The quickest way to get on the bad side of a new mother was to wake up a sleeping baby.

She opened the screen door and rapped lightly on the door, then waited, hoping Carly was close enough to hear the knock. A couple minutes later, she saw someone moving inside the house, but couldn't make out whether it was man or woman through the thick white sheers covering the front window. Seconds later, the door swung open and a pretty woman with a short brown bob looked out at her.

"Carly Boudreaux?" Shaye asked.

"Yes."

Shaye handed her a card. "My name is Shaye Archer, and I'm a private investigator. I wondered if you could spare some time to talk to me."

The girl took the card and frowned. "What's this about?"

"It's about a young woman who went missing six years ago from the French Revival. I believe you were working there at the time."

"Oh, yeah. That was awful. Please come inside."

Shaye stepped inside and followed Carly through a living room cluttered with baby stuff and into an even more cluttered kitchen.

"Sorry about the mess," Carly said. "I had no idea babies required so much stuff. I'm convinced it multiplies when I'm sleeping, which isn't often. Please have a seat at the counter. It's the only place in here with a clear spot."

Shaye smiled and sat on the stool. "How old is your baby?"

"Two months. I just put her down for a nap, so your timing is perfect. Do you mind if I fold clothes while we talk? I live in a perpetual state of behind."

"Please do whatever you need to do."

Carly lifted a laundry basket from the floor and dumped a stack of baby clothes and rags on the counter. Shaye reached for some rags and started to fold.

"The least I can do is help," Shaye said.

"Thanks," Carly said and pulled up another stool. "I swear it never ends. How does such a small person go through so many clothes? That's rhetorical, mind you. So what did you want to ask me?"

"Jenny Taylor, the sister of the missing woman, has asked me to look into her disappearance."

"I guess the police gave up, huh?"

"It's a cold case, but it's still unsolved. Unfortunately, unless some new evidence is introduced, they feel there's nothing left for them to do."

Carly nodded. "There's not a worse time to go missing in New Orleans than during Mardi Gras."

"It definitely adds another layer of difficulty. Anyway, I talked to Alyssa Hebert yesterday and she said you were the one who told Jenny that her sister, Caitlyn, had gone out the back door."

"That's right. I was on break myself and went out back to take a quick smoke. I stopped, by the way, long before I started trying to get pregnant. No desire to start again. Anyway, I was leaning against the wall out back when the woman—Caitlyn—came out the back door. She was moving so fast, I don't even think she saw me when she came out."

"Was there anyone else in the alley?"

"Just me and Caitlyn. She was wearing a mask but pulled it off and stopped right there in the middle of the alley, breathing hard. I figured she was going to get sick. She wouldn't be the first or the last that night. But she just stood there for a bit, mumbling to herself."

"Could you understand what she was saying?"

"No. It was too low. Anyway, she turned around and saw me and froze. Then she said 'Sorry. I didn't mean to disturb you.'"

"I told her she wasn't disturbing me at all and besides, it wasn't like I owned the alley."

"What did she say?"

"She laughed and said it was a shame everyone didn't have my same view of things. By that time my break was almost up, so I told her good night and headed back inside to get in a quick bathroom visit before going back to work. Her sister was coming from the bathroom, and I had to do a double take at first, thinking it was the same person."

"I've seen pictures," Shaye said. "They definitely looked like mirror copies."

Carly nodded. "And they were dressed exactly alike, too. College sweatshirt, jeans, white Keds. Probably on purpose. Hot blonde twins attract the guys, you know? The only difference was the one outside had a pink mask and the one inside was holding a turquoise one."

"And you talked to Jenny? The sister inside?"

"Yeah, she asked if I'd seen her twin sister, and I said she was out back and pointed to the door."

"Did she say anything else?"

"No. She just ran by and went out the door." Carly frowned. "But she looked upset. Maybe. Or maybe she was drunk. I don't know. We were so slammed I admit I didn't pay much attention."

"And you never saw either of them again?"

"No. Not until the police came the next day. They showed pictures of Caitlyn and told me she was missing." She stopped folding and looked directly at Shaye. "It spooked me. Bad. So bad I almost quit. One of the older waitresses talked me out of it, and I'm glad she did, because it was good money. Not all the bars are. But after that, you can bet I had one of the guys walk me to my car every night. It still bothers me. I mean, how does someone just disappear that quickly? And no one saw anything?"

Shaye nodded. "It is scary. Most people don't think about the things that can happen until it's too late."

Carly looked down at the counter, then back up at Shaye. "She's probably dead, isn't she?"

"The odds aren't good that she's alive."

Carly nodded. "She's better off if she's not, right? I mean, six years..." Her eyes widened. "Oh my God, I'm so sorry. I mean, I know what happened to you. I didn't mean to imply you'd have been better off..."

"That's okay. Trust me, there were so many times that I would have been. And even when you're no longer captive, you're still never really free."

Carly's expression filled with sympathy. "I can't imagine. How do you deal with it?"

"One day at a time. An awesome mother and the best therapist in the world. But most of all, I think you have to have a purpose, a reason to get up every day and do something with your life. My job does that for me."

Carly gave her a small smile and sniffed, and Shaye could see tears brimming in her eyes. "I think you're the bravest person I've ever met. And if anyone can figure out what happened to Caitlyn, it's you."

SHAYE LEFT Carly's house and stopped at the nearest café, where she ordered a coffee and Danish and opened her laptop to make some notes. She'd scanned the police file that morning and had all the documents in a folder for easy access. When she finished making notes from her interview with Carly, she compared them with the police report, as she had her interviews with Cody and Alyssa. And just as she thought, the stories matched. They had in every instance.

The only difference in Carly's story was the tiny comment about Jenny looking upset when Carly spoke with her in the hallway. But as Carly said, she could have been mistaken. She was young and green when she went to work there, and Lord only knew how many people she'd served that night. She might have misinterpreted Jenny's expression or even attributed someone else's look to Jenny.

And even if Jenny had looked upset, did it matter?

Upset could mean anything, depending on how dramatic a person was. What Shaye had seen of Jenny lent to the hugely dramatic category, but it wasn't fair to assess her now. She needed to know how Jenny was before Caitlyn disappeared. According to Rick, Jenny had never been "tough" but she had no way of knowing what Rick's definition of tough entailed. She needed to make a trip to Ponchatoula and talk to Jenny's parents and have a much longer conversation with Marisa.

But she'd wanted to talk to all the ancillary players first, because she knew Marisa would ask straight off what she'd done so far. And she wanted to see if anything else popped up that might lead to other questions she needed to ask Marisa and Jenny. There were two more on her list—Sam Lofland, the friend who'd left the group early, and Garrett Trahan, the ex-boyfriend who'd fought with Caitlyn in a different bar earlier that night.

She'd lucked out on both accounts as they worked in the city. Garrett lived downtown in one of the expensive high-rise condos she'd looked into before buying her apartment. Sam lived across the river in Algiers Point. Both were probably at work that day and she figured she'd try them there first, and if she struck out, then that night at home.

Sam's office was the closest, and her research had pegged him as a marketing manager for an apparel company. Garrett was an attorney with a high-powered law firm—one of the firms her grandfather had kept on retainer. Given all the things that had recently come to light about her grandfather, Pierce, Shaye wasn't certain what her reception would be at the firm, but it wouldn't stop her from giving it a shot.

She polished off the Danish and the rest of the coffee and headed out to Sam's place of business. The company was in the warehouse district and had that updated, trendy look that apparel manufacturers aimed for. A young woman at reception looked up at her when she entered, then jumped up from her chair.

"You're Shaye Archer," she said. "Oh my God. I followed everything about you on television. You're totally my hero."

Shaye felt a blush creep up her neck. The woman's enthusiasm was flattering but also a little overwhelming. "Thank you."

"Seriously, what you did for those kids and catching that awful man that was selling them. And all the while dealing with all your own shit—sorry, stuff. It's like super-hero level."

"I don't know about that, but I appreciate the compliments. I was wondering if I could see Sam Lofland, but I don't have an appointment."

"Let me call him. I know he hasn't gone to lunch yet because he always stops by and asks if I want him to pick me up something. He's super nice that way." She punched some numbers on her phone. "Mr. Lofland? This is Cherise. Shaye Archer is here and would like to speak with you. Yes, that Shaye Archer. No, she didn't say. Can I send her up?"

She hung up the phone and beamed at Shaye. "He said go on up. The elevator's right behind me on the left. Third floor. His office is all the way at the end of the hall. You can't miss it."

"Thanks," Shaye said and headed for the elevator. She could feel the young woman watching her until she was out of sight.

The elevator opened on the third floor with a hallway stretched straight ahead of her. She went to the door at the end and knocked. A couple seconds later, the door opened and a handsome young man peered out at her, looking slightly confused.

"Hello," Shaye said, and extended her hand. "I'm Shaye Archer."

"Of course. I recognize you from TV. I'm Sam Lofland." He motioned her inside and pointed to a pair of chairs in front of his desk. "Cherise said you wanted to speak to me. Is there some charity event you're working on?"

Shaye shook her head. "No. I leave all those types of things to my mother. She's the expert. I'm actually here on business. I wanted to talk to you about Caitlyn Taylor."

His eyes widened and he leaned back in his seat and shook his head. "It's been a lot of years since I've heard that name. Can I ask why?"

"Her sister hired me to go over the case. See if I can

find something the police didn't."

"That makes sense. Jenny was always the one trying to pick up the pieces in Caitlyn's wake."

It was something about his tone that made Shaye pay closer attention to him. There was an undercurrent there that didn't come just from the words. And it was the first time she'd heard it when talking to people about the missing woman.

"Did Caitlyn make a lot of waves?" Shaye asked.

"Definitely her share. Probably more. Looking back, I don't guess she was any worse than a lot of college girls, but then college guys aren't much of a prize either, right?" He smiled. "We don't realize it at the time, but we all have a lot of growing up to do."

Shaye smiled back. "That's a mature attitude for someone who hasn't even hit thirty."

"Self-reflection is my hobby," he said. "That and fishing, which allows plenty of time for all that reflecting."

His voice was light, but even though she was certain he'd meant for her to take it as a joke, she would bet her trust fund that Sam Lofland was a serious man.

"How much reflection have you done about Mardi Gras night six years ago?" she asked.

His expression grew serious, then sad. "More hours than I can count. I keep thinking, maybe if I hadn't left early. Maybe things would have been different."

Shaye studied him for a moment. It was typical for those left behind in the wake of a tragedy to speculate about how things could have been if they'd done things differently. Survivor's guilt. It was a very real and very powerful thing. But Shaye got the impression there was more to Sam's regret than just leaving the group early.

"You left before they went to the French Revival, right?" Shaye asked. "Marisa said the party scene wasn't really your thing. I'm surprised you even went on the trip if that's the case. Mardi Gras is pretty much the biggest party ever."

"True, and this year, as I have every year on Mardi Gras, I worked from home. All of the staff who can, do so. The entire company closes at noon to let the warehouse workers get out of downtown before it becomes too much of a zoo."

He shook his head and stared at the wall behind her, and Shaye knew his mind was going back in time. Back to that night six years ago.

"I don't know how many bars we'd gone into," he said. "Five, maybe more. We'd stay for a while and everyone else would drink and dance, and then we'd move on when the rest wanted something new. Then Caitlyn suggested karaoke, and we headed to a bar she'd seen with an advertisement for karaoke on the sign."

"The French Revival?"

"That's the one."

"I didn't realize you'd gone to the bar with them," Shaye said. "I thought you'd left before then."

"I never went inside. When we got there, I told the others I was worn out and was going to head back to the hotel."

"And that was the last time you saw Caitlyn?"

He frowned and looked down at his desk. "I saw her once more."

Shaye perked up. That definitely wasn't in the police report. "When?"

"Not even a minute later. My friends headed into the bar, and I started to leave when Caitlyn came back and grabbed my shirt. I stopped and asked her what was wrong and she...well, she kissed me."

"Kissed you? I didn't realize you were seeing each other."

"We weren't. It wasn't exactly something I wanted."

"So what happened then?"

"I pushed her away and told her it wasn't going to happen and she should join the group. She gave me a look that should have brought lightning down on me, then stalked back into the bar. Then I left. And until now, I've never told a single other person that story."

"Why not?"

"Because it didn't matter in regard to Caitlyn's disappearance and it would have only hurt Jenny. She was already in enough pain over Caitlyn. I didn't see any reason to add more to that when it didn't accomplish anything."

"Why would knowing that hurt Jenny?"

A blush crept up his neck, and he looked slightly embarrassed. "Jenny had a crush on me. Since junior high. I liked her as a friend, but it was never going to be anything else."

"Did Caitlyn know about Jenny's crush?"

"Everyone knew. But people didn't say anything. Jenny was, I don't know how to explain it...delicate, maybe? She had a lot of health problems, and she wasn't the strongest person emotionally either. Things that wouldn't even faze a normal person were like the cut of a knife to her."

"It doesn't appear as if she's improved since," Shaye said. "But I find it surprising that young people didn't use it against her. Kids are often known to be cruel, not kind."

He nodded. "That's true, and if it had been anyone else, I'm sure someone would have rubbed her nose in it. But Jenny was different. Special. She was the nicest, sweetest person you'd ever meet. Hurting her would be like kicking a puppy. It's hard to explain, but the effect she had on people made them want to protect her, not lash out. The blond hair and blue eyes and completely innocent look probably helped things. When we were little kids, I thought she looked like an angel."

Shaye smiled. "It sounds like you really cared for her. I take it you don't see her now?"

"No. I tried, after...but every time I saw her, she got so agitated, and her mother finally said I should stop visiting. That she'd call me when things improved."

"I take it that call never came?"

"I'm still waiting. Based on what you said earlier, I guess it's never coming. I pushed for tests—brain scans and such, especially after that incident with the car. But

Jenny had developed a phobia about closed places, and they never could get a good MRI."

"What incident with the car?" Shaye asked.

"It was about two weeks after Caitlyn went missing. Jenny was crossing the street in downtown Ponchatoula and wasn't paying attention. A car clipped her, and she fell and hit her head on the curb. She was unconscious for several minutes and complained of headaches for days. She went straight home and went full-on hermit for months."

"Well, it doesn't appear to me that Jenny has ever gotten over Caitlyn's disappearance. According to Rick, she's gotten worse."

Sam shook his head. "I'm sorry to hear that. Really sorry. I always wanted the best for Jenny. Instead, she got the exact opposite. You've heard that expression that someone can light up a room with a smile? That was really Jenny. She had a way about her that could make you feel good no matter what you were dealing with."

Shaye studied him for a moment. His grief over Jenny's condition seemed genuine and deeper than a casual friend would express. "Pardon me for saying so, but it seems like you really cared for Jenny. Can I ask why you didn't think there was any chance of a relationship?"

He gave her a small smile. "Simple. I'm gay. Of course, no one knew that back then. It's okay to be gay in New Orleans, especially when you're the marketing director for a women's apparel company. It's almost expected, actually, although completely cliché. But in a small town, it wasn't optimal, and my folks were big church people."

"I understand," Shaye said. And it provided another reason why Sam had stopped visiting Jenny. Given her fragile emotional state, she was less capable of dealing with her feelings for him when he couldn't return them. "Are your parents still there?"

"No. My dad got a better job when I was in college, and they moved to Houston. My mom hates the humidity but loves the shopping." He sobered. "I keep thinking if I hadn't pushed Caitlyn away, or at least gone about things in a better way, then maybe things wouldn't have gone down the way they did. Then I think it's totally vain to assume I was the difference when she could have walked out that back door for any number of reasons that had nothing to do with me."

"I think it's a completely normal thing to wonder about, but I also don't think anything that happened was your fault. Caitlyn had been drinking and singing karaoke in a crowded bar. A more likely guess is that she just wanted to get some fresh air. She might have been dizzy or felt a little ill. And even if she was still mad and went outside to pout, the only person responsible for what happened to Caitlyn is the person who did something to her."

"So you think she's dead. You don't buy the police theory that she took off?"

"You knew her much better than me. Do you buy it?"

His brow scrunched. "No. I don't think so."

"But you're not certain. Why?"

"I think she was seeing someone, but she was keeping it real secretive, and that wasn't like Caitlyn. Usually when she was dating a guy, she paraded him around like a prize—probably her way of warning other girls off."

Shaye perked up. A secret relationship was something the police didn't uncover, but if there was a guy in the wings, Caitlyn might have taken off with someone that night. Maybe she intended on coming back. Maybe things went wrong and she didn't get the opportunity.

"What do you mean by secretive?" Shaye asked.

"She was checking her cell phone all the time. Don't get me wrong, that was normal, but sometimes I'd see her smile. That smile like she had a secret. If someone asked what she was smiling about, she immediately put her phone away and changed the subject. And she'd started doing less with the group on weekends but was vague about her plans. There were other things, too—she'd been dieting, something she didn't normally do, and she'd done some babysitting to get money for highlights. She didn't like kids at all, so that was unusual."

"You're very observant. Most people wouldn't have put all those things together."

He shrugged. "Maybe I was observant or maybe it was just years of knowing her. Either way, I'd bet money that she had someone new."

"Why keep him a secret? Not the kind of guy her parents would approve of?"

"Her parents didn't approve of much, so that wouldn't

be a stretch, but they also had no way of knowing what Caitlyn was up to at the university. Jenny certainly wasn't going to tell them. She spent her entire life covering and making excuses for Caitlyn. No, I think it must have been something different. More like someone her friends wouldn't have approved of."

Shaye nodded. "And you think she might have left the bar to meet him?"

"It makes as much sense as anything else. That would explain the text the next morning and the money taken out of her account. Someone had to have her PIN to get it. After that, your guess is as good as mine. Clearly, at some point, something must have gone wrong. But the only reason I can think of for the text and money is if she left voluntarily."

"Did you mention this theory to the police?" It certainly hadn't been in the file she'd read, but the files rarely contained anything but official statements. An officer's notes about witnesses' feelings on things were usually kept in their personal notes and not entered into official record.

"Sure, I told them," he said, "but I don't think they took me seriously. I mean, what proof did I have? A hunch? Some behavior that was fairly typical of a woman her age? Anyway, they never turned up anything, and I'm sure they got her cell phone records."

"That's true," she agreed. But Caitlyn wouldn't be the first or the last person to have a second phone in order to hide a relationship. It was a long shot, but it was definitely something to look into. And something to ask Jenny, Marisa, and Rick about when she talked to them next.

"Caitlyn had been dating a man named Garrett Trahan," Shaye said, "and I understand they broke up right before you went to New Orleans? Could she have been talking to him?"

He frowned. "Maybe."

"You didn't like him?" Shaye asked, taking a cue from his expression.

"No. But he had no shortage of girls chasing him. His family has money and connections. He was an ass, but he fooled a lot of people. I imagine, in the beginning anyway, Caitlyn thought he was a catch. Hell, maybe she still did after they broke up."

"You didn't think so?"

"I think men like Garrett Trahan see women as an accessory, and Caitlyn was a pretty accessory that he didn't want to lose. Plus, guys like Garrett are used to doing the dumping, not being dumped."

"If Caitlyn thought he was a catch, why would she break up with him?"

"Caught him with another girl, if I had to guess. He wasn't exactly known for monogamy."

"But you think he might have been trying to weasel his way back in?"

"It wouldn't surprise me. I assume you know that we ran into him that night at one of the bars. Caitlyn accused him of following us."

"Was he?"

"Maybe. I wouldn't put it past him to try, but there were so many people in the French Quarter that night. I'm not sure if that would have made it harder to follow us or easier to do it without being seen."

"Could have gone either way. I understand they had a fight."

"It wasn't much of a fight. Mostly Caitlyn called him a stalker and he called her some choice names and we high-tailed it out of the bar before they threw us all out."

"Did you see Garrett again?"

"No. But I always wondered if she didn't go out of the bar to meet him."

"Even though she'd accused him of stalking her?"

"Caitlyn always was dramatic. That's why she was a theater major. But maybe she thought about what she'd said afterward and realized she was wrong. Or maybe they staged the whole fight just to keep us from thinking they were seeing each other again." He shook his head. "You know, when all this went down, he was the first person who came to mind. But then the police said he had an alibi, so I figured I was wrong."

"Why was he the first person you thought of?"

"I think he was violent. Caitlyn had a black eye one time that she claimed she got from running into a bathroom cabinet door in the dark, but I never believed her. I don't think any of us did. Marisa asked a couple times, but Caitlyn shut her down right quick."

"That's unfortunately typical."

"Yeah. I have a cousin whose husband abused her. I'd still like five minutes in the room with that guy."

Shaye rose from her chair and pulled out her card. "I really appreciate you talking to me. If you think of anything else—even another wild theory—please give me a call."

He rose, took the card, and nodded. "I hope you figure out what happened. Maybe if Jenny knew for sure, she could get help. You know, get past this."

"I hope so too."

"Would you...I mean if you find out something, would you let me know?"

"Of course."

He was still standing there, staring off into space, when she turned around and left. Shaye wasn't sure what she'd been expecting when she'd walked into Sam Lofland's offices, but she knew the man she'd met wasn't it. She also hadn't expected to get a new line of investigation to follow, but Sam had presented her with an interesting idea as well as a side of Caitlyn that the police reports didn't reflect.

If Caitlyn had a secret relationship, was it Garrett Trahan or someone else? The fight with Garrett could have been staged for her friends' benefit. And someone with Garrett's means could have easily provided Caitlyn with a second phone. Maybe it wasn't a new man that Caitlyn was hiding. Maybe it was an old one that her friends didn't like.

Either way, her next stop was Garrett Trahan's office.

8

JACKSON LAMOTTE STRUGGLED TO CONTAIN HIS ANGER, but he knew it showed in every square inch of his tense body and tight face. It made him somewhat happy to see Grayson wasn't doing a much better job hiding his disgust.

"Sir," Grayson said. "All due respect, but we've been working this case from the beginning and if you do a review, you won't find something we missed. I assure you."

The man behind the desk was the temporary police chief, pulled out of retirement and asked to fill the position until a new one could be selected, something that was taking a long time to do given all the bad publicity the department had recently experienced. He was a fair enough man but strict about protocol. Jackson didn't have any problem with him, personally or professionally, but he had a problem with the words that had just come out of his mouth.

"No one is saying you missed anything," the chief said and sighed. "Look, this is out of my hands. The grandfather has a friend in Congress who made a call to the FBI and they agreed to put some agents on it. None of that is a reflection on me, you, or this department. It's just a grief-stricken grandparent using every resource to find the people who attacked his son and daughter-in-law and kidnapped his granddaughter."

"She doesn't fit the 'tender years' definition," Jackson said. "And we have no reason to believe she's been transported across state lines. They can't claim jurisdiction."

"I'm aware of that and so is the FBI, but they also informed me of a case in Alabama with a similar MO."

"They think the two are related?" Grayson asked. "Because we conducted a check of other cases and couldn't find anything that was a good match."

"It's a murder of a parent and the kidnapping of a child," the chief said. "Look. It's a reach. You, I, and the FBI all know it, but this is not something any of us get to take issue with. If you told me you had something new, something solid, I might be able to raise enough stink to keep you on. Can you tell me that?"

Jackson looked over at Grayson, almost wishing that his partner was capable of lying. But Grayson would never risk his job and his pension over a case he'd probably be yanked off of regardless.

"No, sir," Grayson said. "I can't tell you that."

The chief gave him a sympathetic nod. "I'm sorry. Truly, I am. The two of you are some of the finest we have here, which is why I put you on this case to begin with. But my hands are tied."

"I understand why we have to allow the FBI to take point," Jackson said. "But why can't Detective Grayson and I remain on the case?"

"Simple numbers. You're too valuable to play administrative assistant to the FBI. You'll have an information exchange in a couple hours when the agents arrive and make yourself available to answer questions after that. I'll assign two junior detectives to work with them."

Jackson's jaw was clenched so hard he knew it would be sore the next day. Because he was afraid of what he might say if he spoke again, he just nodded.

"May I ask what we're doing that's a more valuable use of our skills?" Grayson asked. Their slate had been cleared when they got handed the kidnapping and all their current cases reassigned so that they could focus on that one investigation.

The chief handed Grayson a sheet of paper. "Murder. Just came in. Get over to Metairie Cemetery. A patrol officer will meet you there and take you back to the crime scene. Forensics is already on their way."

The chief picked up his phone, and Jackson and Grayson rose, knowing that indicated their dismissal. They remained silent as they walked down the hallway and continued the quiet game as they collected their wallets and weapons and headed out to the parking lot. Once they were in the car, Jackson exploded.

"Son of a bitch!" he shouted and slammed his hand on the dash.

Grayson didn't have to say a word. His expression as he put the car in gear and squealed out of the parking lot said it all.

"This is a little girl we're talking about," Jackson continued to rant. "Not some political power-play bullshit."

"You won't get any disagreement from me," Grayson said.

"There's nothing we can do about it, is there?"

"Not a thing. If there was, we'd be doing it now instead of driving to Metairie Cemetery."

Jackson blew out a breath. He knew Grayson was right. Had known there was nothing to be done about the situation when they were sitting in the boss's office. The chief wasn't about to make waves with a congressman, because that would cause problems for the mayor and the governor, ultimately culminating in a storm of shit landing squarely on the New Orleans Police Department. And if he and Grayson kept investigating, the FBI would find out and their jobs would be on the line.

But knowing all of that didn't make the pill any less bitter to swallow.

"We did good work on this," Grayson said. "The FBI has resources we don't. Maybe they'll be able to break something. Maybe comparing it to that other case."

"You know that other case is just a bullshit excuse for them to pull rank. The best chance that girl has is if whoever took her decides to make a ransom request. I was praying for that call before. I'm going to pray even harder now."

Grayson nodded, but Jackson knew that the more time that passed without the phone ringing, the less likely it was that this was a case of a kidnapping for ransom and more likely it was something personal against the father or mother and the girl was simply in the wrong place at the wrong time.

"Grab that paper the chief gave us and see what we have to start with," Grayson said. "Get us up to date while I drive. This victim deserves the same level of investigation as Brianna LeBlanc, regardless of what we think we ought to be working on."

Jackson grabbed the paper from the dash where Grayson had tossed it. The senior detective was right. Again. Putting less than a hundred percent into this case wouldn't do any good for Brianna LeBlanc or the family of the current victim.

"Let's see," Jackson said as he scanned the printed sheet. "Victim is a white male, midthirties. Found in Metairie Cemetery by a photographer taking some pictures for a local publisher doing a book on New Orleans sightseeing spots."

"Probably not what they had in mind for people to see," Grayson said.

Jackson nodded. "Photographer freaked and called

the cops. Patrol took the call, got a look at the body, and called downtown. Wounds on the back and front of the head and no apparent weapon. That's it."

"Okay. Forensics should be there by now. We'll see what they have to say, then get an address for the vic and check out his place."

The patrolman who took the initial call was waiting for them in the parking lot. Jackson recognized him as Keith Walker, one of the younger guys. He was an up-and-comer who had his sights set on Homicide one day. He'd asked Jackson to lunch a couple months before to get his advice on the career path, and Jackson had found him serious but likable, and decided he would probably accomplish everything he had set out for.

"Detectives," Walker said, looking slightly confused.

"The FBI moved in on the LeBlanc case," Grayson said. "So we're up."

Walker's eyes widened. "Wow. I'm sorry. I mean, not sorry to work with you but sorry about the FBI."

"Everyone's sorry," Grayson said. "Except the FBI."

"One would argue they're the sorriest of all," Jackson grumbled.

Grayson shot him a look, and Jackson forced himself to focus on the case they were now assigned. "Regardless, the decision is above all our pay grades, including the chief, so here we are. What can you tell us?"

"The victim is a white male, midthirties. Found approximately an hour ago by a photographer taking pictures for a book. He got one look at the body and ran.

I was first on the scene. The body was facedown across a crypt slab, and I could see the wound on the back of the head. I checked for a pulse, but he was gone. The body was cold and the blood already clotted. I immediately radioed in for the forensics team and secured the scene. Forensics arrived about ten minutes ago, and I came up here to wait for you guys."

"That's good work securing the scene," Jackson said. "If you can take a few more minutes from patrol, you're welcome to observe."

"Really?" Walker could hardly contain his excitement. "That would be great. I mean, not great that someone died, but to watch you two work a scene would be awesome."

Grayson shot an amused look at Jackson, but Jackson knew his senior partner hadn't forgotten working his way through the ranks to homicide detective, and how much any little peek into that world meant when you were writing tickets for speeding and jaywalking.

Walker motioned them to a path on the left, and they headed out. Several minutes later, they arrived at the scene, where the assistant medical examiner greeted them.

Grayson looked at the body, still slumped over the crypt marker. "Messy one."

The AME nodded. "Head wound. Lots of blood."

"I assume that's cause of death?" Grayson asked.

"Can't see a better one, but of course, I'll do an autopsy," the AME said. "In any event, it wasn't accidental. No blood on any of the crypts or other objects he could have fallen on. Whatever hit him left the scene, and since weapons don't walk away on their own..."

Grayson nodded. "I don't suppose we got lucky enough to find an ID."

"Buy a lottery ticket on the way home tonight, Detective," the AME said. "His wallet and cell phone were still in his pocket. The victim's name is Cody Reynolds. Age thirty-six. Home address in the warehouse district. We'll do a quick sweep on the items at the lab, but I don't anticipate they hold any forensic evidence. You should be able to pick them up in about an hour."

"Hmmm, now I don't know whether to be happy about that or not," Grayson said.

Jackson nodded. Robbery would have been the easy way out on motive, but harder to find the perp. When it was personal, that meant poking into every avenue of the victim's life, hoping to find that one person mad enough to kill them. And in this case, lure them into a cemetery and kill them.

"Perfect place to kill someone," Jackson said. "No cameras. No witnesses."

Grayson sighed. "Yeah. Perfect. Well, let's find out where Mr. Reynolds lived. Maybe our luck will hold, and we'll find the reason someone wanted him dead."

Jackson nodded. "I'll get him run through the system. See if anything pops. He has a military tattoo on his arm."

"Big guy, too."

"Someone got the jump on him," Jackson said. "Given that it's impossible to walk silently on all these dead leaves, I'm going with he knew the person he came here to meet and didn't feel threatened or he wouldn't have had his back to them."

"That narrows down the field, at least."

"Maybe. Or our luck might run out, and Mr. Reynolds might have been one of those popular people with a football stadium of friends."

"Then we best get going. It will take a while to alibi them all."

JENNY RUSHED out the back door of the bar and past the dumpster. Then the alley went fuzzy and Marisa was there, trying to get her to go back inside. But Marisa's voice was all wrong. Not the calm, soothing voice she usually had. This time she sounded panicked. Jenny saw the back door to the bar open, and she went inside. Rick was there, and Marisa whispered something to him. His eyes widened, and he pushed past them, headed for the back door.

Then it all faded to black.

JENNY WOKE up from her nap as exhausted as when she'd gone to sleep. It had been that way too much lately. No matter how tired she was, or how quickly she fell asleep, it wasn't restful. She awakened feeling as though she'd been ill or run a marathon instead of been asleep. Her body ached and her legs cramped sometimes. Her mother gave her potassium for the cramps and it helped some but didn't take away the pain completely.

And then there were the dreams. No matter how tired she was, they always came. At first, it had been only one every week or so. Then every week had turned into every night, and finally, she couldn't sleep at all without memories of Caitlyn occupying her subconscious. Somewhere in all that jumbled mess was an answer. She just had to remember the right thing.

She pushed herself up into a sitting position, trying to think about what she needed to do that afternoon, but she couldn't remember what day it was. Not that it mattered much. Nothing mattered much since Caitlyn had disappeared. She'd dropped out of school her last semester. Her parents had been supportive, of course, but they were also grieving. It was hard for three devastated people, all living in the same space and sharing the same sorrow, to be much comfort to one another. And her parents had never been the huggy, feely type.

It had taken her a year before they managed to get her back to school to finish. The university had accommodated her back into the classes and dorm, and she'd managed to fumble through the semester with barely passing grades. But she'd graduated, and that was all that mattered. At the time.

She knew her parents had hoped that going back to school meant she was healing. That she was making the move to going out on her own, but every time she thought about leaving her parents' house and being responsible for her own home, bills, meals—not to mention having a job and all the responsibility that came along with that—she started to panic. Then she started having panic attacks.

So she stayed. Right there in the house she'd grown up in. In her childhood bedroom.

And for a while, she'd worked at the local hardware store as a clerk. She wasn't setting the world on fire, but it was low stress and within walking distance, which was important since she'd never learned to drive and still wasn't interested. She'd changed up her bedroom—a fresh coat of paint in a sunny yellow on the walls and new linens for the bed and bathroom. She'd even picked up some good used bedroom furniture from a family who was moving.

And then her father had died.

The coroner said it was a heart attack. That he had a family history of heart problems, but Jenny knew he'd never been right since Caitlyn disappeared. She'd never heard of someone actually dying of a broken heart, but maybe that wasn't as impossible as it sounded. Her mother said she couldn't manage the upkeep on the big house they lived in, nor could she afford it. So they'd moved from the one place of stability she had into a tiny old structure that had once served as a church but had been remodeled into a home decades before.

Unlike their other home, this one was outside the city

limits and came with some land. The previous owners had kept chickens and horses and maintained a decent-sized garden, but Jenny's mother hadn't wanted any of that. She'd grown up poor with her hands in the dirt and never wanted to live that way again. She sometimes said she might be poor now but at least her hands were clean. Jenny knew her mother didn't like the house all that much, but it had been cheap. The money she'd banked from the difference in price between the old house and the new one would take her through retirement. And Jenny too, assuming she stayed. What happened after that was a huge question mark and something Jenny worried about as her mother seemed to slip away a little more every day. The house and the retirement account would come to her, but the Social Security that made up the difference in their bills would go along with her mother.

Unfortunately, the move meant Jenny was also dependent on her mother or friends for a ride. She had an old bicycle that she used to pedal into town sometimes. When the weather was nice, it wasn't a bad ride. In fact, Jenny enjoyed it. But her grief over her father and the situation with the commute both pushed her to quit her job. She wasn't reliable, and the owners needed someone they could depend on. So now she sat out here with her mother. Mostly silent. Both of them lost in their thoughts.

She pushed herself out of bed and reached for her shoes. She hadn't bothered to take off her clothes before she'd lain down to rest and she was sure they were all rumpled, but with only her mother to see her, it hardly mattered. And her mother barely acknowledged she was there. She headed downstairs into the kitchen and pulled out some items to make a sandwich. Her mother was on the back porch in her rocking chair, the place she spent most of her waking hours, staring out into the woods as if a better life were going to materialize from the trees.

Jenny pushed open the back door and stuck her head out. "Momma, I'm making a sandwich. Would you like one?"

Her gray hair was pulled in a tight knot on the top of her head, leaving her face completely exposed. The wrinkles and sun spots made her look even older than she was. She'd aged at least twenty years in the past six.

"Momma?" Jenny called out again when she didn't get an answer.

Her mother slowly shook her head but never spoke and never turned to look at her. Jenny closed the door and went back to the counter, guilt rushing through her. She knew her mother blamed her. Blamed her for going to New Orleans. Blamed her for letting Caitlyn go outside the bar alone. Blamed her for not remembering what happened afterward.

And Jenny blamed herself.

Not for all of it. She wasn't foolish enough to believe she could have prevented Caitlyn from doing anything she was determined to do. Caitlyn had never once listened to Jenny's cautions, and that trip was no exception. But she did blame herself for her lost memory.

She'd always been the sickly one. The one who needed more attention and care. It had frustrated Caitlyn because she got stuck doing a lot for herself while everyone waited on Jenny hand and foot. It frustrated Jenny because she lacked the independence that seemed to ooze from every pore of Caitlyn's body. She'd tried to go about things like a normal girl, but she'd never been able to match even a quarter of Caitlyn's energy and activity. Even trying often left her bedridden for days. Finally, she'd just stopped attempting to be normal at all. She lived her life by halves and forced herself to accept that was the way it would always be.

Now she wasn't even living at half. Some days not even a quarter.

She carried her sandwich to the breakfast table and sat. Her mother's rocker was in front of the window. Jenny always wondered why her mother had picked the rocker, because she never bothered to rock it in. Not that Jenny had seen. Instead, she sat every day, both feet planted firmly on the warped porch wood, forearms on the armrest, and sitting upright, the same way she did in church every Sunday. She wore black polyester slacks and a black blouse with a black sweater. For church, she replaced the slacks with a long black skirt that hung to her ankles. She hadn't altered from that look since the day Jenny's dad died.

Sometimes Jenny thought that if she could remember

what happened—if they could find out what happened to Caitlyn—it might bring her mother back to her, at least in some small way. She'd hoped the dreams would help, but so far they'd done nothing but tease her with her failure. Then Marisa had shown her a story about Shaye Archer in the local newspaper, which spawned the idea of hiring her. Shaye had solved cases that the police hadn't been able to solve. In fact, she'd uncovered crimes they hadn't even been aware of.

Most importantly, she knew what it was like not to know. To have your memory betray you.

If anyone could help, Shaye Archer could. Jenny was counting on it.

9

The law firm Garrett Trahan worked for was housed in the French Quarter in a historic building that was probably worth more than the entire rest of the block. Everything in it had been maintained or restored to the original architecture. Even the furniture and decor were period-accurate. Shaye took note of a vase in the reception area that her mother had priced out when it was for sale at a local gallery. It had cost more than Shaye's SUV. Corrine had great taste and wasn't cheap, but that price had been too high for even her to go along with.

The receptionist was an older woman, probably in her sixties, who had worked for the firm as long as Shaye could remember. She looked up as Shaye approached and smiled.

"Ms. Archer. It's been a long time. I trust you're well."

Somewhat surprised at the genuine tone and expression from the receptionist, Shaye nodded. "Very well, Mrs. Marlowe. Thank you for asking. How are your grandkids?"

The receptionist broke into a smile. "Growing like weeds. My grandson is senior year and wide receiver. His father hasn't stopped grinning since he got the position. My granddaughter was accepted to MIT and started last fall. She's smarter than the rest of us put together."

"That's so good to hear."

"It's been a good year for my family." Her smile faded. "I'm so sorry about everything that happened with yours. I won't linger over words. I just wanted you to know that."

"Thank you."

"Now, how can I help you today?"

"I'd like to speak to Garrett Trahan, but I don't have an appointment."

Mrs. Marlowe frowned. "I don't mean to doubt your selection but are you sure you wouldn't rather talk to one of our older and more experienced counselors?"

"Actually, I need to talk to him about a case I'm working on, not a legal matter."

Mrs. Marlowe's eyes widened. "Oh! I hope he hasn't involved himself in something that would disgrace the firm. I've lodged my own complaints but you know how the good ole boy network takes things."

She picked up the phone. "Mr. Trahan. Shaye Archer would like a moment of your time. She doesn't have an appointment, but if you could spare—yes, she's here now. Of course."

"He can see you now," Mrs. Marlowe said after she hung up the phone. "Third floor, first office on the right."

"Thank you." Shaye started to walk off, then paused. "Would you mind telling me what kind of complaints you lodged against Mr. Trahan?"

Mrs. Marlowe pursed her lips. "He's a bad egg. If there's a spoiled-rich-boy cliché you can think of, he fits it. I don't doubt he's as clever as the partners contend, but he's got a mean streak that one, and a smart mouth. I'm afraid that one day, he's going to cause more problems for this firm than justifies the money he brings in."

"So he treats staff badly?"

"Female staff. If you get what I'm saying."

"I do. Thank you for telling me, and it was good seeing you."

"You too."

Shaye headed for the elevator, mulling over Mrs. Marlowe's insinuations. Bad treatment could run the gamut from denigration and yelling to sexual harassment. Mrs. Marlowe hadn't specified and based on her demeanor, Shaye hadn't figured she would provide more details than she already had, so she hadn't pressed for any. Mrs. Marlowe might not like Garrett Trahan, but she was loyal to her longtime employer. If Shaye decided it was a relevant line of pursuit, she could probably find any number of young female staffers who wouldn't have the same conflict.

Shaye got off the elevator on the third floor and before she could even lift her hand to knock on the office door, it swung open and a young man gave her an up-and-down look, lingering a little too long on areas aside from her face. Shaye held in a sigh. No need to talk to other employees. In less than two seconds, she'd already zeroed in on the problem with Garrett Trahan.

"Shaye Archer," he said, and extended his hand. "The woman, the legend."

Other people had given her this type of compliment and meant it. But based on his tone and the half smirk he wore, Shaye knew he was merely amusing himself. Garrett Trahan had probably never been impressed with anything a woman had done. His ego wouldn't allow it.

"Woman, yes," she said. "I guess legend remains to be seen."

"The century is early yet," he said, and motioned her to a chair. "How can I help you? I know the firm did a lot of work for your grandfather, but I understood your mother recently divested your interest in those holdings. Are you looking to start up your own empire with the proceeds?"

Shaye struggled to maintain a placid expression. She would rather throw the money from an airplane into a brush fire than let the man in front of her get his hands on even one dollar. "I'm afraid I don't have any interest in empire building," she said. "I actually wanted to speak to you about a case I'm working on."

He shifted in his seat and frowned. "What kind of case?"

She held in a smile. He was probably worried he'd harassed the wrong woman and she'd decided to call him on it. "I was hired by Jenny Taylor to look into her sister's disappearance."

His eyes widened. "Wow. That's a blast from the past."

"I understand you were in a relationship with Caitlyn while you were both attending LSU and that she broke it off with you right before her trip to New Orleans?"

"I don't know that 'relationship' is the right word. I mean, we went out, but it wasn't serious. There were always other girls." He gave her a lazy smile that was probably supposed to be sexy.

"I see. Then Caitlyn was also seeing other guys?"

The smile disappeared. "Not that I know of."

"Then I'm confused. I thought it wasn't serious, but if she stopped dating other guys...I mean, my understanding was that Caitlyn had no shortage of pursuers. One only has to look at a picture to see why."

"Yeah, she was a looker. And maybe I spent more time with her than I did with the others, but it's not like we were engaged or anything. It was college, you know? Dating a cheerleader got you points on campus, but she didn't have the family connections I'd need after school. I'm thinking about politics long term."

"You're married now?"

"Still shopping...if you're in the market, I know a place that has great lasagna."

"So do I. My boyfriend's house."

He shrugged. "If that doesn't work out, give me a call. Anyway, what is it you need to know? I've got a meeting with a client in fifteen minutes and I have to prepare."

Clearly, if he couldn't get his hands on her money or her body, Shaye was of no interest to Garrett.

"You ran into Caitlyn and her friends in a bar in New Orleans the night she disappeared. They said you fought."

"We called each other a few names and she left. It was no big deal."

"You were there with friends?"

"I'd ridden in with friends, but we got separated for a bit in the French Quarter. The place was a zoo."

His statement was perfectly reasonable, but Shaye knew he was lying. Garrett Trahan was smooth enough to fool most people, but he didn't fool her. If he got separated from his friends, she had no doubt it was intentional, and likely had everything to do with tracking down Caitlyn.

"Did Caitlyn tell you where she was?"

"Why would she do that? We weren't dating anymore."

"One of her friends thought you might be firing up the old flames again. Just keeping it a secret this time."

"Her friend is smoking something. I don't care what Caitlyn or anyone else says. I didn't follow her to New

Orleans. I didn't have anything to do with her disappearance, and I have no idea what happened to her. But it doesn't surprise me."

"Why do you say that?"

"Because Caitlyn always did whatever she wanted, and what she wanted was usually on the other side of that line that most people walk."

"She took chances?"

He looked her straight in the eye. "Women have to be careful, you know. There's no telling what can happen to them if they're not careful."

"What do you think happened to her?"

"I think she ditched her friends and hooked up with a guy, the same way she did the night I met her at a fraternity mixer. Just this time, she wasn't as lucky."

Shaye heard the buzz of a cell phone and glanced at the phone on his desk. Garrett rose from his chair.

"If that's all," he said. "I have to get ready for my meeting."

Shaye rose from the chair and placed her card on Garrett's desk. "Thank you for your time, Mr. Trahan. If you think of anything else, please give me a call."

He gave her a single nod and she left.

But she could feel his eyes on her as she walked.

It gave her the creeps.

Even more interesting was the call he received right before he rushed her out. The buzz was definitely a cell phone, but the display of the phone on his desk was completely black. And the sound seemed to come from his pants pocket.

Why would Garrett Trahan need two cell phones?

JACKSON GAVE the apartment manager a nod and stepped inside Cody Reynolds's apartment. He gave it a once-over and looked over at Grayson. "It's not what I expected."

"Me either," Grayson agreed.

Jackson had reviewed the background on Reynolds on their way to his apartment. He was originally from Baton Rouge. Had dropped out of school at fifteen and had a sealed juvenile record. Got his GED and did an eight-year stint in the army when he turned eighteen. Was honorably discharged and came to New Orleans, where he'd been ever since. Had bounced around from job to job until he landed at the French Revival, where he'd stuck for the last eight years.

His first four years in New Orleans, he'd been a guest of the NOLA PD several times. Drunk driving, possession of a controlled substance, and three cases of assault, all bar fights. Then his behavior had tapered off into the occasional speeding ticket. He wouldn't win any Man of the Year awards, but his past read like a million other young men who rebelled, went a little wild, then grew up and started taking some responsibility.

Still, the apartment was a lot nicer—and cleaner—than Jackson had expected.

The building was one of those old warehouses that had been converted into apartments. It had that industrial look that appealed well to masculine clientele. High ceilings. Exposed brick and pipes. And huge windows that offered a clear view of the surrounding area. The furniture was simple as well and didn't detract from the architecture of the apartment. Just standard brown leather couch and chairs, a solid blue rug, and glass-and-iron end tables. A large television hung on the wall over the fireplace. The living room was open to the kitchen and dining area, and the theme continued into each connected space.

"Maybe he hired a professional decorator," Grayson said.

"Housekeeper too," Jackson replied.

"Please. I've been to your apartment. You could eat off the floor. It doesn't look bad either."

"Yeah, but my mother helped."

Grayson laughed. "Well, let's hope all this cleanliness also means organization and not just everything shoved in closets and drawers. It will make our job easier. I'll start in the kitchen. You want to take the bedroom?"

"Sure." Jackson headed for the opposite side of the kitchen toward the door that he figured led to the bedroom. It was a one-bedroom apartment, so not too much space to cover.

The bedroom was just as neat as the front rooms, and

Jackson would bet he could do the military quarter bounce on the bed, the linens were pulled so tight. Maybe that was it. Maybe the things he'd been forced to do in the military had stuck. That would explain the neatness, anyway. The rest was probably due to a woman's influence—mother, sister, girlfriend.

He headed into the bathroom first and checked the vanity and the cubby behind the mirror. Neither contained anything outside of normal bathroom items. The bedroom wasn't large and contained the bed, one nightstand, and a dresser. Jackson dug through the dresser, making easy work of the neatly folded and stacked underwear, socks, and tees. Then he moved to the nightstand, which contained cough drops, a television remote, condoms, and a Bible.

Jackson frowned as he looked at the large book in the bottom of the drawer, the condoms perched on the top corner of it. It seemed an odd choice to keep next to his bed, because Reynolds didn't appear to be the type of guy who'd read the Bible before sleeping. At least he didn't seem that way on paper. Family heirloom, maybe?

He reached in to grab the Bible and knew immediately what was going on. It was much heavier than it should have been. He opened it up and pulled a nine-millimeter from the cutout inside.

"Take a look at this," Jackson called out.

When Grayson walked into the room, Jackson showed him the Bible and the gun.

"Interesting," Grayson said. "So he had a gun, but he didn't take it with him to the cemetery."

"More proof that he knew who he was meeting and didn't think he had any reason to fear them. He was wrong about that one. You find anything?"

"Just neatly stacked dishes and a pantry that looks like the one from that movie with Julia Roberts."

"*Sleeping with the Enemy?*"

"That's the one."

"Maybe that's it. Maybe it was an ex who took him out."

"If he'd been shot, I'd be on board with that theory, but what kind of woman risks a head shot to a guy Reynolds's size? She'd have to take him down with the first blow or he'd kill her."

"Why are you assuming the ex is a woman?"

"Well, hell. I don't know, but you're right. Anything to indicate a relationship in here?"

"Just condoms, but that doesn't clarify things either. I still need to check the closet."

Grayson nodded. "Let's get it done and head over to the bar. Maybe his coworkers can shed some light on things."

Jackson pulled open the closet doors and started checking the pockets of pants, which were all hung on the left. Grayson began with shirts, all hanging on the right. The shoes were lined neatly across the bottom and a review came up with nothing inside them. The top of the closet held spare pillows and blankets and two shoeboxes. Jackson pulled the shoeboxes down and placed them on the bed.

"This looks like receipts," Grayson said. "I'll bring it with us to go through later. What do you have?"

"Looks like personal items. Some newspaper clippings about his service with the military. His discharge papers. Passport. And a stack of photos." Jackson pulled the photos out and handed Grayson half the stack.

"He's got names on the back," Grayson said. "Maybe we can narrow down that ex thing."

Jackson flipped through the photos, mostly featuring Reynolds with his army buddies and several with Reynolds and some children. No children had popped up in the background check so Jackson assumed they belonged to a relative or friend, but he'd ask Reynolds's coworkers and dig a little deeper into things just to be sure.

He flipped past a picture of Reynolds posing with fish and stopped when he saw a pic of Reynolds with a pretty blonde. She was younger than him and looked vaguely familiar. He flipped the photo over and read the inscription.

Me and Caitlyn.

Shit! That's why the girl looked familiar.

"What's wrong?" Grayson asked. "You have that look like you ate something bad."

Jackson showed Grayson the picture. "The woman in this photo went missing from the French Revival six years ago. She was never found."

"Wow. You remember a missing person from six years ago? That's some serious facial recall."

"No. I remember her from a picture from a case file Shaye showed me last night. This girl's sister hired her yesterday to look into this. It went cold with the department years ago."

Grayson's look of dismay reflected exactly how Jackson felt. Most cops were past the situation that had been exposed regarding their former police chief, and most had never really blamed her for what happened. But many held a grudge because she'd been the catalyst, even though they knew the truth needed to come out. Still, the mandate forbidding police involvement with civilians regarding investigations had been made clear almost daily for weeks. And everyone knew why.

Intentionally or not, Shaye had set forward the chain of events that exposed some unpleasant things about the police department. The last thing the new administration wanted was to give her an inroad to do it again.

"Does Shaye know anything about Reynolds?"

"I don't know. I was so tired I wasn't awake for long. She only told me that she'd taken on a missing persons case, and I saw the photo paper clipped to her file. I think she questioned a bartender last night, but I can't remember the details. Which is why Reynolds's name and the bar didn't raise a red flag. My mind was kinda shot."

"We're going to have to bring her in for questioning," Grayson said. "I'm sorry, man."

"Don't apologize. Shaye won't mind. She knows how it works. Besides, she's going to want to know who killed Reynolds as much as we do, maybe more."

"You said her client was the missing girl's sister?"

"Twin. Shaye said she's been a mess ever since."

"Let's just hope being depressed is all she has to deal with."

Jackson nodded. He'd already thought the same thing. The timing of Reynolds's death and Shaye's investigation was definitely suspicious. And if Reynolds had known more than he'd told the police, then someone could be cleaning house.

Which meant Jenny Taylor might be in danger.

10

SHAYE WALKED INTO THE POLICE STATION AND SMILED at the desk sergeant, Robert Royer. He'd been a fixture at the station for thirty-two years and at the desk since his knee sidelined him from the more active aspects of police work. He returned her smile. Sergeant Royer had remained one member of the department who was always happy to see her.

"Ms. Archer," he said. "How are you doing?"

"I'm good. Thank you. How is Susan?"

"She's taking a pottery class, and we're overrun with ashtrays. The fact that no one smokes is apparently lost on her. She says she's working her way up to a vase."

Shaye laughed. "Please tell her I said hello. My mother was asking about her the other day. You know she's starting up her own corporation to help kids? I think she was hoping that Susan would be interested in helping with some of the setup, particularly the rules for the living quarters."

Sergeant Royer and his wife had fostered children and knew the complications one experienced taking on kids who had issues to address. "I'm sure she'd be willing to do anything to help," Royer said. "We're very excited about what Corrine is doing. It's going to make a huge difference for the children in the community."

"That's the plan. I'll remind her to give Susan a call. I'm here to see Detective Grayson."

Royer nodded. "They're in room two."

"Thanks," Shaye said and headed down the hallway. She'd been in the station enough times to know exactly where she was going. The burning question in her mind was why she'd been called there. She hoped her new case hadn't ruffled feathers already, but she'd crossed no legal or ethical lines and neither had Jackson. Still, getting the phone call from Grayson earlier had her worried, and the two-hour delay she'd had before the meeting had left her even more worried.

The fact that Jackson hadn't contacted her reinforced her thought that somewhere, somehow, her actions had crossed into police territory. Shaye had made Jackson promise to never risk getting on management's radar with his relationship with her. That meant no contact about police work, especially when he was on the clock. Their interaction during the day was mostly limited to texts and then only what time they were meeting. If the department subpoenaed Jackson's phone records, they wouldn't find anything to complain about.

Jackson and Grayson were already in the room when she entered, both sitting and talking low over some papers. When she walked in, Jackson jumped up and pulled out a chair for her, motioning to her to sit.

"Thank you for coming down here," Grayson said. "I know it's a disruption to your day but unfortunately, this couldn't wait."

"What's wrong?" Shaye asked. Grayson's tone was serious, not aggravated. Something had happened. Something that involved her. "Is it Clancy? Did they find something else in the records?"

"It's not Clancy," Jackson said. "It's Cody Reynolds."

"The bartender at the French Revival?" Shaye asked, completely confused. "Did he file a complaint? He agreed to talk to me."

"He's dead," Jackson said. "Murdered."

Shaye's mouth dropped open. Of all the things she'd imagined she might hear, that wasn't even in the dark reaches of her thoughts. "When? How?"

"This morning in Metairie Cemetery," Grayson said. "Jackson said he thought you interviewed him last night. Can you tell me about that conversation?"

"Sure." Shaye recounted her exchange with Reynolds, including her observations on his behavior before, during, and after the interview, because she knew that was part of what Grayson wanted as much as the actual dialogue.

"And you didn't notice any nervousness?" Grayson asked when she finished.

Shaye shook her head. "If he was worried about anything he certainly didn't show it."

"The other employees at the bar have him labeled a 'cool customer,'" Grayson said. "Apparently, they had trouble getting a read on him too, and some of them had known him for several years. No one seems to know much about him. At least not that they're saying."

Shaye nodded, still trying to wrap her head around the fact that the man she'd just talked to the night before was now lying on a slab in the morgue. What wasn't lost on her at all was everything that Grayson wasn't saying.

"Do you think it has something to do with my case?" she asked.

"His wallet was intact, so it wasn't robbery," Grayson said. "Our guess is he went there to meet someone. He had a pistol in his apartment that he left behind, so we're also assuming it was someone he knew."

"And wasn't afraid of," Shaye said.

Jackson looked over at Grayson, and he nodded. "We found this when we searched his apartment."

Shaye took one look at the photo and gasped. "That's Caitlyn. Or Jenny."

"The back says 'Me and Caitlyn,'" Jackson said. "There's no date, so we have no way of knowing when it was taken. But even if Reynolds is telling the truth about that night, he lied about recognizing the photo you showed him. Clearly, he knew Caitlyn, and the body language in this photo doesn't look like the kind between people who are just friends."

"No," Shaye agreed. "It looks like they were involved. One of Caitlyn's friends thought she was seeing someone on the sly—someone they probably wouldn't approve of —but Reynolds never crossed my mind. How could I have missed this?"

"I wouldn't take it as a reflection of your ability," Grayson said. "The employees at the bar were all surprised when I showed them the photo, and I don't think any of them were faking. If Reynolds was involved with Caitlyn, it appears it was so well kept that no one who knew either of them was aware."

Jackson nodded. "And after Caitlyn disappeared, Reynolds probably figured it was in his best interest to keep his mouth shut permanently."

"Well, he did a stellar job then," Shaye said. "I completely bought his act."

"I think everyone did," Jackson said.

"Apparently, one person didn't," Shaye said. "But the question is why? I get Cody keeping his mouth shut so that he didn't become a suspect in Caitlyn's disappearance, but why was he killed now? And if it's because of my investigation, then that tells me he knew something or was part of something, but he wasn't the only one."

"We're looking at other avenues, of course," Grayson said. "There's always a chance his murder has nothing to do with your case."

"But that's not what your gut tells you, is it?" she asked.

"No," Grayson said. "I think we all have the same opinion on the matter, which is why we're giving you information. If hiring you prompted this, then it might not stop with Reynolds."

Shaye nodded. "Jenny and her friends could be at risk for hiring me."

"Or one of them knows something they're not telling you," Jackson said. "Cody Reynolds certainly wasn't forthcoming with his answers. Maybe he's not the only one."

"I'm sure you dumped his phone," Shaye said. "Did he contact someone? Did someone contact him? What about the phone at the bar? The meet at the cemetery had to be arranged sometime, and if they went to such trouble to avoid being seen, I can't imagine the person who killed him waltzing into the bar to set it up. Or risking being seen at Reynolds's apartment, for that matter."

"We dumped his cell and the phone at the bar," Grayson said. "One number was called from both places, and the first call was shortly after you questioned Reynolds. There were no text messages. We've subpoenaed them from the phone company but that will take a while. Unfortunately, the number belonged to a prepaid phone and it's turned off."

"It's probably at the bottom of a bayou now," Shaye said.

"Probably," Grayson agreed. "Anyway, we don't have anything else to go on, but I thought you needed to know about Reynolds. I assume you'll be questioning your clients more about their knowledge of Caitlyn and Reynolds's relationship, and I needed to make you aware that we will be as well. I'm not asking you to step back from the case. Caitlyn's disappearance is not our primary concern. Just how it relates to Reynolds's murder."

Shaye nodded. "I get it. I'm sorry our paths had to cross this way. I know it makes things more difficult for both of you." She frowned. "What happened to the kidnapping? Weren't you supposed to be on that day and night?"

"That's a long story that I'm sure Jackson will share with you later," Grayson said. "But the short explanation is a congressman and the FBI."

"Oh," Shaye said, immediately understanding the implications. "I'm sorry. I think it's a mistake to take you off the case. I know that doesn't help, but it's the way I feel."

"I appreciate that," Grayson said. "Well, Jackson and I need to get out of here. We need to make the drive to Baton Rouge to speak with Reynolds's parents. We want to make the notification in person."

"Hey," Shaye said. "There's someone you need to talk to—Garrett Trahan. Caitlyn had just broken up with him before she disappeared, and they fought in a bar earlier that night. She accused him of following her, but his friends alibied him, although I doubt they're telling the truth. I talked to him this morning and was less than impressed."

She told them about her conversation with Garrett and the phone buzzing before she left.

Grayson nodded. "We'll have a talk with Mr. Trahan tomorrow."

Shaye nodded. "Stay safe. Both of you. And if there's anything else I can do..."

She rose from her chair and gave Jackson a small smile as she headed out, their entire exchange running through her head. So many unanswered questions. If Cody didn't know anything about Caitlyn's disappearance, then why was he killed? And assuming the killer had known about Cody's involvement or knowledge all along, why wait six years to kill him? Because of her investigation? That seemed weak. Cody had managed to keep it all a secret this long. Why take the risk to kill him now, when his murder would immediately be associated with her case? If someone thought he was a liability, it would have been easier to kill him years ago, when Caitlyn's case was collecting dust.

SHAYE LEFT the police station and directed her SUV onto the highway toward Ponchatoula. Jackson and Grayson's priority was interviewing the victim's parents in Baton Rouge, which left her client and friends for the next day. But Shaye didn't want to wait a day for them to receive word of what had happened. They needed to be on alert that Reynolds's death might have something to do with the investigation, and Shaye needed to give them an opportunity to change their minds about moving forward. She wouldn't really blame them if they did. It was a horrible feeling, walking around with a target on your back, constantly looking over your shoulder and unable to trust anyone. For six years, they'd been left to grieve in silence. Shaye didn't believe for a moment that Reynolds's murder was unrelated to her case. The timing was too exact.

She checked her GPS as she drove through the quaint downtown and directed her vehicle down one of the farm roads outside of town. Houses were spaced by rolling acres of farmland and woods now, each so far from the other that they enjoyed complete privacy. Shaye could appreciate the sprawling land and the way the stars looked at night when there were no city lights to dim their glow, but she couldn't see herself living that far away from everything. As much as she was an introvert who preferred to avoid social events, she also liked living in the center of anything she might need. Especially restaurants. Cooking was likely something she was never going to take a liking to.

The GPS indicated she'd reached her destination and she slowed, almost missing the narrow dirt road on her right. The sun was starting to set, and the woods cast dark shadows over the overgrown land. She could see a house about a hundred feet into the property and figured that must be the place. She drove slowly, attempting to dodge the worst of the holes, and finally arrived at what appeared to be an old church, complete with steeple. The white paint was peeling and some of the siding was loose and had slipped but with a little work, it could be charming. Of course, that work also required money, and since Marisa had covered Jenny's retainer, that was probably where the gap existed.

She knocked on the door and waited. Light shone through the sheers covering the front window, and there was an old Cadillac out front, so she hoped that meant Jenny and her mother were at home. She waited a bit, then knocked again. When no one answered, she stepped off the porch and decided to walk around to the back of the house. They might have livestock or some other chore to handle in the evening.

The grass, what there was left of it, needed mowing, but she picked her way through the lawn to the back of the house. There was a structure that looked like a chicken coop some ways from the house and an old barn even farther, but neither looked as if it'd been used recently. A shed sat closer to the house, but there was an outside latch and it was drawn. She heard a noise to her left and looked over to see an elderly woman sitting on the back porch in a rocking chair. Grandmother, maybe?

She headed for the steps and walked up, noticing that

the woman never bothered to look at her, just kept staring directly out at the woods behind the barn.

"Excuse me, ma'am," Shaye said. "I'm looking for Mrs. Taylor."

The woman shifted her eyes to Shaye but never moved her head. "You found her. Ain't got no money for what you're selling."

"I'm not selling anything. I'm a private investigator from New Orleans. I'd like to talk to you about your daughter."

Virginia sighed. "What's Jenny done now?"

"I meant Caitlyn. Jenny hired me to look into her disappearance."

That comment got more than a tired response. She looked up at Shaye, her brow scrunched. "Jenny don't drive. Never has. And she don't have money."

"Her friends brought her—Marisa and Rick—and Marisa covered my retainer."

Virginia shook her head. "Marisa was always a good girl and she's a good woman, but she needs to let this go. Needs to let Jenny go and move on with her own life. No need in Jenny keeping all of us in the past. Well, if you're going to keep talking, sit on that bench there. Hurts my neck to look up at you."

Shaye took a seat across from Virginia. "Do you mind my asking about Jenny's health? I get the impression she's not well and hasn't been for some time. I don't want to make things worse."

"Can't make something worse if it's already at rock

bottom. Jenny's been unwell since the womb. The doctors said Caitlyn was taking more than her share of nutrients and such and it left Jenny sickly. Spent two months in the hospital before we could bring her home. Never quite got right. If someone in the next parish sneezed, she caught their cold. If she fell, she'd bruise and her muscles would knot quicker than other kids. Probably could have paid for a new Cadillac with all the money I spent on doctors and medicine."

Shaye nodded, the comments others had made about Jenny's health now making sense. "That must have been difficult for you. Jenny lives here with you and Mr. Taylor now, right?"

"She lives here, but there ain't no Mr. Taylor anymore. He went into the grave a year after Caitlyn disappeared. Heart attack. Men of his generation didn't talk about feelings and such. Maybe he'd have lived longer if he did."

"You think the stress killed him?"

Virginia shrugged. "His heart wasn't great to begin with, and he was almost a decade older than me, so no spring chicken. Neither am I, for that matter." She looked at Shaye. "You're wondering about my age, aren't you? Probably thought I was Jenny's grandmother when you set eyes on me."

Because that's exactly what she thought, Shaye elected to remain silent.

"People always did, mind you," Virginia said. "Even when they was little, it was clear I was a lot older than most mothers. Roy and I tried for years to have a baby and it never happened. Finally, we gave up and figured it wasn't God's will. Then I turned forty-two and I came up pregnant. Could have knocked me over with a feather. Heck, I was sick for two months before Roy made me go to the doctor. Didn't even guess..."

Shaye quickly did the math and put Virginia's age at sixty-nine or so, which was older than what she expected to find, but still younger than Virginia looked. Shaye would have guessed the woman was closer to eighty than seventy.

"I suppose after all that time you wouldn't guess you were pregnant," Shaye said. "It must have been a shock."

"That's one word for it. And not just pregnant but pregnant at forty-two with twins. Heck, by that age, I was supposed to be worrying about college or weddings. Never thought I'd be chasing toddlers long after the time I was fit to go chasing anyone. But I'm sure that ain't what you came for, so go ahead and ask your questions."

Shaye pulled out her phone and showed Virginia a picture of Cody Reynolds. "Do you recognize this man?"

Virginia looked at the picture for a couple of seconds, then shook her head. "Should I?"

"I think he was someone Caitlyn dated. Might even have been dating when she disappeared. He was a bartender at the bar she disappeared from and was working that night."

"I don't know nothing about him, but Caitlyn did a lot of things I probably don't know about. We did our best with her, but she was a willful one. If she wanted it, wasn't God or nobody getting in her way."

"The reason I'm here tonight is because this man was murdered today, and I think it might have something to do with Jenny asking me to look into Caitlyn's disappearance."

Virginia stared at Shaye as if she didn't quite believe what she'd heard. "Murdered?"

"Yes, ma'am. I interviewed him yesterday and he called someone right after, but the number he called can't be traced. He went to Metairie Cemetery this morning—the police think to meet someone—and that someone killed him."

"Lots of people get killed in those cemeteries. Lots of crime in the city. That's why I live out here."

"It wasn't a robbery. His wallet wasn't taken, and he had cash inside. The police also agree that the timing of his death and my investigation are suspicious. They'll probably be here at some point to ask you and Jenny some questions, but I felt you needed the information as soon as possible."

"Well, I appreciate your sense of responsibility, but I don't know what I'll do with that information. I'm sorry the young man was killed, but I can't see as how it matters to me."

"It's possible that this man knew something about Caitlyn's disappearance. Something the person who killed him didn't want us to know. But it's strange that he waited all these years to eliminate Reynolds as a threat. If my taking this case has someone spooked, then it's possible that person could come after Jenny, Marisa, or Rick, or even you."

"I see. You're worried she's done stirred up a hornet's nest." She sighed. "Sometimes it's better to let sleeping dogs lie. My daughter is gone. Knowing how it happened doesn't change a thing."

The sadness in her voice made Shaye's heart clench. This woman had lost her daughter years ago and had decided that the cause didn't matter. Although Shaye had never felt that way about her own unanswered questions, she understood how some people did. Everyone had their own way of coping and Virginia's way was blanket acceptance. Unfortunately, Jenny couldn't follow the same path and had kept them both mired in the past.

"I'm really sorry for what happened," Shaye said. "I can't imagine the pain of losing a child."

Virginia tilted her head to the side. "But you know a thing or two about loss yourself. I seen you on the TV. You had a hard time of it. The fact that you came out of it like you did speaks to your own convictions and that of the people around you. I sometimes think if I'd done things different...but then, I don't know what different would have been."

"I'm sure you did everything you could. Jenny is lucky to have you to care for her."

Virginia nodded. "I worry about what will happen when I'm gone, but then I guess I'll be cold in the grave and it won't matter. Not to me."

"Is Jenny home?"

"Upstairs in her room. Been quiet most of the day. Guess now I know why."

"I don't want to upset her, but I feel like she needs to know the risks of my continuing to work on the case. I want to give her the opportunity to stop the investigation."

"Go ahead in and try, but I doubt she'll change her mind. Once it's made up, that's all she wrote."

Shaye thanked the woman and headed into the house, through the tiny kitchen and toward the front of the house where she found the stairs. They were narrow and somewhat steep and ended at a small landing with a single door. Shaye knocked on the door and called out.

"Jenny? It's Shaye Archer. I'd like to talk to you if that's all right."

She heard movement inside and a couple seconds later, the door swung open and Jenny looked out at her. Her hair was disheveled and although she was fully dressed, her clothes were rumpled as if she'd been asleep in them.

"Do you want to talk here?" Shaye asked when Jenny stood silently. "Or would you like to go downstairs?"

"Here is fine," Jenny said. "I have a chair you can sit on. I'll just sit on the bed if that's all right."

"Whatever you'd like," Shaye said.

Jenny stood back and allowed Shaye to enter the room. If it hadn't been so run-down and if there wasn't an oppressive air to the place, it could have been charming.

Instead, it was what Shaye would describe as sparse. The basics of furniture and linens and that was it. No frilly pillows. The only things hanging on the walls were two sad-looking floral paintings.

Shaye took a seat in the chair Jenny had indicated and watched as Jenny perched on the end of the bed, still not meeting Shaye's eyes.

"How are you feeling today?" Shaye asked.

"A little tired, but that's no different from any other day."

"I'm sorry. Everything is so much harder when you're not feeling well."

Jenny shrugged. "Got nothing to do but sit here anyway. Being tired doesn't make a difference. Sleeping makes the time pass quicker besides."

"I wanted to ask you some questions about Caitlyn. Is that all right?"

Jenny looked up at her and nodded. Shaye pulled her phone out and rose from the chair, approaching the bed. She held the phone up so that Jenny could see the image of Cody Reynolds.

"Do you recognize this man?" Shaye asked.

Jenny looked at the image for a bit, frowned, then finally shook her head. "I don't but I feel like I should."

"His name is Cody Reynolds. Does that name ring a bell?"

"I don't think so."

"He was a bartender at the French Revival and was working the night Caitlyn disappeared."

"Oh. Maybe that's why I thought I should recognize him. I probably saw him there that night, right?"

"It's possible. But you've never seen him any other time?"

Jenny shook her head.

"Did Caitlyn ever mention his name?"

"Not that I can remember. Why?"

"Because I have reason to believe that Caitlyn and Mr. Reynolds were involved."

Jenny's eyes widened and she looked at the image again. "You mean, like dating?"

"Yes."

"But he lived in New Orleans, right?"

Shaye nodded, and Jenny frowned.

"What are you thinking?" Shaye asked.

"I remember Marisa saying something about Caitlyn disappearing on weekends. I guess we figured she was with Garrett. Caitlyn stayed pretty busy with boyfriends. She usually had one or two."

"Did she have a boyfriend when you went to New Orleans?"

"I don't think so. I mean, she'd been going out with that awful Garrett Trahan, but she swore that was over. I never liked him. None of us did. He always thought he was better than the rest of us. And he was using Caitlyn. I'm sure of it. He followed her to New Orleans. Did you know that?"

"I know that's what Caitlyn accused him of. I talked to Mr. Trahan earlier today, but he denies her claim."

"Did you believe him?"

"I'm not sure. I *am* certain I didn't like him."

Jenny gave her a rueful smile. "That's because you've got good taste."

Shaye studied Jenny for a bit. Her skin was even paler than it had been in Shaye's office, and the circles under her eyes were darker. Jenny might be getting plenty of sleep, but it didn't appear restful. Could she handle what Shaye needed to tell her? Or should she talk to Marisa about it and let the other woman decide? Virginia didn't seem all that worried about the potential for danger and certainly showed no interest in attempting to tell Jenny what to do.

It can come from you or Detective Grayson.

She held in a sigh. Ultimately the decision wasn't whether or not to let Jenny know what had happened, because that was going to happen one way or another. The decision was whether to deliver that news herself tonight or let the police do it later. As much as Shaye hated putting additional stress on the already-frail young woman, she couldn't in good conscience leave there tonight without telling her what had happened. She had an obligation to her client.

"I have some bad news," Shaye said.

Jenny sat up straight, looking slightly distressed. "You're quitting, aren't you?"

"Not unless you want me to."

"Why would I want that? I just hired you."

"The man I showed you—Cody Reynolds—was

murdered this morning. The police think it has something to do with my investigation."

Jenny's eyes widened. "Do you think he's the one? Did he do something to Caitlyn?"

"I don't know, but if he did, he wasn't alone. And that other person didn't want him to talk. Jenny, I interviewed Cody yesterday. The police don't think the timing is a coincidence."

"You interviewed him? Did he say he was dating Caitlyn?"

"He claimed he'd never seen her before the police showed him a picture the day after her disappearance when they came to question everyone in the bar."

"But you said they were dating."

"The police found a picture of Mr. Reynolds and Caitlyn in his apartment. They looked like a couple."

"He lied. All this time...but why?"

"I think if we knew that, we'd know what happened to Caitlyn. And I'm not trying to scare you, but there's a chance that the same person who hurt Mr. Reynolds might come after you or Marisa or Rick to try to stop the investigation."

Jenny grabbed Shaye's hand. "You can't stop. Promise me you won't stop until you're certain you can't get me answers. If you can't, well, I'll figure out how to handle that."

"I won't quit unless you ask me to, but I need to be certain that you understand you might be in danger."

"Then that means you are too, right?"

"Yes. But that's part of my job, and I'm trained to protect myself against that kind of threat. You're not."

"I'll be okay. What's the worst that can happen? He gets me too? Either way, my problems are solved."

"You can't think that way. It's not productive, and I know you want answers."

"I do. And sometimes I think I'm going to get them, then I wake up disappointed again."

"Are you still dreaming about Caitlyn?"

"All the time. But lately, it's different. I'm starting to see things at the bar—things I never remembered. Today I remembered going into the alley and Marisa pulling me back inside and talking to Rick, but I don't remember anything she said or what happened in between. That's got to be it, right? The thing that will answer all of it?"

"Maybe. But there is no guarantee. For all we know, Caitlyn might have left the bar and walked down the street. Whatever happened to her might have been in a completely different location than the French Revival."

Jenny looked disappointed. "I guess that's true. But I still feel like it's there, you know?"

Shaye nodded. "I know exactly. And I also know you can't force it to happen. When you're ready, the memories might come. Or they might be gone forever. It's impossible to know."

"But yours came back, right?"

"Yes, but even now, I'm still remembering things I didn't before. I'll have no way of knowing if I've remembered everything. Each time I think it's all come out, I dream about something new or a previously unrecalled memory is just there, like a flash of lightning."

"Does it frighten you?"

"Yes. Then I remind myself to breathe and force myself to remain calm. Your memories can't hurt you unless you let them."

"Thank you for being honest. Most people would have lied to make me feel better, which is nice but not helpful. I'm sorry, but I'm really tired. Can we talk again later? I need to rest."

"Of course." Shaye headed out of the room, glancing back as she pulled the door shut behind her. Jenny was already laying back on the bed, curled into a ball like a child, her shoulders shaking. Shaye wanted to comfort her, but she had no idea how and was afraid anything she did right now would only embarrass the distraught woman.

She headed downstairs and almost collided with Virginia, who was turning on the porch light near the front door.

"Couldn't change her mind, could you?" Virginia asked.

"No. She's upset, even though she didn't want me to know it. You might want to check on her."

"Always have. Always will."

She sounded as exhausted as Jenny looked.

"Good night," Shaye said. "And thank you for your time."

Virginia nodded and walked past Shaye toward the

kitchen. Shaye took that as her cue to leave and hurried out to her SUV, beyond ready to get out of that house. It felt as if a dark cloud hung over the structure and everyone in it. She started her vehicle, trying to put her finger on what it reminded her of. Then it hit her.

The morgue.

11

JACKSON WALKED UP THE SIDEWALK NEXT TO GRAYSON and waited while he knocked on the door of Cody Reynolds's parents' house. It was a small brick home, built in the '70s, with overgrown landscaping and peeling paint on the trim. A quick background had shown that Reynolds's father, Peter, was a mechanic at a locally owned auto repair shop and his mother, Sue, was a waitress at a nearby café. Neither had a police record, and Jackson figured they were probably a typical blue-collar family.

The background check also revealed that Cody was an only child, which made Jackson even more sad about what they were about to do. Not that having multiple children diminished the loss of another, but when there was only one and they were lost, there was nothing left at all. Grayson rang the doorbell and shifted to his professional face. He'd done family notification more times than he could probably count, but based on his huge lapses into silence on the drive there, Jackson knew it hadn't gotten any easier, even if the senior detective had gotten more proficient at it.

The door swung open and Peter Reynolds looked out at them. Grayson pulled out his badge. "Peter Reynolds? My name is Detective Grayson and this is Detective Lamotte from the New Orleans Police Department. We need to speak with you."

Peter looked back and forth between the two of them, and then his shoulders slumped as he stepped back for them to enter.

He already knows.

The older man's body language told the entire story. Two detectives from New Orleans showing up at his front door could only mean something had happened to Cody. Jackson's gut clenched as he thought about what kind of devastation Grayson's words would deliver. Seeing what had happened to the victims was the worst part of his job, but this was definitely second.

They followed Peter to the rear of the house, where Sue was pulling a mixing bowl out of a kitchen cabinet. She frowned when they walked in, then looked at Peter and set the bowl down. It was impossible to ignore the general feeling of gloom that had descended over the room.

"These are detectives from New Orleans," Peter said to Sue. "They need to talk to us. You best come sit down."

Sue stiffened, then left the kitchen and joined her husband on the couch. Grayson and Jackson sat in two chairs placed in front the fireplace. One of the first things Jackson had learned was to sit when delivering this kind of horrible news. It was more human, less domineering.

"I'm sorry to have to tell you this," Grayson said, "but your son, Cody, was killed this morning."

Sue cried out and covered her face with her hands, immediately sobbing. Peter put his arm around her and pulled her close, burying his face in her hair. Jackson could hear him mumbling but couldn't make out what he said. Jackson and Grayson sat silently, giving the grieving parents some time to process the shocking information. It rarely took more than a minute or two before they started asking questions, but every minute felt like an hour to Jackson. Finally, Sue lowered her hands and Peter kissed her forehead.

"Can you tell us how it happened?" Peter asked.

Unfortunately, there was no gentle way to deliver that information.

"Your son was murdered," Grayson said.

Sue gasped and clasped her hands to her chest. Peter's eyes widened, and he stared at them in disbelief, then slowly, his expression shifted to one of anger.

"I told him working in a bar would be nothing but trouble," Peter said. "And in the French Quarter? So much crime down there."

"He wasn't killed at the bar," Grayson said. "In fact,

we don't think his death had anything to do with his work."

"Robbery?" Peter asked.

"No," Grayson said, and described the circumstances of Cody's death.

When he was finished, Peter shook his head. "I don't understand. Why would Cody meet someone who was threatening him?"

"Cody had a pistol in his apartment," Grayson said. "Our assumption is that he didn't think the person he went to meet was a threat."

"Then why?" Peter asked. "None of this makes sense."

"I agree," Grayson said. "We talked to all of Cody's coworkers earlier and his landlord, but no one has offered an explanation for what might have happened or a guess as to whom Cody went to meet. We'll check the background of everyone he worked with, and their alibis, and we'll push them all again to see if they know more than they said. But you might be able to help."

"I don't see how. Cody left for the service as soon as he was eligible and went straight to New Orleans when he got out. He came by to visit from time to time and he called every week, but he never shared much about his personal life. The truth is we have no idea what he might have been mixed up in."

"Out of curiosity," Jackson finally said, "why do you assume Cody was mixed up in something?"

"Habit, I guess," Peter said. "He wasn't an easy child,

and he was an impossible teen. Stubborn and defiant. Wouldn't listen to a thing and thought rules were for suckers. That's exactly what he'd tell me when I tried to discipline him. Shocked the hell out of me when he joined the army. I figured he wouldn't last a day, but he surprised us all by sticking it out. I thought maybe he'd grown up but when he got out, he bounced around from bar to bar, nothing ever sticking. And I know he was in trouble with the law a time or two. That sort of thing is public, and we've got friends with kids in New Orleans. Word gets around."

"Especially when it's negative gossip," Sue said.

Jackson nodded. It was an unfortunate truth that a lot of people took great satisfaction from the misery of others, especially if they got to contribute to it.

"If you don't mind," Grayson said, "I'd like to ask you some questions anyway. I understand if you don't have answers."

"We'll do anything to help," Peter said, and Sue nodded.

Grayson pulled a photo of Caitlyn Taylor from the file he held and showed it to the couple. "Do either of you recognize this young woman?"

They both looked at the photo and shook their heads.

"Did Cody know her?" Peter asked.

Grayson nodded. "We found a photo of the two of them in his apartment." Grayson pulled out the photo and showed them the picture as well as the inscription on the back. "The body language suggests they were in a relationship."

"Appears so," Peter said, "but we never met anyone he dated and he never talked about it. Do you think his death has something to do with this girl? Maybe he was meeting her and that's why he didn't take his pistol?"

"The woman in this photo is Caitlyn Taylor. She disappeared six years ago on Mardi Gras from the bar where Cody worked," Grayson said. "Her disappearance remains unsolved."

Peter's eyes widened. "And you think Cody had something to do with it? Why?"

"Possibly," Grayson said. "Or it's possible he knew something that he never told the police. The sister of the missing girl hired a private detective yesterday to look into this. That PI questioned Cody last night at the bar. He made a call from the bar and later from his cell phone to a prepaid cell phone that we can't trace to anyone."

"And then he went to a cemetery and was murdered," Peter said and blew out a breath. "That's not good."

"No. It's not," Grayson agreed. "And it could be a coincidence, but the timing is highly suspicious."

"I don't think any of us thinks it's a coincidence," Peter said, his voice weary. "He's worked in that bar for all these years without incident, then after being questioned by a PI, he calls someone on a number you can't trace, likely to set up that meeting, and was killed. I'm no detective, but that seems pretty straightforward to me."

"I'm very sorry," Grayson said.

"Don't be," Peter said. "If Cody had something to do with that woman's disappearance, then he made his own bed."

"How can you say that?" Sue cried, choking on the last words. "We lost our son."

"I can say it because it's the truth," Peter said. "Another family lost their daughter, and everything points to Cody having a hand in it. Besides, the truth is, we lost Cody a long time ago. I'm really sorry, Detectives. I wish I knew something that could help, but we didn't have insight into our son's life. Haven't for a long time."

Grayson nodded. "I understand. Did Cody have any friends from high school that he stayed in touch with, or perhaps someone who served with him? Someone who might know more about his personal life?"

"There was one guy," Peter said. "Came here with Cody once when they were delivering an AC unit to me that Cody had bought cheap from the bar when they replaced one in an office upstairs. First name was Brennan but I never got a last name. Had that posture like he'd served, you know?"

"I do and it will make him easier to track down," Grayson said and handed Peter cards for himself and Jackson. "If you think of anything else, please call us. Anytime."

Peter took the cards and stared at them for a couple seconds. "What about...I mean, I guess I need to make arrangements..."

"The coroner will contact you when he can release the body," Grayson said.

Peter nodded. "Thank you for coming here to tell us in person."

"Of course." Grayson rose from his chair and Jackson followed him outside.

"You think they're telling the truth?" Jackson asked as he climbed into the passenger's seat.

"Yeah. Everything he said fits what we know of Reynolds's history."

Jackson nodded. He thought the facts fit the parents' story as well. "Let's hope this Brennan knows something. Because his coworkers didn't appear to, and I didn't get a feeling any of them were hedging things either."

"No," Grayson agreed. "It appears that Mr. Reynolds had a secret life that very few knew about."

"Maybe no one."

"At least one person knew. Because that person killed him."

SHAYE PULLED up in front of the small home that Rick and Marisa rented and walked up the sidewalk. The SUV they'd been driving when they came to her office was parked in the driveway along with a late-model sedan. Shaye had called on the way over, and Marisa had said she'd be at home but Rick was working late. Either he'd finished up earlier than he thought or he'd been too curious about Shaye's visit to miss it. Regardless, she was happy she would only have to have this conversation once. If she thought one of them was holding back, she'd address it with them individually later.

The front door swung open before she knocked, and Marisa motioned her inside.

"Is your daughter napping?" Shaye asked. The house was quiet, which wasn't common with a toddler about.

"No. I'd just left the grocery store when I got your call, so I dropped her off at my parents'. I figured it would be easier to talk that way. Rick's in the kitchen."

Shaye followed her through the small but neat living room and into a room that served as both kitchen and dining room. Rick pulled a beer from the refrigerator and held it up.

"I've got beer, soda, and water," he said.

"Water would be great," Shaye said.

Marisa pointed to a square table in the breakfast nook. "Would it be okay to sit there? I need to pop a lasagna in the oven."

"Whatever is most convenient for you," Shaye said and took a seat at the table. Rick set a bottled water in front of her and slid into the chair across from her. Marisa placed a tray in the oven, then grabbed a diet soda and sat in between Rick and Shaye.

"Have you found something?" Marisa asked.

"It's only been a day," Rick said.

"I'm sorry," Marisa said. "You're probably here because you need to get information, not give it."

"Both, actually," Shaye said and showed them the image of Cody Reynolds. "Do either of you know this man?"

Rick shook his head. Marisa frowned, her brow scrunched, then shook her head as well.

"His name is Cody Reynolds," Shaye continued. "Does that ring a bell?"

"Yes," Marisa said. "His name is in the police file. He was working at the bar the night Caitlyn disappeared."

"But you have no other knowledge of him aside from that?" Shaye asked.

"What's this about?" Rick said, his suspicious tone reminding Shaye she was dealing with an attorney. They always preferred to ask the questions.

"I interviewed Mr. Reynolds last night at the bar," Shaye said, deciding the direct approach was best. "And someone murdered him this morning."

Marisa's hand flew over her mouth. "Oh my God. You don't think...I mean, why would anyone..."

"The police found a photo of Mr. Reynolds and Caitlyn in his apartment," Shaye said. "Their body language in the photo suggests they were in a relationship."

"I knew it," Rick said. "I told you she was seeing someone. She would have never flaked out on that pool party unless it was over a guy."

Marisa frowned. "And if you recall, I said you were probably right, but I figured she was seeing that ass

Garrett again and didn't want to hear what we'd have to say about it."

Shaye thought it was interesting that not one but two men who were friends with Caitlyn both had the same impression.

"Did you think she was seeing Garrett again as well?" Shaye asked Rick.

He shrugged. "I don't guess I thought about it much beyond making the observation that she was sneaking around, and with Caitlyn, that usually meant a man was lurking somewhere in the background. It could have been Garrett or whatever other loser she decided to take up with."

"Some might consider him a success—nice job with a big law firm," Shaye said, wanting to get Rick's take on the other man but knowing he'd probably hedge if she asked outright. She'd met plenty of men like him, and it was just in their nature.

Her comment hit home. A flush started on Rick's neck and began to creep up his face. "Money doesn't give you class. And trust me, Garrett Trahan is in such a deficit on that end of things that he'll never make enough money to dig himself out. He wouldn't even have that job if it weren't for his father's connections."

Shaye nodded, Garrett's continued employment despite his alleged harassment of female employees now making sense. If his father had called in a favor, he'd have a longer leash than someone hired on merit alone. But

Garrett better be careful. That leash was probably just long enough for him to hang himself from it.

"I understand you ran into him that night and that he and Caitlyn argued," Shaye said.

"She accused him of stalking her," Marisa said.

"Was he?" Shaye asked.

Marisa shook her head. "I don't know. Maybe. I mean, he claimed he was there with friends, but I didn't see any of his frat brothers or the other guys he was always with."

"What do you think?" Shaye asked Rick.

"I think he was mad as hell when Caitlyn dumped him. He's used to getting what he wants, and women are no different than a car or a pair of tennis shoes."

"Do you think he was responsible for her disappearance?" Shaye asked. She didn't ask outright if they thought Garrett had murdered Caitlyn, but she knew they would understand the implication.

Marisa glanced at Rick and bit her lip. Rick took in a deep breath and blew it out. "It's definitely crossed our minds," Rick said. "And more than once. He was pissed. And I think his fixation with Caitlyn went further than she thought. He seemed unhinged that night. I mean, I'm not saying he did something..."

"But you think he was capable," Shaye said.

Rick looked at her. "I think under the right circumstances, we're all capable."

Shaye agreed with him, but there was something about his tone that made her wonder. Then she remembered—attorney. And based on a law school interview that she'd turned up in her background check, Rick had set his sights on criminal defense. He didn't have much to go on in Ponchatoula except drunk driving and shoplifting and other minor offenses, at least minor in the big scheme of things. But Shaye knew he wanted more, and for defense attorneys that meant the big cases. The ones that splashed your name across the news and brought in boatloads of money.

"I agree with you," Shaye said to him. "But what I'd like to know is your opinion based on knowing Garrett and the situation. I am well aware that it's not evidence, but you know that a perceptive person can get a feel for certain things. I think you're one of those people."

She added the deliberate flattery, hoping it would get him talking, but didn't layer it too thick because he'd probably clue in to it. Rick Sampson might be stuck in a small town, but Shaye would bet he had big-city instincts and smarts.

He nodded. "I guess given what you do, and especially given your own experiences, you understand that better than most. And you're right. Some people get a feel for things that others don't clue in on. I pick up on things that Marisa doesn't. I always say it's because I'm cynical and she's sunny."

He gave her a small smile, then it faded. "My honest impression of Garrett is that I absolutely think he's capable of violence. Caitlyn had a shiner once that I'd bet he gave her even though she made up some story about a door. You know, the total bullshit excuse of every battered spouse. And a lot of girls complained about him having grabby hands and a foul mouth when it came to sexual suggestions. The question is do those flaws add up to something bigger?"

"And your answer?" Shaye asked.

"I think that they could have," Rick said. "Not premeditated, but in a fit of anger...I think he could easily cross lines."

Shaye nodded and looked over at Marisa. "What do you think?"

Marisa glanced at Rick and swallowed. "I didn't like him. He was mean in a way that undermined people, you know? He loved finding someone's flaw and poking at them about it until they lost it." She took a deep breath, then looked directly at Shaye. "The truth is I was afraid of him. I didn't like the way he watched Caitlyn when we were in social settings. It was creepy, not romantic. I know that sounds silly, but I don't know any other way to explain it."

"It's not silly," Shaye said. "And I understand exactly what you mean. I think most women would."

"Doesn't matter what we think, anyway," Rick said. "Trahan has an alibi. Likely bought and paid for, but you'd have to prove that. And that would only be the start. There's nothing to connect him to the French Revival that night. Even with motive and opportunity, it would be impossible to make a case with no forensic evidence, especially given all the random crime that happens on Mardi Gras."

"That's true," Shaye said, "but now there's been another murder and this one won't be shelved along with Caitlyn's disappearance."

"The connection is still circumstantial," Rick said. "They won't give Caitlyn's disappearance anything other than a cursory review."

"Perhaps," Shaye said, although she knew Jackson and Grayson well enough to know that wasn't the case at all. "But the fact remains that a man was killed who had a connection to Caitlyn that none of you were aware of. I don't think the timing is coincidental, so I'm going with it being motivated by Jenny hiring me. The real point of my visit was to let you know that the situation surrounding the investigation has changed, and there's a chance that you might be in danger."

Marisa's eyes widened. "Why us? I don't understand."

"You're funding the investigation," Shaye said. "Jenny is my client, but it wouldn't take much poking around for someone to figure out she's probably not footing the bill. I'm not saying that will happen, but I felt it was my responsibility to give you and Jenny the information and the possibilities it could create because you need the opportunity to cancel my investigation if you are not comfortable with the risks."

"Oh my God," Marisa said. "I never thought...you don't really think someone would come after us?"

"I don't know," Shaye said. "Logically, the smart thing

to do would be for the guilty party to lie low, but murderers are rarely rational. My investigation caused a reaction—one we weren't anticipating. I have no way of knowing how far this individual will take this."

Rick nodded. "I understand your concern, and I appreciate you coming here in person to lay it out. Even with my cynical outlook, I don't know that I would have taken it as far as you have, but I can see why you did. I would have felt an obligation as well if I were in your position."

"What did Jenny say?" Marisa asked.

"She wants me to stay on the case," Shaye said. "But I don't think I have to tell either of you how fragile Jenny appears to be emotionally. I'm not sure she can make the best decisions for herself, and it's not fair for her to make them for you. After all, you are paying the fees and that puts you at risk as well. If that's something you're not comfortable with, I understand completely and will be happy to turn over my notes and refund the balance of the retainer."

Marisa looked at Rick. "What do you think?"

"I don't like it," he said, "but I'm leaving it up to you. It was your decision to support Jenny on this in the first place. I'm not going to be the one to call it quits."

"Do you think we're in danger?" Marisa asked him.

He shrugged. "I think the risk is low, but I'm not willing to say it doesn't exist. Someone has been murdered. That's about as serious as it gets."

Marisa looked back at Shaye. "Wouldn't that mean you're in danger as well?"

"Perhaps," Shaye said, "but that's part of my job. It's not part of yours as a friend."

Marisa looked at Rick again, who didn't say another word, clearly putting the entire thing in Marisa's lap. Finally she looked at Shaye and nodded. "Keep going," she said. "We'll be careful, and I'll make sure Jenny is. If anything looks odd, I'll rethink it."

"Okay," Shaye said. "There's something else you should know. Something Jenny told me."

"What is it?" Marisa asked.

"She's starting to remember," Shaye said.

Marisa sucked in a breath. "Really? I mean, I knew she was having dreams, but they didn't seem to correspond with anything from the past."

"I think they started out as something else," Shaye said, "but she told me today that she'd dreamed about the bar. She remembers going outside and you taking her back inside, then talking to Rick, although she can't remember what was said. But what happened in between is still a blank. I have to tell you that what she's going through is very similar to what happened to me."

"And did you remember everything?" Marisa asked.

"I remembered a lot," Shaye said. "And pieces are still coming. Usually a new one every week or so."

Marisa looked over at Rick. "If she remembers...I mean, we always thought she was just in a panic because Caitlyn was missing, but maybe she saw something."

"It's possible," Shaye said, "and it's also possible that her panic was simply because she couldn't find Caitlyn. My understanding is that her coping skills never have been as good as the average person's."

"That's true," Marisa said. "She's always gotten upset rather easily. But still..."

"Anyway," Shaye said, "I thought you should know because Jenny will need someone to lean on if her memory ever returns full force, especially if she did see something horrible in that alley. And I get the impression that her mother isn't going to be the shoulder she needs."

"That's sort of an understatement," Marisa said.

Shaye rose. "I'm going to let you get back to your dinner. I'll be working on the investigation tomorrow. But if you change your mind about it, just give me a call and I'll halt everything. I'm afraid, given the situation, the New Orleans police will likely want to talk to you."

Rick nodded. "That's to be expected. Again, we appreciate your delivering this news personally."

"Be careful," Shaye said. "And let me know if there's anything else I can do."

She headed out of the house and climbed into her SUV, then pulled away, reflecting on the conversation. Rick and Marisa had backed up Sam's thoughts on Garrett Trahan and his potential for abuse, so that was three people with the same impression of Trahan. Four if she counted herself. She wondered what Trahan would say when Grayson and Jackson talked to him tomorrow. Unfortunately, Jackson wouldn't be able to tell her and she wasn't about to ask. That wasn't fair to either of them.

She shook her head. As much as she could picture Garrett Trahan as an abuser and potential murderer, the one thing she couldn't find a reason for was his associating with Cody Reynolds. If anything, Trahan would have hated Reynolds if he'd known about his involvement with Caitlyn. Or maybe it was something even more sinister.

Maybe she'd been playing both men.

Maybe they'd found out.

MARISA LOOKED out the blinds and watched as Shaye Archer drove away, then walked back into the kitchen where Rick was on his second beer. "Oh my God," she said and sat next to him. "Someone was murdered."

"I told you this entire thing was a bad idea."

"You told me to stop indulging Jenny's fantasies of Caitlyn being alive somewhere, and that's what I was trying to do. When Shaye Archer didn't come up with anything more than the police did, I figured she'd have to face facts. I never expected anyone to die. I just don't understand. Why would someone kill that bartender?"

"Who knows? It's New Orleans and he wasn't exactly an accountant. Lots of bartenders are involved with all sorts of shady side business—drugs, prostitution."

"But Shaye said the police don't think the timing was a coincidence and neither did she."

"Cops hate coincidence and private detectives are no different, but that doesn't mean it doesn't exist."

"Is that what you think? That it's just some horrible chance of timing?"

"Maybe."

"But what about the picture? Caitlyn was involved with him and none of us even knew."

"I think there were probably a lot of things we didn't know about Caitlyn. It wasn't unheard of for her to duck out, and you said yourself that a couple of times she claimed she was spending the weekend with Garrett you saw him out with his friends."

Marisa nodded. "You think she was seeing the bartender then?"

"That makes the most sense. Remember, it was Caitlyn who suggested that bar."

Marisa's eyes widened. "That's right. I bet it was to see him. But I never saw them talking, did you?"

"I don't remember him at all, but it was wall-to-wall people, and we'd been drinking for hours. The whole night sorta ran together. Besides, Caitlyn talked to everyone she met. No way I could remember them."

"What about her phone, though? If she was taking calls from him then wouldn't his number have shown up on her phone records? I know she had a prepaid phone because of not having credit and all, but would that matter?"

Rick shook his head. "The police can still get a log of the calls and texts from the service provider as long as they know the number and have a subpoena. But if she had one phone, what makes you think she didn't have another? Especially if she was hiding something from us. I know you were friends and you were brought up with that whole 'not speaking ill of the dead' thing, but you and I both know that the only time Caitlyn wasn't scheming was when she was asleep."

Marisa sighed. "I know. You're right. This whole thing has been a nightmare from the beginning. I swear I was just trying to make it stop by suggesting Jenny hire Shaye. I figured she'd cover all the same ground the police did and come to the same conclusions, then I could convince Jenny to let it go. Instead, I've probably made it worse."

"It's not your fault. You were just trying to help, like you've always done. Don't worry about it. The cops will probably come up with something he was involved in that got him killed."

"You really think so?"

He took another drink of his beer and stared at the wall, not answering.

She started to talk again but bit her lip instead. Once Rick got broody, as he looked now, he wouldn't participate in a discussion. But she couldn't help but worry about all the implications. Sure, the timing could be a coincidence, but was it? There were a million chores Marisa needed to complete before she could pick up

Maya and eventually climb into bed, but the thought of trying to finish up dinner or fold socks made her stomach clench. It was so trivial when someone had been murdered.

She'd hoped hiring Shaye would end their long nightmare. Instead, it might have just fired it up even more.

12

CAITLYN AWAKENED TO DARKNESS. FROM THE TINY window, she could see the tip of the sun as it disappeared over the trees. The last thing she remembered was the morning sun streaming in and then...she strained to recall what had happened since the sunlight but it was all a blank. How could she lose an entire day? She checked the room and saw a paper plate on the nightstand that hadn't been there before. A few bread crumbs were all that was left.

Clearly, she'd eaten at some point, but why couldn't she remember?

Her captor was poisoning her. She was sure of it. Something that ate away at her memory.

But why not just kill her? Why was she being punished this way?

So maybe she hadn't always been the nicest person. Maybe she'd treated people badly.

But this? What was the endgame?

She walked to the door and tried to turn the knob, as she always did, but this time she was shocked when it spun around. She heard a *click* and the old door creaked open. Her heart leaped into her throat. This was her chance.

She inched out the door, pausing every time the floorboards creaked. She took the steps one at a time, stopping on each one, her pulse shooting up every time the old wood groaned. Every few steps, she had to remind herself to breathe. She listened for noise downstairs, but all she heard was the wind outside. At the bottom of the stairs, she peered around the wall and scanned the dark room. A tiny bit of light filtered in from a light outside a door.

That must be the front of the house!

She took three steps toward the door, her hand shaking as she reached for the dead bolt and slid it back. Praying that the hinges didn't squeak, she inched the door open and peered outside. The lone light bulb didn't illuminate much, but she knew from her view out the window that somewhere ahead of her was a dirt road. She stepped outside and walked down the cement steps.

Thunder rumbled around her, and lightning flashed off to her right. The smell of rain was in the air. She had to hurry because of the storm, but to where? She had no idea where she was or how far away help might be, and the weather would make it even harder to see lights from other houses.

She set off in the direction she thought the road would be. It didn't matter. Being lost would be better than being captive. She only needed to survive one night in the dark. If she didn't find anyone who could help her, she'd do it when daylight came. There had to be a town nearby. The food and bathroom supplies came from somewhere. If she could just get to a phone, she could call the police.

She'd gone maybe twenty yards when lightning flashed right above her, causing her to duck. Thunder boomed so loudly her ears vibrated, and she felt a flash of pain in her temples. She pressed her hands to her head as the rain began to pelt her face. Had she been struck by lightning? The pain in her head was so bad her vision blurred.

No!

She staggered forward, determined to get far enough away from the house that no one could find her. If she could just find a place to hide. She could get help tomorrow. Surely they wouldn't come looking for her in the storm.

One hand pressed to her head, she forced herself forward, but three steps later she stumbled and fell to the ground, her head feeling as if it would split in two. Desperate, she started to crawl, but before she'd even moved forward one foot, she collapsed on the ground, eyes clenched and praying for all of it to be over.

13

VIRGINIA TAYLOR STEPPED OUT ONTO THE BACK porch. It was close to 11:00 p.m. and the rain was really coming down now. The thunder raged so hard it shook the walls of the tiny house. It had been a bad year for storms. So many of them sweeping through the area. Lots of flooding. Lots of damage from lightning. Sometimes, Virginia thought it was the apocalypse. That God had grown so dissatisfied with his creation that he was going to send it all back to dust. Maybe start over. Maybe abandon it altogether as a lost cause.

Jenny had finally come out of her room at some point and was sitting on a footstool on the far end of the porch, watching the storm. She'd always been fascinated with them, ever since she was a little girl. In a fancy way, it mirrored her childhood. Jenny was always the one watching the storm. Caitlyn was the storm.

"You're going to get wet," Virginia called out.

Jenny turned to look at her. "Already have. I got caught in it checking the mail after my walk. And the wind is blowing the rain in sheets. It's come under the porch a couple times."

Virginia nodded. The only real activity Jenny committed to was walking. Some days she'd walk for hours, returning with blisters on her feet. On really good days, she'd ride her bicycle into town and visit Marisa. Those days had gotten more and more scarce, but the walking had been a constant.

Virginia started down the porch and stood beside her daughter. "That detective you hired talked to me today."

Jenny looked up at her. "I'm sorry I didn't tell you about it, Momma. But I knew you wouldn't approve."

"You need to let it go," Virginia said.

"Is that what you did?"

"Yes. You have to. Either you let it go or it eats you alive, like it did your daddy."

"Don't you want to know what happened?"

Virginia stared out into the darkness for a bit, considering the question. Finally, she spoke. "I don't think I do. Nothing the Archer woman can find will change what happened. Nothing can bring back the past. Thinking something will is how you lose the present and the future. I'm going to bed. Remember to lock the door when you come in."

Virginia turned and headed back into the house, glancing back at her daughter before she closed the door behind her. Whatever had happened hadn't just cost her family one life. It had cost all four.

As she walked into her bedroom, the letter she'd received in the mail that day crinkled in her pocket. She sat on the bed and pulled it out, staring at the words her doctor had told her earlier that week. He'd said a lot of other things, but only two words had mattered.

Six months.

She reached for her Bible and turned around, using the bed to help her lower herself down on her knees.

Lord, I ain't asked for something in a long time but I got to now. You know I ain't got much longer here and you know the situation I got with my daughter. I think I know what I need to do, but I have to be sure. Give me a sign. Let me know it's your will.

She looked up at the ceiling and waited. Then a flash of lightning bolted through the sky, striking the weather vane on the top of the old barn. Immediately, all the lights went out and Virginia rose.

"Your will, Lord."

WEDNESDAY, February 17, 2016
French Quarter, New Orleans

SHAYE AWAKENED after a night of fitful sleep. The storm had raged for hours, which had contributed to her general unease, but mostly thoughts of the case kept her mind too active to allow her to drift off into restful slumber. And if she was being honest, she was still reeling a bit from Cody Reynolds's murder.

When she'd taken this case, she'd expected to cover the same ground the police had, verifying the interviews and seeing if she could formulate a theory, even if she couldn't provide enough proof for an arrest. Given the circumstances surrounding Caitlyn's disappearance, she hadn't really expected to find much. Her biggest hope had been that her investigation would allow Jenny to put the past behind her and work on a healthy future. For herself and for the others she'd locked in the past with her.

Then Cody Reynolds was killed. And that had come as a total shock.

Shaye believed in coincidences but she didn't believe this was one. She could be wrong, of course. Reynolds could have been involved in something else entirely. Maybe he simply got nervous because her poking around might uncover something else he was involved in. Maybe whomever he met in the cemetery thought he wouldn't be able to play it cool and decided to eliminate the possibility of exposure to whatever they were involved in.

In a way, that made more sense. Because if Reynolds had been involved in Caitlyn's disappearance, there had been ample opportunity to kill him before now when it wouldn't have drawn scrutiny directly related to Caitlyn's disappearance. First thing this morning, she was going to review her notes from yesterday, then she was going to be at the French Revival when it opened and have a chat with the employees.

One of them had to know something about Reynolds's life, even if it was just suspicion. There was no way he'd worked with people for years and they'd never observed something they thought was odd. Or something about his life outside the bar. Jackson had said his apartment was nicely decorated. Had he had help? His mother maybe? What were his parents like? Jackson and Grayson had gone to speak with them yesterday, but they wouldn't be able to share information concerning an open investigation. And she wouldn't intrude on the parents' grief unless she had no other option. But perhaps she could find someone who grew up with Reynolds who was willing to talk.

She headed into the kitchen and fired up the coffeepot, then sat down at the counter with her laptop. It should be easy enough to locate Reynolds's high school classmates. Baton Rouge was a bit of a drive, but maybe she'd get lucky and find one locally. Worst case, she could call, although she hated to do anything but cursory information-gathering over the phone.

She found a couple yearbooks online and cruised through the group photos, looking for Reynolds and making a note of the other students he was pictured with. Three stood out because they were in more than one photo. Two women and one guy. She did a quick search on those names, and located the two women on

Facebook, both married and both still in Baton Rouge. She scanned the feed on their profiles to get a feel for them and discovered that one had recently passed away from a long bout with breast cancer. She deleted that name from her notes and did a broader search for the guy, Eric Pellerin, and found him on LinkedIn, his profession listed as loan officer.

"Yes," she said when she saw his current employer was a company in New Orleans. With any luck, the profile was up to date. It was just past 8:00 a.m. so she looked up the company, a mortgage lender, then called the main number.

"Hello," she said when the receptionist answered. "I'm interested in a home mortgage and a friend recommended Eric Pellerin to me. Can I make an appointment with him?"

"I'd be happy to make an appointment," the woman said. "When would you like to come in?"

"As soon as possible. I don't suppose he has anything this morning?"

"Let me check...I'm afraid he's already scheduled for later this morning. He has an eight-thirty opening. Can you make it here by then?"

"That would be great. I'll see you shortly."

She hung up before the receptionist could ask her name. If news of Reynolds's death had circulated back to Eric, she didn't want him ducking out of their appointment. One thing she'd learned quickly is that a lot of people didn't want to talk to private investigators any more than they did the police. Even if they didn't have anything to hide. So many people simply didn't want to be involved in anything sordid. This way wasn't exactly honest, but she'd apologize when she got there. If he told her to get lost after that, then so be it.

She headed into her bedroom to throw on some clothes, and her phone rang. It was Jackson.

"Good morning," she said.

"I'll agree with the morning part," he replied.

"Long night, huh? What time did you get in?"

"We got back from Baton Rouge around ten but went straight to the station to make some notes and see if forensics had left anything for us. It's not breaking the rules to tell you there's nothing to tell. No trace evidence on Reynolds's body. Death was due to blows to the head."

"It really sucks when all this cool technology we have now doesn't yield anything."

"Tell me about it. Especially when you have victims' families watching television and thinking we can solve cases in the time it takes to make dinner."

"How were Reynolds's parents? Emotionally, I mean." She knew Jackson would never presume she was asking for case information, but it didn't hurt to clarify.

"Shocked. His mother is devastated. His father is upset but also angry that Cody might have been involved in something that brought it on. He didn't cut him much slack in that area. I get the impression he was strict when it came to morals and ethics."

"It's got to be a difficult thing to reconcile—losing a

child but because of bad choices he made. Assuming that's what this shakes out to be, of course."

"At this point, I just want an answer. As long as this file doesn't go on a shelf next to Caitlyn's, I can live with whatever that answer is."

Shaye put the phone on her dresser and pressed the Speaker button. "I have an interview in twenty-five minutes, so I'm dressing and talking, if that's okay."

"Anyone interesting?"

"A guy Cody was friends with in high school. It's a long shot, but he's in New Orleans so I figured why not."

"Reynolds's father gave us the first name of a guy they met once—a friend from New Orleans, probably military buddy. I'm going to try to run him down today."

Shaye pulled on jeans and a New Orleans Saints T-shirt and sat to put on her tennis shoes. "I talked to Jenny, Marisa, and Rick. None of them want me to stop the investigation."

"We'll probably talk to them today or tomorrow. Did any of them know about Caitlyn and Reynolds?"

"No. Unless they're all professional actors, they seemed shocked. Jenny was probably the calmest about it all, but I don't think she's running at full capacity. Marisa was shaken and I don't think Rick liked it at all, but he's going along with what Marisa wants to do. I think he just wants it all over."

"Based on what you've told me about his situation, I get that. I'll let you go so you can make your appointment. I have no idea what my day will look like, but I'd like to see you tonight if I get off at a decent hour and don't think I'll fall asleep within five minutes of walking in."

"I'll take the five minutes if I can get it. Take care of yourself today. You and Grayson are both running on near empty."

"Job-related hazard, right? I know I don't have to say it, but I'm going to anyway—be careful. I'll call later and let you know how tonight looks."

"Sounds good." She grabbed her phone off the dresser and hurried into the kitchen, lifting her keys and purse from the counter as she went. She had twenty minutes to get to Pellerin's office. It was only five miles or so away, but that was five miles in the French Quarter in work traffic. Every second counted.

She pulled away from the curb, trying to decide on the route of least resistance, and took a right at the end of the street. This was the longer way around, but she was fairly certain the shorter way had a piece of street under construction. That was a sure way to up your aggravation level, and the last thing she wanted to do was arrive at Pellerin's office rushed and frustrated.

Her choice proved to be a good one, and she parked across the street from the building with five minutes to spare. She crossed the street and headed inside, smiling at the receptionist, who looked up from her paperwork, her eyes widening.

"You're Shaye Archer," the young woman said.

"Yes. I have an appointment with Eric Pellerin."

"Of course. We spoke earlier but I forgot to get your name."

Shaye smiled. "That was my fault. I was in such a hurry to get out the door that I completely forgot and hung up."

"Oh, that's okay. I just told Eric I'd let him know when you were here." She picked up the phone and had a brief conversation, then sent Shaye through the door behind her and down a hall to his office.

He rose from his chair as she walked in and extended his hand. "Eric Pellerin, and you're Shaye Archer. Sorry, I recognized you from the news."

"That's all right. A lot of people do."

He waved at a set of chairs in front of his desk and she sat. "I imagine that gets tiring. It seems that those who want the spotlight constantly struggle to get it and those who value their privacy sometimes have a hard time getting out of it."

She studied him for a moment. "That's very perceptive."

He shrugged, looking slightly embarrassed. "I had a cousin I was close to. She had an, uh, situation that brought unwanted attention. She'd always been such a private person, and I saw how difficult it was for her."

"I hope she's all right."

He smiled. "She's fantastic, thank you for asking. She was a fighter, like you. Sometimes the human spirit amazes me. She's a big fan of yours. I can't wait to tell her I met you in person."

Shaye smiled. "Well, you might not be as thrilled when I tell you I'm not really here for a loan."

"I didn't figure. You could probably write a check for most anything in the city. Given your profession, I assume you're here about an investigation, but I can't imagine what I might know. Frankly, the anticipation is killing me."

"The truth is, you're a long shot, but I don't have a lot to go on. I'm going to take you back in history for a bit. Back to high school, as a matter of fact. I'd like to talk about Cody Reynolds."

Pellerin leaned back in his chair. "That is taking it back a bit. Is he under investigation for something? I guess you can't tell me that, right?"

"If that was the case, then no, I couldn't tell you. But in this case, it doesn't apply. I'm sorry to say that Cody was murdered yesterday in Metairie Cemetery, and I think his death might have something to do with a case I'm working. But since I don't know much about him, I'm hoping to get more information to help determine whether his death is related to my case or something else entirely. He seems to have been one of those private people we were just discussing."

"Murdered? Wow. I take it the motive wasn't obvious, so that lets out robbery and any other common crime." He shook his head. "I don't really know what I can tell you. Cody and I were friends in high school until he dropped out. He started running with an older crowd then, and they were mostly up to no good. I had my sights set on college and an easier life than my blue-collar parents, so we drifted apart. To be honest, I don't even know that he noticed I was gone."

"You haven't seen him since high school?"

"I've seen him twice since high school. Once was in a bar down in the Quarter, but I can't remember the name."

"The French Revival?"

"That might have been it. I was doing a pub crawl with some college buddies who were here for the weekend, and I'm somewhat embarrassed to admit that parts of the night aren't all that clear. He was tending bar. We recognized each other and shook hands, but the place was busy and we got a table afterward. I didn't see him again."

"And the second time?"

"Actually, that was the second time—probably a year or so ago. The time before was a ways back. I haven't thought about it in forever, although it bothered me at the time. It's been at least five years, maybe more."

"What about it bothered you?"

"I took a girl I was dating out to dinner at Crescent City Brewhouse—you know the place?"

Shaye nodded. "My stomach and my waistline know it well."

"Yeah, it's great. Anyway, we had a table outside in that courtyard area, and I saw Cody sitting at a table in the corner with a young woman. I excused myself from my date, figuring I'd say hello, but I wasn't planning to linger. Hadn't seen him since high school so I thought a quick 'how you doing' wasn't out of line."

"Sure. I take it Cody wasn't happy at the intrusion?"

"Not at all. I could tell as soon as I stepped up to the table that something was off. I'm pretty sure they'd been arguing, and I popped up right in the middle of it. Anyway, Cody shook my hand and asked about my parents, but I could tell he just wanted to get rid of me. I told him to give my regards to his folks and skedaddled."

"Did you know the young woman he was with?"

"Never seen her before and he didn't bother to make any introductions."

It was a long shot, but Shaye had a feeling about Pellerin's story. She pulled a photo of Caitlyn out of her purse and showed it to him. "Is this the woman?"

Pellerin took the photo and studied it for several seconds before nodding. "I think so. I mean, it's been a long time but it could have been her. She was definitely younger than him. Didn't look much past high school, if that, but then a lot of women don't these days. Gotta be careful on the dating scene."

He handed the photo back to her. "Did something happen to her? Was Cody involved?"

"The woman's name is Caitlyn Taylor. She disappeared from the French Revival six years ago on Mardi Gras."

Pellerin's eyes widened. "The same bar Cody worked at? Really? Was she killed?"

"No one knows. She simply vanished."

"That sucks. I know it happens—probably more here than some places given all the bayous and stuff—but I feel sorry for her family. I can't help but think that a bad answer is better than none at all."

Shaye nodded. "I think so too. Caitlyn's twin sister hired me to look into her disappearance. The case went cold for the police a long time ago and without answers, my client is having a tough time moving on."

"So why do you think Cody's murder might be related?"

"Several reasons. Some I can't divulge because the police are investigating, but I questioned Cody the night before he was killed, and he claimed no knowledge of Caitlyn aside from when the police questioned all the bar employees the day after her disappearance. I found out later that he was probably involved with her."

Pellerin nodded. "Then he turned up dead. I'm not even a PI and I find that suspicious. I wish I knew something that could help."

"You said it looked like they were arguing before you walked up. Did you hear anything they said? Even small bits of the conversation might help."

"Not when I walked up. Cody saw me coming and said something to her. I figure he told her to get quiet because she never said a word, even though he didn't introduce us. But when I was walking away, she said something about never making him any promises. I didn't get any more than that."

"And what was your take on it?"

He frowned.

"It's nothing I would hold you to," Shaye said. "And it's not like an opinion can be entered into evidence. Besides, I'm not the cops. I find that people's intuition about something is often correct, and sometimes it leads me down a path of investigation that provides the answers I'm looking for."

"Okay, I guess I can see that. Honestly? My first impression was that she was dumping him, and he was mad as hell about it."

"Any idea why you got that impression, or was it just a feeling?"

"Body language and their expressions. He was pissed. You could see it on his face, and his hands were clenching the chair arms. She had her arms crossed and this...I don't know, kinda defiant look on her face. Then there was the general feel. I've been dumped when I was really into the girl. Walking up to that table reminded me of it straight off."

Shaye nodded. "And there's a strong chance you're right."

Pellerin shifted nervously in his chair. "You don't think Cody killed that girl for dumping him, do you?"

"I don't know what happened. But if Cody's murder had something to do with Caitlyn Taylor's disappearance, then Cody wasn't the only one who knew what happened."

Pellerin's eyes widened. "Oh shit." He held up a hand. "Sorry. But I hadn't even thought of that."

Shaye rose from her chair. "That kind of thinking is what I'm paid to do." She handed him her card. "If you remember anything else, please give me a call."

"Sure," he said as he took the card. "And good luck. I'm sorry to hear about Cody's death. Maybe I'll send his parents a card." He looked at Shaye. "What the heck do I say to them?"

"You seem like a nice man. You'll figure it out. Thanks for your time."

Shaye headed out of the office and hopped in her SUV. Pellerin seemed like a credible witness, and she was willing to trust his impression of the situation between Cody and his date in the restaurant. She was even willing to go out on a limb and say he was probably right in identifying Caitlyn as the woman. But all that did was reinforce the theory she was already working with—that Cody had been involved with Caitlyn and something had gone wrong.

But who else was involved?

Because there was one thing she was certain of. Cody was murdered because of something he did or something he knew.

Or both.

MARISA SLUNG her purse over her shoulder and started to lift her daughter off the couch where she sat playing with her toys. Then she glanced out the front window and silently cursed. Usually Rick was long gone before her in the mornings, but this morning, he'd claimed he wasn't feeling well and was going to go into work later. That meant his SUV was parked behind her in the narrow drive.

Her options were to move the car seat from her car to his SUV and take the SUV, or play the car shuffle. Deciding the car shuffle was less hassle than wrestling with the seat, she went back into the kitchen for his keys and headed out.

"Mommy will be right back," she said to Maya as she closed the front door.

She jumped into the SUV, her frustration level already high, and that frustrated her more. Starting off the day in the hole didn't bode well for the eight hours of work that stretched in front of her. Especially when her job provided enough aggravation for ten people. Added to that, her parents were taking Maya to a children's event in New Orleans and she was supposed to have met them at the café for breakfast ten minutes ago.

She started the SUV and put it in Reverse, then backed out of the drive and parked it on the curb. As she was about to climb out, she looked down and noticed a coffee cup in the center console cup holder. Normally, such a thing wouldn't make her pause, but this one was bright blue with red-and-white lettering and she immediately knew it had come from a café they usually stopped at when they were in New Orleans.

Except they hadn't stopped at it when they were in

New Orleans to see Shaye, and they hadn't been back since.

Don't jump to conclusions.

Maybe a client had left the cup in his car. Rick often drove clients from the office to the courthouse. Someone could have had the cup in his car and transferred it to Rick's. She leaned forward and looked at the mileage. Two hundred miles put on the vehicle since they'd made the trip to New Orleans.

She sat back in the seat and blew out a breath. Rick's norm was maybe ten miles a day on the vehicle. No way could he put two hundred miles on the car in a day just doing work driving in Ponchatoula. And she was certain about the mileage because she'd checked so she could make a note of when the SUV was due for service. Since she worked next door to the service station, she usually drove it when service was due and left it for them to handle while she was at work.

She wrapped her hands around the steering wheel and clenched. Rick had left home before she'd even gotten out of bed yesterday morning, claiming he had to prep for an early client meeting, but when she'd called around eight to ask him a question about scheduling a dentist appointment for the three of them, the receptionist had said he wasn't in the office. Marisa had assumed his meeting was at a client's home or he was at the court-house, but Rick didn't have clients that required a two-hundred-mile commute to meet.

So where was he yesterday morning? And why did he lie to her?

She thought about Shaye Archer's visit the night before, and her stomach rolled. All indications were that Rick had been in New Orleans early yesterday morning, which is when Cody Reynolds was murdered.

Calm down. You're losing it.

She took a deep breath and slowly blew it out. It was a huge leap to assume Rick's keeping something from her meant he'd murdered someone they didn't even know. This entire mess had put her on edge, and now she was imagining things that were ridiculous. She hopped out of the SUV and hurried for her car.

But as she walked, she wondered.

14

JENNY STARED AT THE STAGE, WATCHING A DRUNK FRAT guy do a horrible rendition of a Maroon 5 song. The entire night had been one casualty after another. First that disastrous run-in with that loser Garrett and then one lame bar after another. Now it was bad singing and watered-down drinks and the same crowd of drunks that filled every bar and street in the French Quarter.

She had no idea why she'd come here. The entire trip had been a mistake.

Then the room tilted and began to spin and when it stopped, she was in the alley outside the bar. Her chest tightened, and she drew in a ragged breath. Something was wrong. She glanced around, trying to remember what she was doing here. Where was her sister? Wasn't she just there? Something had happened. Something she'd seen but couldn't quite remember.

She squeezed her eyes together, trying to force her mind to recall what she knew was there, but all she got was a blur of the *hallway from the restroom to the back door. A flash of her sister smiling at her, then nothing.*

JENNY BOLTED UPRIGHT, her heart pounding in her chest. She'd almost had it. It was there, buried in the recesses of her mind, but it was trying to come out. It was something important. She just knew it.

Something that would change everything.

⸻

JACKSON LOOKED up as the desk sergeant led a man into the interview room. He knew from the man's driver's license picture that this was Brennan Murphy. He lived in New Orleans and worked for a small local oil company. Fortunately, he was on shore and available for an interview.

"Brennan Murphy?" Grayson asked as he stepped forward to extend his hand. "My name is Detective Grayson. We spoke on the phone. This is Detective Lamotte. Please have a seat."

Brennan glanced at Jackson, then back at Grayson before sitting in a chair on the opposite side of the table. Grayson hadn't explained why they wanted to speak to him, just that they would like to ask some questions and he could come down to the station or they would be happy to schedule an appointment to meet at his apartment. Grayson had reassured him that he was not a suspect and that they were only looking for information, but Jackson supposed an invitation to chat with the police always caused a bit of trepidation.

"Thank you for coming down," Grayson said.

"I didn't want to worry my girlfriend," Brennan said. "What's this about?"

"Is Cody Reynolds a friend of yours?" Grayson asked.

"Yeah. I mean, he was. We haven't hung out in years, but we served together and then we hung out when I first got to New Orleans. Cody helped me get my job. Had a regular at the bar who worked on a rig. He got me an interview. Why? Did he do something?"

Grayson shook his head. "I'm sorry to tell you, but Mr. Reynolds is dead."

Brennan straightened in his chair. "Dead? How?"

"He was murdered early yesterday morning in Metairie Cemetery," Grayson said.

Brennan's eyes widened. "Okay. Man, that's...I don't know what to say. I mean, if you'd said some crazy popped him in the bar or something, but the cemetery? What was he doing there? He doesn't have any family buried in New Orleans that I know about."

"That's what we're hoping you can help us with," Grayson said. "The day before his murder, a private detective talked to him about a cold case she'd been asked to take on by a missing woman's sister. The missing woman's name was Caitlyn Taylor."

"Oh, shit." Brennan shook his head. "I told him that

girl would be the death of him. You say those sort of things, you know. You never think..."

"Why did you tell him that?" Grayson asked.

"Because she had him going," Brennan said. "He was obsessed with her and she played him every minute."

"Played him how?" Grayson asked.

"You been to his place, right? To search and stuff?" Brennan asked.

Grayson nodded.

"Did Cody look like the kind of guy who'd live like that? Assuming it's all the same as last time I saw it, the place looks like one of those renovation shows on television that my mother insists on playing every time she visits."

"That's a pretty accurate description," Jackson said.

"Before Caitlyn, Cody had a secondhand recliner, a TV tray for a dining room, and a television on top of an old suitcase. Everything you see now was Caitlyn. He emptied his bank account and ran up every credit card he had over that girl. Even bought her a cell phone and paid to keep minutes on it. He was probably still paying off all the debt. Just the running back and forth between Baton Rouge and New Orleans had to cost a dime or two."

"People do strange things when they're in love," Jackson said.

"I get that," Brennan said. "And I'm not saying classing yourself up a little is a bad thing, but in his case, there was no point. That girl was never serious about him. A complete stranger could have seen it. But Cody was blind to everything where Caitlyn was concerned."

"If she was never serious, then why bother classing him up?" Grayson asked.

"I think it was a game to her," Brennan said. "Like she was trying to see how far he'd go."

"So how did their relationship play out?" Jackson asked.

"I don't know the details," Brennan said. "I'd cut out a couple months before. Couldn't take watching him lose his mind over that wh—" He gave them an apologetic look. "Sorry. I have some strong feelings about the situation."

Jackson frowned. It was one thing to believe a friend was a fool, but Brennan seemed to take it almost personally. "Can I ask why you feel so strongly? I mean, everyone has had a friend who acted a fool over a woman at some point. Why did this one bother you so much?"

"She came on to me," Brennan said. "At a party one weekend at Cody's. He was damn near passed out drunk, and she suggested we go to the bedroom and, uh, have some fun." He shook his head. "I was military. I've seen and heard some shit, especially with women chasing a paycheck or citizenship. And Cody and I had been talking earlier that night about him ditching the bar and working rigs with me because I was making so much money. But it still floored me. Not just hitting up his good friend but right there in his home with him in it?

That's a level of crazy I don't have any desire to tangle with."

"That's pretty blatant," Jackson said. "I assume you told Cody about it."

"Damn straight," Brennan said. "The next day, as soon as he was up and sober, I laid it all out for him."

"And let me guess," Jackson said. "He didn't believe you."

Brennan scowled. "Called me a few choice names and had the nerve to say I was just jealous. Jealous of what? That idiot was bankrupt over some bitch who was using him and running around with God knows how many other guys, looking for a bigger take. That was it for me. I told him that if he got rid of Caitlyn and got his common sense back, to give me a call. I was done with it."

"I don't blame you," Jackson said. "So when did you hear from Cody again?"

"I didn't. I mean, not deliberately. A couple weeks later, I ran into him at Harrah's. He was sitting alone at the bar, so I walked up and asked how he was doing. He told me he'd asked Caitlyn to marry him. You can about imagine I was ready to call in the white jacket people. Not that I was worried she'd say yes, mind you. I just couldn't understand why he didn't see what everyone else did."

"Clearly, she said no," Grayson said.

"Not just no. She laughed at him. Told him he was just her bit of fun and she had her eye on someone with money and connections. I didn't say 'I told you so' but man, I was thinking it. Thinking it hard. But he was so broken up about it I didn't have the heart to rub it in, even though he'd called me some pretty awful things. Dude looked bad. Like he had been sitting on that stool for days, drinking one after the other."

"Was that before she disappeared or after?" Grayson asked.

"A couple weeks before. I called him a time or two and tried to get him to come out for a drink but he always turned me down. When I asked about Caitlyn, he'd clam up, and I figured he was making a last-ditch play for her and didn't want me knowing. So I let it go."

"How did you learn about Caitlyn's disappearance?" Grayson asked.

"The news. Was sitting at home having dinner and up pops her face on my television."

"Did you talk to Cody after that?"

"Yeah. I picked up the phone and called him straight off, but he brushed me off, saying his parents were visiting and he'd call me when they left. He never did, though. Truth is I doubt his parents were there at all."

Jackson leaned forward and looked Brennan straight in the eye. "Do you think Cody had something to do with Caitlyn's disappearance?"

Brennan took a breath and leaned back in his chair. "I didn't want to think so, but yeah, I'll admit it crossed my mind. More than once and for longer than a second or two, if you know what I'm saying."

"So you think he was capable?" Jackson asked.

"Before Caitlyn I would have said no. I mean, Cody was no saint, but he wasn't violent. Not beyond your basic male scrap in a bar or something. But that girl had him twisted up so tight that anything could have happened when he started to unravel."

Jackson nodded. "Is there anything else you can tell us? Anything about Cody's relationship with Caitlyn or Caitlyn herself?"

"I didn't really know her," Brennan said, "and didn't want to. What I saw was enough for me to make up my mind. The girl was trouble. And I don't know how she plays into Cody's death, but you can bet your ass, whatever it is comes back around to her."

"Do you think there's a chance she ran off with another man and is still alive somewhere?" Grayson asked.

Brennan raised one eyebrow. "Do you?"

His tone clearly relayed that he didn't think that for a minute. Grayson didn't bother to answer. He didn't have to. All of them knew the score.

When Brennan had gone, Grayson threw his pen on the table and blew out a breath. "What do you think?"

"I think everything he said fits with part of our theory and it explains Cody's apartment decor. Also provides motive. Opportunity was already in place, just risky."

Grayson nodded. "But it doesn't explain who killed Cody. What are we missing? On the surface, this seems straightforward but when you try to line things up, there's a big hole."

"Yeah. Who killed Cody and why."

"Okay, so let's run down the potentials. Start with Caitlyn's friends. Maybe one of them found out Cody did something to Caitlyn and decided to make him pay for it."

"But how did they find out? And why would Cody have their prepaid cell number? If the calls had come in to Cody's phone, then I could make a case for one of them calling and asking him to meet. But Cody initiated the call. If one of Caitlyn's friends was mad enough to kill someone over Caitlyn, then why would they have been exchanging phone numbers and calls with Cody to begin with?"

"I agree that it doesn't track logically. Okay, what about Garrett Trahan? If he was following them he could have seen them go into the bar. There's opportunity. And if he was infatuated with Caitlyn, that night might not have been the first time he followed her. Shaye said people have already suggested Trahan was abusive. Maybe he took it to the next level."

Jackson nodded. "So let's say Trahan saw Caitlyn with Cody because he followed her one weekend when she came here to meet up with him. Trahan follows her again during Mardi Gras and after their run-in, tracks them to the bar where Cody works. Trahan sees Cody and it puts him right into the stratosphere with anger. But if Garrett did something to Caitlyn and Cody knew about it, why not turn him in? Flip side, if Cody did something to Caitlyn and Garrett figured it out, why wait all this time to do something?"

"I don't know. But we need to talk to Trahan."

"Yep. And what about Brennan Murphy? We can't dismiss him, either."

"No," Grayson agreed. "He knew Caitlyn and Cody, and all we have is his word that things went down the way they did. We didn't ask him to alibi Mardi Gras night but if he was out partying, he probably couldn't anyway."

"He definitely had strong feelings about her and not in a good way. What if she didn't hit on him? What if it was the other way around and she blew him off?"

"That might be a motive for killing Caitlyn, albeit somewhat flimsy, but why kill Cody? And more importantly, why now?"

Jackson sighed. "So many options and every one of them only works halfway."

"We're missing something," Grayson repeated.

"Yeah. I guess we better get out of here and go looking for it."

As they started out of the room, Grayson's phone rang. He looked at the display and frowned. "It's Victor LeBlanc."

They both stopped walking as Grayson answered the call. Jackson listened to the one side of the conversation, wondering what the man could possibly want with them. He'd already pulled strings in DC to get the FBI assigned to his granddaughter's kidnapping, effectively removing

Grayson and Jackson from the case. They'd turned over all their case files and done a thorough debriefing with the FBI agents. What could he want now?

Grayson slipped the phone back into his pocket. "He wants to meet with us."

"About what?"

"I have no idea, but everything about it sounds strange. He said he'll be in a café in the French Quarter in fifteen minutes. Don't go to his home or office and don't call him or anyone else in his family."

"What the hell?"

Grayson shook his head. "Something's up. And I have a feeling it's not going to be good."

"He knows we're not on the case, right?"

"Since he's the reason we're off, I'd have to go with he knows."

Jackson studied his senior partner as he frowned, probably working through all the possibilities and the implications that went with them, not only for LeBlanc but for them as well. It wasn't their case and meeting with LeBlanc wouldn't sit well with the FBI, which wouldn't sit well with the chief. "What do you think?"

Grayson blew out a breath. "I think I should have told him to call the chief if he wanted to talk to us. But I got the feeling he wouldn't have done that. And since I want to know what he's up to, I guess I'm about to break protocol. Sort of. I mean, he asked us to talk and he's not the victim or a suspect, so it's sort of a gray area, but I doubt the FBI will see it that way. Still, it's one thing for me to put myself on the line. I'm not making that call for you."

"To hell with it. There's a little girl's life at stake. I can always find another job."

Grayson smiled. "How did I know you were going to say that? You realize you're a bad influence on me, right? I never would have even considered doing this a year ago."

"Welcome to the dark side."

JENNY HURRIED down the path through the woods surrounding her mother's home. The walls of her bedroom had felt like they were closing in on her, and she'd thought getting outside for a walk would help. But now, with dark clouds circling above, her anxiety was increasing. Why had she walked so far? She'd known a storm was coming. Why hadn't she stayed closer to the house?

Thunder rumbled overhead, and she picked up her pace until she was practically jogging. How much farther now? She couldn't remember. She'd walked this trail before, but it had been long ago and the foliage had grown so much that it didn't look the same. Had she veered off somewhere?

She shook her head. No. There was only the one path, and it hadn't branched.

Why hadn't she taken the bigger trail that she usually

walked? Why pick today to revisit something she probably hadn't been on in six months or better? She slowed and glanced around, making sure she was still on the path. This had to be the way, but it seemed like she should have reached the end by now. Still, there was no break in the foliage as far as she could see. And unfortunately, she had no idea how long she'd walked down the path or how long ago she turned around.

Stupid. The whole thing was stupid.

She stopped for a minute and reached down to rub her ankle, which was hurting a bit. Maybe she'd twisted it. As she straightened back up, she realized that everything had gone still. Not a breath of air stirred the trees. The sound of birds and insects had disappeared as if someone had pressed a mute button. Then off to her left, a twig snapped, the crack sounding like a cannon echoing through the stillness.

She froze.

Whatever broke that twig was too large to be one of the cute, furry creatures that offered nothing to fear. This was something much bigger. She peered into the brush but couldn't see anything beyond a thick set of vines growing up gangly bushes. Her ankle was still sore, and she wasn't much of a runner to begin with, but she didn't care.

She launched down the path, legs churning as quickly as she could force them, her thighs burning with the effort. Pain radiated from her ankle and shot up her leg, but she didn't slow. Her breath came in ragged heaves, like she was drowning, and just when she thought she couldn't make it another foot, she burst out of the woods and into the field behind her home. She staggered to a slow jog, glancing back into the trees.

About ten feet in, something moved. Something tall and thin. It was there one moment, then gone as if it had disappeared behind the tree. She whipped around and forced herself to run again. She was half limping and she wouldn't win any races with her speed, but it was better than hanging around for what was lurking back in those trees. Because there was only one predator she could think of that fit that shape and height.

A human.

The shot from the rifle echoed through the stillness like a canon. Jenny screamed and started sprinting, all thoughts of her sore ankle completely gone. She didn't dare turn around to look behind her because she might trip, but she continued yelling as she ran. Her mother rose from her rocking chair and grabbed the rifle that was never far from her side, then ran down the steps toward Jenny.

Jenny practically vaulted over the rail fence that separated the yard from the fields and never slowed. Her mother ran toward her, gun leveled at the woods behind her, but it was clear from the look on her face that she had no idea what was wrong. Jenny ran right past her and into the house, then collapsed into a chair in the kitchen, struggling to catch her breath.

Her heart was beating so rapidly, she was dizzy, and

for a moment she thought she would pass out. Her mother ran in after her and immediately grabbed a glass of water and shoved it at her.

"Take a drink," Virginia said. "Long deep breaths. In as slow as you can, then out."

Jenny did as her mother had instructed and finally managed a sip of water to wet her dry mouth and throat. She looked up at her mother and managed to get out a "thank you."

"What happened?" Virginia asked.

"Someone shot at me," Jenny said. "I heard someone when I was on the trail. He must have been following me. I started to hurry but when I left the woods, I heard the shot and started running."

Virginia frowned. "Probably some idiot poaching deer. I've seen a herd a time or two just outside of the tree line. I've already told you to be careful walking in there. People don't obey the law. You ought to stick to the road and stay out of the woods."

Jenny knew her mother was right—the woods were full of deer and the fact that it was private property and well past deer season didn't stop people from taking a shot at a nice buck if they could get it. But Jenny hadn't seen any deer or heard them. For that matter, she hadn't heard anything at all except for the person who'd fired the gun.

Still, there was no point in arguing with her mother. Jenny wouldn't be able to make her understand that she knew that he was after her. Everything about it felt off—

not at all like a local poaching deer. And it was all her fault. She'd opened this can of worms by hiring Shaye to look into Caitlyn's disappearance. Of that, she had no doubt. Shaye had even warned her that she might be in danger, but she'd dismissed the investigator's worries as being overly cautious.

She wasn't dismissing them now.

But she wouldn't make a decision while she was frightened. She'd head upstairs and take a shower, then lie down and rest. When she was calm, she'd think it all through and decide what she should do, but of one thing, she was certain.

She wouldn't be walking in the woods again.

15

MARISA WALKED INTO THE ANTIQUES STORE SHE managed a couple minutes past opening time. The clerk, an older woman named Janice, gave her a concerned look.

"Are you all right?" she asked. "You're a bit flushed. And those eye bags have been smaller. Maya not sleeping well again?"

They'd gone through a spell when Maya had turned two where she decided that she didn't want to sleep. And despite being so young and obviously needing to sleep, her daughter had managed to keep them up more hours every night than they'd gotten shut-eye.

"No. She's sleeping fine now," Marisa said as she stuck her purse under the counter and logged onto Quick-Books so she could update the sales information for the previous week. "I'm just worried about Jenny."

"Is something wrong with her? I mean, aside from the usual?"

"She's been having dreams—nightmares really—about Caitlyn. She says Caitlyn is calling to her in them because she's all alone."

"Oh my God. That poor girl. That must be horrifying."

Marisa nodded. "I'm sure it is. That's why I took her to New Orleans to hire a private detective."

Janice gave her a skeptical look.

"Don't get me wrong," Marisa said. "I don't think the detective will be able to find anything beyond what the police did, but I thought if someone else reviewed everything and came to the same conclusions, then maybe Jenny would be able to accept it and move on."

"Do you really think Jenny's going to just accept the word of some detective? She hasn't listened to the police or her parents or you and Rick. What difference is one more person going to make?"

Marisa sighed. "Maybe none. Maybe a lot. I took her to Shaye Archer. You know her story. I figured if Jenny was going to take anyone's word, it would be hers."

Janice nodded. "I suppose if that route is going to make a difference, the Archer girl would be the one to do it. She's sharp and after all she's been through, she's got instincts. If she doesn't come up with something, then my guess is no one ever will."

Janice patted Marisa's hand. "You're a good friend. Maybe this will be the thing that works. I'll say a special prayer for Jenny and Ms. Archer tonight when I make my usual rounds."

"Thank you."

Janice gave her a nod and headed off to tag some china they'd taken in the day before. Marisa watched her walk away and wished that Janice's prayers were all they needed. When Jenny had agreed to hire Shaye, Marisa thought there might be an end in sight. That Jenny might finally be able to come to grips with her loss and make a new life for herself.

But then Cody Reynolds had been murdered. Which changed everything.

And Marisa didn't think all the prayers in the world could fix things now.

Then there was the issue with Rick. He'd lied about where he'd been the day before. She was sure of it. Even worse, the additional mileage on his SUV and the coffee cup both indicated he'd been in New Orleans. But why? They didn't even know Cody Reynolds. Marisa had seen his name in the police file, but she still hadn't made the connection until Shaye pointed it out. It bothered her that Caitlyn had been in a relationship with the man, but that still didn't have anything to do with Rick. So why was he in New Orleans? And why was he keeping it from her?

Then there was this illness of his. The entire time they'd been married, Rick had never missed a single day of work. Not even when he'd broken his foot. He'd simply loaded up on Vicodin and asked her to drive him to court, then hobbled around on crutches all day even though the pain had to be awful. But now he was in bed complaining about not feeling well.

Something was up.

She lifted the store phone and dialed Rick's cell phone, but it went straight to voice mail. Maybe he'd turned it off so he could sleep. Or maybe he was on the other line with his office. Despite Ponchatoula's being a small town, Rick had plenty of work. It just didn't pay him what he could make with the same caseload in a big city. She'd try him again later. And if she never got hold of him, she'd swing by at lunch to check on him.

Everything was fine.

She drew in a breath and blew it out. Maybe if she kept telling herself that, she'd start believing it.

Her cell phone rang and she jumped, then yanked it out of her pocket. She shot Janice an apologetic look for not setting the phone to vibrate as she was supposed to and checked the display. It was Jenny. Despite being a bit emotionally unstable, Jenny rarely called Marisa at work unless something was wrong.

"I need to take this," Marisa told Janice, and hurried to the storeroom. "Jenny? Is something wrong?"

"Someone shot at me," Jenny said, her voice cracking on the last two words.

"What?! When? Are you all right? Where are you?"

"I'm at home and I'm all right. I ran and he missed, but it was so scary."

"Okay. Just stay calm and tell me exactly what happened."

Marisa heard Jenny take a deep breath, then she began to recount what had happened to her in the woods, then the exchange between Jenny and Virginia in the kitchen. When she finished, Marisa tried to quickly process everything. On the one hand, Virginia was right about the poachers. Every year they managed to put a stray bullet through a home or a windshield, hunting off-season and trespassing to boot.

On the other hand, Marisa didn't want to dismiss Jenny's story as poachers because of what had happened with Cody Reynolds. Maybe someone *had* shot at Jenny. She certainly seemed to think so, and putting Jenny's feelings down to her fragile physical and emotional state wasn't fair and might be detrimental to her safety.

"Let me come get you," Marisa said. "You can stay with Rick and me for a while. At least until we figure all of this out."

"No! I don't want to put you at even more risk than I already have. You have Maya to think about. And besides, I don't want to leave Mom alone. I'll be fine here. Mom has the rifle, and I'll stay inside."

Marisa didn't like it, but she couldn't argue the logic of what Jenny said. "Are you sure?"

"I'm sure."

"Okay. But get some sort of weapon and keep it with you. Do you have a baseball bat?"

"We're not exactly a sports kind of family."

"Then get a kitchen knife. Something, just in case. And if you change your mind, call me. Anytime. I'll come get you. I can talk to your mother too, and see if she'll come with us." Marisa knew nothing short of the second coming of Christ would get Virginia to move out of her home, but sometimes you had to go through the motions.

"There's something else," Jenny said. "I'm thinking maybe I should stop the investigation. I never wanted this to happen. I just thought she might be able to come up with something—even if it was just a theory—and I would be able to accept it. But there's no point of any of this if it puts the people I love in danger. Nothing will bring Caitlyn back, and I don't want to lose any more than I already have."

"That's completely up to you," Marisa said. "Whatever you want to do is fine with me."

"You're a good friend. You always have been."

"Take care of yourself. I'll keep my phone on me. Call me if you change your mind."

"I will."

"And Jenny? Be careful. Very careful."

SHAYE WAS JUST POLISHING off eggs and toast and a particularly good vanilla latte when she got a call from Jackson. She answered immediately, already tense. A midmorning call was hardly common, so whatever Jackson had to say was important.

"I'm getting ready to go into an interview, so I only have a minute," Jackson said. "But I thought you should know this as soon as possible."

Shaye clutched the phone. Had something happened to Jenny? Or Marisa and Rick?

"Remember I said I was going to hunt down that old detective whose dad was a family law attorney? Well, I found him last week, and he said he'd talk to his dad and let me know if he came up with anything. He called me a few minutes ago with a name. You ready to take it down?"

Shaye's heart leaped into her throat. For months they'd been trying to locate the attorney who'd brokered the sale of her baby, but everything had been a dead end. Existing family law attorneys weren't willing to talk about the illegal side of their business that some engaged in, probably because they didn't want to be implicated for not reporting their suspicions. And because suspicion alone wasn't enough to put a man's livelihood on the line. Even the hint of that sort of impropriety could ruin someone's career, and the last people who were willing to walk straight into a defamation suit were attorneys.

"Jerry Allard," Jackson said. "The detective's father said he suspected Allard was involved in some shady stuff but there was never any way to prove it. It was all rumor mill. Jerry Allard died last year. His wife divorced him decades ago and he never remarried, but his daughter,

Brenda, lives in the Garden District. She's not married, so same last name. We both know Allard wouldn't have talked to you anyway, but maybe his daughter still has his business records. Maybe she'd let you take a look."

"Thanks. I'll try to get in touch with her today."

"If you need anything from me, call."

Shaye knew what Jackson was saying. If she found anything in those records that upset her or led her down another investigative path, he wanted to be part of it. She checked her watch. A little after 10:00 a.m. The bar probably wouldn't be busy enough to warrant much staff until lunchtime, and she hadn't yet decided where to take the investigation after that, so she accessed the internet to do some research on Jerry Allard.

There wasn't much to find—some old listings for legal services of the usual family court sort. Child custody cases, divorce, adoption. Nothing that stood out, but then if Allard was brokering black-market babies, he would hardly advertise that fact. His assets would be a better indication of whether all his work was legitimate or whether he was pocketing the bigger dollars off the books, but she had no way of accessing those except property records.

She pulled up the property tax database and searched his name. Two properties came up with Allard as the previous owner. One was a house in English Turn valued at a little over a million. The second was a French Quarter penthouse valued at three million. Some attorneys did quite well, but that was a significant amount of real estate. Still, he might have money from other legitimate sources such as inheritance or investment. Or he could be living the American dream and have been mortgaged up to his eyeballs.

She did a quick search on Brenda, but all she found was a LinkedIn profile listing her as a nurse for a local pediatrician. Shaye frowned. As much as she hated manipulation, Brenda's profession might give her the angle she needed to get the woman to cough up information. If she worked with children and mothers, she would probably feel more inclined to help Shaye's search, even if it meant finding out things about her father that she didn't want to know. In any event, it was something Shaye would hold in reserve if Brenda balked at talking to her.

Next, she pulled up the pediatrician that Brenda worked for and was happy to see that his office was closed today because he made hospital rounds. That meant Brenda might be at home. Shaye had always had better success getting an inroad when she spoke to people versus asking them for help over the phone. She knew it was because everyone in the area knew her story and they felt sorry for her and couldn't turn her down to her face, but that didn't bother her anymore. It had at first, and she'd spent many hours arguing with Eleonore over how to handle it, but ultimately, her friend and therapist had won the argument with practicality. It was her usual stance and often annoying. Mostly because she was always right.

So Shaye had rolled with it, and if people helped because they felt sorry for her, then so be it. The outcome was the important thing, and it wasn't as if she were intentionally playing on their sympathy. Just being in the same space with some people had them misting up and apologizing for the things that had happened to her.

She closed her computer and put some money on the table for the food and tip. Then she headed out the door. It was a reasonable time to make a house call. Maybe she'd get lucky and catch Brenda at home. She punched Brenda's home address into her GPS and set out for the Garden District. The location of the home was only a couple blocks away from Corrine's, so Shaye easily drove right to it.

The house was a small colonial with beautiful flower beds. Either Brenda or her gardener had an incredible green thumb. There was no car parked in the drive, but the house had a one-car garage, so that wasn't a good indicator. Shaye walked up the drive, trying to think of what she would say. She'd been thinking of nothing else the entire drive over and still hadn't decided on the best method. When she reached the door, she still didn't know.

She blew out a breath and reached for the button, figuring she'd just wing it. All of this was a long shot anyway, because Jerry Allard wasn't the only attorney in NOLA who'd been suspected of shady dealings. She'd already looked into several whose names had cropped up when she'd spoken to other family law attorneys, but none of them had made her radar perk up. Granted, anyone who could be involved in such a practice probably lacked the emotional depth to give himself away in an interview, but still, Shaye would have expected some reaction when she told them why she was there.

She pressed the doorbell and waited. Just when she was going to ring it again, the door opened and a middle-aged woman with short black hair and green eyes looked out at her.

"Brenda Allard?" Shaye asked, although she already recognized the woman from her LinkedIn profile picture.

"Yes."

"My name is Shaye Archer. I'm sorry to interrupt you but if you have a few minutes, I'd like to talk to you."

"I know who you are, Ms. Archer, and what you do. I've also met your mother on a couple of occasions as well. I can't imagine what you want from me, but please come inside. I just finished making fresh lemonade. I know it's a little early in the season, but I prefer summer and wanted to pretend."

She stood back and motioned for Shaye to enter. Shaye stepped inside and followed her through a formal living room that had been decorated as a library, then down a short hallway and into the kitchen. This room was pretty. White walls, green cabinets with glass fronts, and fresh flowers in several vases dotted the countertops. Probably from Brenda's own beds.

"Your flowers are beautiful," Shaye said. "Were all these taken from your beds?"

Brenda nodded and poured two glasses of lemonade. "I like gardening. It relaxes me. Everyone needs something to help them decompress."

"I agree," Shaye said as Brenda placed a glass onto the bar and indicated for her to sit.

Brenda slid onto a stool next to her and took a sip of the lemonade. "So tell me what I can do for you. I know from the gossip mill that you don't have your mother's interest in charity events, although I'm certain you contribute more than your financial share. I'm guessing it has to do with your work, but I can't imagine what I might know."

"Maybe nothing. But it's a difficult case and I don't have anything to go on but rumor and conjecture. It's actually about your father."

Brenda frowned. "My father? What has he done this time?"

Something in her tone alerted Shaye to the fact that Brenda was already aware of and apparently unhappy with some of the choices her father had made. "My client had a baby eleven years ago, when she was very young. It was an abusive situation, and she was told that the baby died."

Shaye deliberately avoided telling people she was both the client and the detective. The last thing she needed was for the birth and sale of her child to become public knowledge. The press wouldn't stop until they ferreted out the child, and then even more lives would be ruined.

"That's horrible," Brenda said. "But what does my father have to do with it?"

"My client doesn't believe the baby died. She thinks her child was sold on the black market."

Brenda's eyes widened as the implication of what Shaye was saying hit her. "And you think my father could have been involved? Okay. Give me a second to process that. He was a family law attorney and I know he handled private adoption, but I never thought..."

Brenda frowned.

"What's wrong?" Shaye asked.

"Something my mother said back before she left him. I had forgotten about it until now. She was dragging me out of the house. I was maybe eight and crying because I didn't understand what was happening. He said he'd take me away from her. And she said, 'She's too old to be valuable.'"

Brenda's hand flew up to cover her mouth and she looked at Shaye, a horrified expression on her face. "Oh my God. My mother never would tell me why she left him. Just that he made choices she couldn't have on her conscience."

Shaye struggled to remain calm. Just because Jerry Allard might have been involved in shady adoptions didn't mean he had anything to do with *her* baby. "I'm really sorry. I didn't mean to cause you any distress."

"No. It's fine. You have a job to do, and your client deserves answers. What a horrible, horrible thing. I'm a pediatric nurse, and we deal with difficult cases like severe birth defects and terminal illness. I see what parents go through losing a child. I can't imagine..." She took a deep breath and blew it out. "So how can I help?"

"I wondered if you had your father's records from his practice? If so, I was hoping you'd allow me to go through them. But I understand if that makes you uncomfortable."

"I don't think it could make me any more uncomfortable than it already has, but if my father took part in what happened to your client, I want her to get answers. I put everything from his office in storage. I was afraid to get rid of it in case a client needed something. I planned on having it all scanned at some point but haven't gotten around to it."

She jumped off her stool and opened a kitchen drawer and pulled out a key. "This unlocks the storage unit." She handed the key to Shaye. "I'll give you a card with the location and the access code, so you can get inside. And I'll call the manager and let him know you have my permission to be there. I have to warn you. It's rather a mess. The movers just shoved everything into boxes and hauled it off. I don't think they even labeled anything."

Shaye took the key, hardly believing her luck. "That's all right. I'll bring a folding table to work on."

"Don't even bother. There's no overhead light, and it's cold and dark there. Take whatever you need with you. Go through as many boxes as you can haul at a time and then trade them out for another set. I trust you to put them all back."

"I can't tell you how much I appreciate this. And please know that I'm not certain of anything. There's just as good a possibility that your father wasn't the attorney who brokered the deal for my client's baby."

"Maybe not, but he had a lot of money and a couple of high-dollar debt-free properties when he died. I always wondered how he managed to accumulate them, but he claimed he was a good investor. Never saw a single equity statement, mind you." She looked around and sighed. "I guess now I have to figure out how to deal with the fact that my inheritance paid for this house."

Shaye reached across the counter and put her hand on Brenda's arm. "That's not on you, and you shouldn't feel bad about it at all. Trust me. I know what I'm talking about on this one."

Brenda nodded, and Shaye could see the tears brimming in her eyes. "Yes, I suppose you do. I'm sure I'll figure out a way to compartmentalize it eventually but for right now, I'm going to wallow a bit in horrified and angry."

"I'm really sorry to bring this to you."

"I'm not. It's always been there, you know? That thing in the back of my mind telling me that something didn't fit, but I could never figure it out. Then when you started talking, it all fell into place. I have no doubt my father was involved in exactly what you suspect. Maybe not for your client, but for others. Too many things— little snatches of overheard conversation between him and my mother and between my mother and my grandmother—are starting to come back to me. Lining up like little toy soldiers. I hope the answer your client needs is there."

"So do I. And thank you again." Shaye rose from the stool and prepared to leave.

"Ms. Archer?" Brenda stopped her.

"Yes?"

"If you get answers for your client, will you let me know? I don't need to know who the client was or the details of what happened. But I'd like to know that she got what she was looking for. I'll be thinking about her."

Shaye nodded. "If I get an answer, I'll let you know."

It had been a long shot to pay Brenda a visit, but it had turned out so much better than Shaye had ever hoped. Maybe Jerry Allard wasn't the lawyer who'd brokered the sale of her baby. But at least she had the means to prove it one way or another. And she was going to head over to that storage unit and start digging right away.

16

Marisa walked into her house at 1:00 p.m. and headed straight for the bedroom. She'd been calling and texting Rick all morning but he'd never responded. Janice had seen how frazzled she was and had just told her to go home and check on him when the store owner showed up. He'd spent the next two hours barking orders and complaining about all the things that weren't done until she and Janice were both completely spent. There was absolutely no pleasing him but unfortunately, there was also a shortage of jobs in Ponchatoula, especially that let Marisa incorporate her accounting degree a tiny bit. She was still holding on to the hope that the little book-keeping she did get to do would help her résumé when a better position came open somewhere in town.

In the meantime, she was a glorified clerk and number one whipping boy. By the time he left, Marisa was so panicked that Janice insisted she go even though

Janice had been scheduled first for lunch. So she'd broken major speeding laws getting home only to find Rick's SUV still in the driveway. Which only caused her to panic more.

At first, she'd hoped he'd gone to work and simply forgotten his phone at home, but when she'd called the office, they hadn't seen him yet that morning. She'd hoped he was at court or a client's location and his office just had their signals mixed, but seeing his car here totally eliminated a simple explanation. So why wasn't he answering?

She ran straight down the hall for the bedroom and shoved open the door, startling Rick, who looked like he'd been asleep.

"What's wrong?" he asked, bolting up. "Is Maya okay?"

Marisa dropped onto the corner of the bed before she collapsed. "I've sent you a million messages and you never answered. I was afraid something had happened."

"What in the world could have happened to me in my own bed? I know I have a lot of stress but I'm too damned young for a heart attack. Why are you panicking?"

"I don't know. I guess it was foolish. No. That's a lie. I'm panicking because someone murdered that bartender, and Shaye said we might be in danger. Then you never responded to me, and you always respond to me unless you're with a client or in court."

"I was sleeping. I told you I didn't feel well."

"And you're never sick. And even when you are, you never sleep. You never skip work. So sue me for thinking everything was off."

"Okay, well, I'm sorry I worried you." He studied her. "Are you sure that's it?"

Marisa bit her lip. All morning, she'd been trying to decide if she was going to confront Rick over the mileage and the coffee cup. Finally, she decided she wouldn't be able to sit in the same room with him all night without knowing the truth.

"Why were you in New Orleans yesterday?" she asked.

"I was at work yesterday."

"Yesterday afternoon you were, but where were you yesterday morning? If I call your office will they verify you were either in the building, at a client's, or in court? I'm guessing not, because none of those things would have put two hundred miles on the SUV and provided you with a coffee from your favorite NOLA café."

Rick studied her for several seconds, then sighed. "I had an interview."

Marisa blinked and stared. Of all the things she'd imagined, that one hadn't even been on the list. At best, she'd figured he was hiring a divorce attorney. At worst, she thought he might already have a girlfriend who would make the whole process a nightmare, especially where Maya was concerned. But she'd never thought he'd go through with his threat to find a job in the city.

"An interview?"

"Yes. You keep suggesting it, and I don't see things changing here. Mark called last week and said they had an opening at his firm. It's entry-level, but even that pays six figures. If I get the job, I figure I can get a small apartment in the Quarter until I can save enough to buy a house and move you and Maya there. That way, when the hours are really bad, I have a place to stay and you and Maya could come to the city on weekends and we could take her to do stuff...the zoo, the aquarium."

Instantly, Marisa felt guilty. Here she'd been imagining everything from *he was going to divorce her* all the way to *he'd killed a man they didn't even know*, and all he was doing was trying to get a better life for them. Maybe she'd been unfair when it came to a lot of things about Rick. He'd given up a lot careerwise to be here in Ponchatoula and he'd done it all for her, probably thinking that after a year or so Jenny would be better and they could leave. But Jenny hadn't gotten better, and then Maya had come along. A good surprise, but a surprise nonetheless. So he'd continued to stay for Maya.

"Why didn't you tell me?" she asked.

He shrugged. "It's a long shot, you know. There are guys with more experience competing for the job, and I didn't want you to think I was a loser if I didn't get it."

A second wave of guilt washed through her. "I've never thought you were a loser. I know how much you've given up for Maya and me. I just don't tell you often enough how much I appreciate it."

He looked at her, and the hope in his expression

made her heart clench. Rick wasn't perfect, but neither was she. And he was doing the best he could for them. She needed to remind herself of that when he got snippy and she got frustrated.

"Anyway," he said, "I was going to tell you after the first interview, but then Shaye told us about that bartender getting killed and I figured the last thing I needed to do was put myself in New Orleans that morning."

"But we didn't even know him," she said.

"Doesn't matter. I'm part of all of this and if Shaye and the police knew I was in New Orleans, that gives me opportunity in two crimes. The last thing I need is the police questioning the partners at the firm about my whereabouts. No one is going to hire a criminal defense attorney if he's being investigated for a felony."

"Oh God. I hadn't even thought about it that way. So how did the interview go?"

He smiled. "It went well. Really well. They're going to schedule for me to come back and talk to one of the partners who was on vacation. Mark said that I'm on the short list and he thinks I have a good shot."

"That's great." She leaned forward and kissed him lightly on the mouth. "I hope you get it. You deserve it."

"Thanks. I just wish the timing were a little better. This whole investigation could cause me serious problems."

"Oh my God!" Marisa spun her entire body around to face Rick. "I completely forgot to tell you. Jenny called me earlier in a panic. She said someone took a shot at her while she was walking in the woods."

Rick frowned. "That sounds more like poachers to me."

"I know. I thought the same thing, but Jenny insisted she could feel the difference somehow. I couldn't tell her she was crazy, even if she is. Anyway, I offered to let her stay here for a while, but she refused. She's got it in her head that her being here will put us in danger."

He took her hand and squeezed it. "Honey, you know Jenny hasn't been right since Caitlyn disappeared. And when she gets stuck on something, she doesn't let it go. If she thinks she needs to stay at home, then don't push. After a while, she'll realize it was just someone trespassing for deer."

"You really think it was a poacher?"

"Yes. Why would someone shoot at Jenny? What could anyone possibly gain from her dying? This bartender could have been mixed up in all kinds of things, but Jenny doesn't do anything but sit in that house and watch the weeds grow. She's not a threat."

"But what if she's remembering?"

"No one knows about that but us, Jenny, and Shaye Archer. And if she ever remembers something relevant, we'll deal with it then."

"You're right. I'm just getting anxious about everything."

"It's a lot to process. That's normal. But Jenny depends on us to be the calm ones."

Marisa blew out a breath. "That's getting harder by the minute."

"Try not to worry about it. All this will blow over soon enough and either Jenny will accept Shaye's report and make an attempt to get on with her life or she'll go back to the way she was before."

"I'm sure you're right," Marisa said. But she still worried. Things had already gotten worse—more complicated. Exactly what she'd been trying to avoid. "I'll let you get back to sleep. Do you need me to get you anything before I go? Did you eat?"

"I'm fine. If I get hungry, I'll heat up some soup or something. You already have enough to worry about without having to wait on me."

"Okay. I'll call before I leave work in case you need me to pick something up at the drugstore. And if you need anything before then, call or text. I'm keeping my phone in my pocket just in case Jenny changes her mind."

Rick nodded and slid back down into the bed. Marisa headed out of the room, giving him one lingering look before she closed the bedroom door. Despite claiming he didn't feel well, Rick didn't look sick, and his hand hadn't been sweaty or clammy, the way they usually got when he came down with something. What he looked was worried, but then that was probably because of the interview. She knew how bad he'd wanted something like this. If it didn't pan out, she wasn't sure he'd try again.

She headed through the kitchen and into the utility room, figuring she'd take some chicken out of the freezer to thaw for dinner. The chicken was at the back of the freezer in the corner, so she had to balance over the edge to reach it. When she raised back up, she glanced over at the door into the backyard and frowned. There was a mat next to the door that she kept their rubber boots on.

After their last fishing trip, she'd scrubbed the boots and washed the mat, but she could see flecks of mud in the middle of the mat. She picked up one of Rick's boots and looked at the bottom. It was clean, but it was damp. Their last fishing trip had been over a week ago. No way the boots were still wet from that cleaning. She put the boot back down and hurried out of the kitchen.

Now more worried than ever.

VICTOR LEBLANC SAT at a table in the back of the near-empty café. A cup of coffee sat in front of him, but the level of liquid indicated that he hadn't touched it. He looked up at Jackson and Grayson as they approached, and Jackson could see the extreme anxiety in the man's expression. He rose from the table and extended his hand. Jackson noticed it was shaking when he reached out. During the time Grayson and Jackson had been in charge of the investigation, Victor had remained steadfast. The strain and worry had shown in his expression, but they had never been this pronounced.

Something had happened. Something that had shaken the unshakable Victor LeBlanc.

Jackson glanced over at Grayson, who gave him a look that said he saw the same things. Jackson had no doubt that whatever Victor LeBlanc was about to say, it was going to be something neither of them could have predicted.

"Mr. LeBlanc," Grayson said.

Jackson shook the man's hand and they all sat. After several seconds of silence, Victor reached for a sugar packet and pulled it open, but he yanked too hard and spilled most of it on the table. He dumped the rest in the cup and stirred, not even seeming to notice.

"Thank you for coming," Victor said. "I was afraid you wouldn't, given what I did with the whole FBI thing."

"You did what you thought was best for your granddaughter," Grayson said. "In your position, I would use all the resources I had at my disposal as well."

Victor nodded. "I just want her back and unharmed. I mean, as much as a child can be after something like this. But as long as she's alive, we can get her the help she needs to deal with...with whatever might happen."

"Of course," Grayson agreed.

"So that's why I called you here," Victor said. "I made a mistake. A huge mistake getting the FBI involved."

"Why do you say that?" Grayson said. "Are they not handling things to your satisfaction?"

"It's not that," Victor said. "I'm sure they're the best at what they do, but when I called in this favor, I didn't know...there were things..."

"Sir?" Grayson said. "Clearly you called us here because you think we can help you, but we can't do that if you don't tell us what's wrong."

Victor looked up from his coffee mug, all the color drained from his face. "I know who's behind this. I know who's behind all of this."

"Who?" Grayson asked.

"My son," Victor whispered.

Jackson glanced over at Grayson, who looked as shocked as Jackson felt.

"Your son?" Grayson repeated. "You're sure?"

Victor nodded, clearly miserable. "Do you think I'd be here talking to you if I weren't? But I can't tell the FBI what I know. They won't handle it correctly."

"Even if you don't have hard evidence, I assure you that the FBI would take such an accusation seriously," Grayson said. "Kidnappings are all those two agents do. I'm afraid there's probably very little they haven't heard or dealt with before."

"I'm sure that's true," Victor said, "but what would they do with that accusation if I made it? Talk to my son, right? Launch an investigation of him. And that's exactly what I can't afford to have happen."

"Why not?" Jackson asked.

Victor ran a hand over his head. "I made a mistake. A terrible mistake, long ago, and I've compounded it by thinking I could force something that was never going to be. The truth is my son is not a good man. Not a moral man. But he knew my standards and he wants to inherit, so he's toed the line all these years because of that. I guess I thought if I forced him into acting the part that he would change, but I was wrong."

"I don't understand," Grayson said. "What do you think caused this?"

"Greed and lust," Victor said. "Pure and simple. Ian has a mistress. I didn't like it, but I overlooked it, figuring she would pass the way of others before. But this one is different. He's obsessed with her."

"Then why doesn't he divorce his wife?" Grayson asked.

"Because I told him that if he left his wife, I'd cut him off," Victor said. "My mother was abandoned by her rich husband—the sperm donor that gave her me. I know what it's like to grow up without a father, and I swore I wouldn't let that happen to my granddaughter. But I never thought he'd take it this far. That the money meant more to him than his own child."

"Did he intend for his wife to die?" Grayson asked.

"I don't know," Victor said. "I'd like to think not, but I'm beyond assuming anything when it comes to Ian. I absolutely think he wants ransom money—enough to run off with his mistress."

"If you think the ransom is his goal, why haven't you gotten a ransom call?" Grayson asked.

"I have. This morning, only it wasn't a call. The FBI has my lines tapped and my son knows that. I think my involving the FBI is why the request has been delayed. The note was delivered by a street person who said he was paid to do it. I didn't show it to the FBI because it verified what I already suspected."

Victor pulled a piece of paper from his suit pocket and handed it to Grayson. Jackson leaned over to see the note.

If you want your granddaughter back alive, wire 10 million to this account tomorrow at 10 am. If you notify the police, she dies.

Below the message was the account information.

"It's an account in the Cayman Islands," Victor said. "I recognized the routing number because a few weeks ago, my accountant pointed out some discrepancies in our investments. Money was being funneled out of the US and into that bank. The amounts were so small in relation to the normal amount of movement that no one had noticed."

"How much was moved?"

"About five hundred thousand over the course of two weeks."

Grayson frowned. "And I guess your son knows that the accountant reported the discrepancy to you."

"I'm afraid so," Victor said. "I think that's what prompted all of this. There are only ten people or so, including him, who could have managed this, and he knew I wouldn't stop digging until I figured out which one it was."

"So he's making the play for the big payoff," Jackson said. "The one that will set him up for life."

"You'd think so," Victor said, "and I'm sure that's

what he thinks as well, but if Ian got his hands on that money, I would give him a year, probably less, before it was all gone."

"Do you plan on sending the money?" Grayson asked.

"That's why you're here. I don't know what to do. Obviously, I want my granddaughter back, but I don't know who Ian hired to do this. Given the way they beat my daughter-in-law, they're evil people. What if I send the money and Ian skips town without giving them their cut? What will they do to my granddaughter?"

Jackson felt his stomach roll. "You think Ian would do that—leave his own daughter at the mercy of hired killers?"

Victor shook his head. "At this point, I just don't know. But I can't risk it. I can't risk my granddaughter. Not when all of this is my fault. Ian is my son and I should have never stuck my head in the sand where he's concerned."

"This is not your fault," Jackson said. "Some people are just born different than the rest of us. You did what you could to keep Ian on the straight and narrow."

"And now my granddaughter is in the hands of madmen," Victor said.

"Okay," Grayson said, clearly rattled by the situation. "Do you have any suggestions? Any way that we might track who Ian hired to do this?"

Victor nodded and pulled a photo from his pocket. "After the accountant discovered the discrepancy, I put a detective on my son. He took that photo five days ago. I don't know the men he's with, but they don't look like the kind of people my companies do legitimate business with, and Ian had no meetings on his schedule for that time."

Grayson took the photo. "We can run it through our database and see if we get a hit. But technically speaking, we are not on this case."

Victor nodded. "And what I'm asking you to do jeopardizes your careers. I realize that, and I'm sick about it, but I don't know what else to do. If the FBI goes straight at my son, everything could go in a very bad direction. And they'd only need to ask him questions for him to suspect. But if you're investigating and the FBI is in the dark, then he won't know someone is onto him. There's a chance you can get my granddaughter back before my son figures out that I know."

Jackson's heart clenched for the man, unable to imagine what he must be feeling. The worry for his granddaughter coupled with the guilt that his own son could have put the child in this situation. All over money.

Victor rose from the table. "I have to get back home to my wife. I told her I had to run for a quick meeting but if I'm gone too long, she'll start looking for me and I'm afraid the FBI agents and my son will as well. I know I don't have the right to ask for your help, and I'm aware of the risk you run if you agree to do it. But as a grandfather, I'm begging you. Whatever it takes to make things right after my granddaughter is safe I'll do, even if it means paying off every city official in New Orleans."

Jackson and Grayson rose as well and Grayson nodded. "How can we keep in touch with you?"

Victor handed him a business card with a number written on the back. "It's a prepaid cell phone. I picked it up on the way over here."

"I'll text if I need to talk," Grayson said.

"I'll await your decision," Victor said. "And thank you for meeting with me."

He headed out of the café, and Grayson dropped back into his seat. Jackson did the same and signaled to the waitress. His throat was dry, and he needed something to drink. Probably something to eat as well, although he wasn't feeling all that hungry.

"Do you think he's got it all right?" Jackson asked.

"Yeah. I do. I don't think he'd have called us unless he was sure."

"Me either. So what are we going to do about it?"

Grayson leaned back in his chair and blew out a breath. "It's just a pension, right?"

"Maybe. But you heard the man. If we get his granddaughter back, I have no doubt he'll go to bat for us, through whatever means necessary. And he has the pull. We've got the FBI here to prove it."

"It's still a huge risk, especially with everything that's gone down in the department lately."

"True."

"What do you think?"

"You know what I think, but I'm not the one with a

wife and kids and three-quarters of the way to full pension."

"To hell with it," Grayson said. "That girl is my daughter's age."

Jackson nodded. "Then let's get some lunch and figure out how we're going to get that picture run without alerting the chief that we're up to no good. And we can't drop the Reynolds investigation. He's going to ask for an update before we clock out today."

"Who says we have to? That photo isn't going to trace in a minute. After we eat, we'll go by your place, crop the two men out of the photo and upload each of them as suspects in the Reynolds case. If anyone asks, the images were taken from pictures from regulars in the bar."

"It's thin but it might work."

"It only has to work for a day. Come tomorrow, if the men holding Brianna don't have money in their hands, this all goes south and misclassifying data is going to be the least of our regrets."

17

Caitlyn awakened with a start, gazing wildly around, trying to figure out where she was. Pain shot through her head, and she grabbed it with both hands, the pressure easing the worst of it. Something had happened. Something important. Then she remembered.

She'd escaped.

But where was she now? Wherever she was, there was a draft and she was lying on dirt. Next to her hands was something cold and hard. She ran her fingers along the edges of it and decided it was a crowbar. She pushed herself up and, figuring it might come in handy, took the crowbar with her. She reached out with her empty hand and felt around. There was a storm—that part she remembered—and she thought she'd been struck by lightning. She fell and then...she couldn't remember what had happened afterward. Only that she was determined to find a place to hide until she could locate help.

Her fingers brushed rough wooden slats, like something used for a storage shed or a barn. She followed the slats to a corner, then around another side until she felt a doorframe. Gently, she ran her hands over the door, trying not to get a splinter in her search for the knob. Finally, her hand brushed against the cold, hard metal and she twisted, expecting it to be locked. But it moved freely in her hand.

She'd done it! She'd actually gotten away.

She cracked open the door and peered out. The sun was starting to set over the tree line, which meant she'd been blacked out for at least a day. There was a house in the distance. The house she'd been held captive in maybe? She couldn't be sure because she'd never had the opportunity to see it from the outside until last night and last night, she'd never looked back. And since she'd blacked out, she had no way of knowing how far she'd gone. For all she knew, this shed could be miles away from the place she was held.

She inched out and took a couple steps toward the house. If she could get close enough to see inside, she'd know if it was people who might help. Strangers. Not her captor. Or maybe there was a vehicle she could take. That would be safer. Steal a vehicle and drive far, far away. One of the guys she'd secretly dated had shown her how to boost a car. Granted, she only knew how to boost that one kind and she didn't have any tools, but she might be able to figure something out. Maybe the keys would just be sitting on the counter and she could lift them.

She inched forward toward the house, listening for any sound of voices inside, but only the sounds of the insects coming alive in the woods echoed throughout the still air. When she got to the edge of the house, she crept around the side and peered in a window. It was a kitchen. A dingy, poorly furnished kitchen, but it was empty and there was probably food inside.

Another bolt of pain shot through her head, and she struggled not to cry out. She clenched her head as she had in the shed and counted until the pain started to subside. Then everything began to whirl. She blinked and let go of her head to clutch the window ledge. What was happening? It was as though her mind was on fast-forward. As if someone had rewound the tape, then let it go. She saw the bar, the karaoke stage, the alley.

And she saw who had hurt her.

Suddenly it all flooded back, like a tidal wave washing over her. She dropped to the ground, eyes clenched, hands pressing her head. It was too much. She couldn't handle it. Couldn't believe it. Then everything stopped, and she took a deep breath as the pain subsided. And she thought about everything that she'd just remembered— played it back in her mind over and over again. And it suddenly made sense.

And the more she thought about it, the angrier she got. Then all thoughts of escaping slipped away.

They were going to pay for what they did to her.
They were all going to pay dearly.

18

SHAYE WALKED OUT OF THE FRENCH REVIVAL, FEELING frustrated. Cody Reynolds's coworkers were more than a little shaken up over his murder and were happy to talk with her, but no one knew anything helpful. She'd spent all afternoon engrossed in the records in the storage unit. When she'd realized how much time had passed, she'd loaded as many boxes as she could haul into her SUV to bring home. Then she'd driven straight to the French Revival.

But even after spending over an hour talking to the five employees on shift, she didn't know anything more about Reynolds's personal life than she did before walking in the bar. They all liked Reynolds, but no one seemed to know much about him. And all of them expressed shock and dismay upon learning he was likely involved with Caitlyn before her disappearance. For the life of her, Shaye didn't think any of them were lying.

After exhausting his coworkers with her list of questions and getting nowhere, she took her show to a couple of regulars at the bar. Like the coworkers, they were more than willing to talk, but didn't have anything to offer. Apparently, Reynolds had been the only bartender in the world who didn't stand around talking about life with the customers.

She climbed into her SUV and sat there, trying to figure out her next move. Jackson and Grayson would be talking to Marisa, Rick, Jenny, and Virginia at some point, and they would check into Garrett Trahan. Jackson had also mentioned a potential military buddy that they were going to attempt to trace and question, but even if they located him and got anything of relevance, Jackson couldn't share the information.

Briefly, she considered driving to Baton Rouge to talk to Reynolds's parents, but she didn't think they'd be able to help. And the last thing she wanted to do was intrude on their grief. Besides, her job was to figure out what happened to Caitlyn, not find out who killed Reynolds. And even though she had no doubt the two were related, they called for slightly different approaches.

And maybe that's what she needed to do—try a different approach. Or the original one.

Reynolds's murder had sidetracked her into looking into his life, but her original line of investigation had been to explore Caitlyn's past in order to formulate a theory about what had happened. And no one knew Caitlyn like her sister.

It was time for another conversation with Jenny.

Shaye called Jenny's number but never got an answer. Figuring she might be napping, she directed her SUV to the highway and headed for Ponchatoula. An hour and a half later, she pulled onto the long drive that led to Jenny's home. The car she'd seen before was parked out front, which was a good sign. If Jenny wasn't here, then Virginia probably was. Shaye had found the twin's mother to be direct but not necessarily forthcoming with a lot of details, but maybe another conversation could push her to open up more.

Or maybe Virginia really didn't have any answers.

Caitlyn and Jenny had been away at college, which automatically limited what their parents knew about the things they did. Shaye had already gotten the impression from others that Caitlyn was the outgoing one who pushed limits, even stepping over them, and Jenny was the quiet one who covered for her sister and tried to clean up her messes. Sam and Marisa weren't the type to have tattled to the twins' parents about what they were doing, and Rick wasn't from their hometown and likely had never even met their parents until Caitlyn disappeared. So it was unlikely that Virginia knew what Caitlyn had been up to at college.

Still, if the opportunity presented itself, Shaye wouldn't mind taking another run at their mother. She parked next to the car and made her way up to the porch to knock on the front door. When no one answered, she walked around to the back of the house, as she'd done before, figuring she'd find Virginia on the back porch in her rocker. She was a bit shocked to see Jenny sitting there, drinking a beer and reading a romance novel. Jenny smiled as Shaye approached.

"I knocked up front," Shaye said as she sat on the bench across from Jenny. "When no one answered, I figured I'd find your mother sitting back here."

"She doesn't like it when I drink," Jenny said. "She really doesn't like when I read romance novels. She thinks they're sinful."

"You mother has strict convictions. Honestly, I'm a little surprised myself. You seem to be feeling much better."

"I am. Something happened today. Something that grabbed me by the shoulders and shook me. It was like waking up from a long coma."

"What happened?" Whatever it was had made a huge improvement in Jenny's appearance. Color was back in her face and the dull look was gone from her eyes. Now she had a bit of fire in them.

Jenny shook her head. "That story can wait. First, I want to know if you have any news."

"I'm afraid not. I've talked to a lot of people, but no one was aware of Caitlyn and Cody's relationship."

"That doesn't surprise me. I mean, not on Caitlyn's end, anyway. I think she kept a lot of things from the rest of us, especially me."

"Really? I thought twins were close. You know, shared clothes and all of that."

Jenny smiled. "My sister and I didn't exactly have the same idea about things. We looked alike, but that's where most of the similarities stopped. And we definitely didn't have the same taste in clothes. Caitlyn would never have worn something like this. Not even at home."

She waved her hand over the baggy gray sweatshirt with flowers on it and the navy sweatpants.

"She wouldn't have wanted to share my wardrobe then," Shaye said. "I prefer comfortable to fashionable, much to my mother's dismay."

"Mothers never have good ideas about what their daughters should wear. If Momma had her way, I'd be wearing dresses down to my ankles like one of those girls from *Little House on the Prairie*." She stared off into the woods. "Sometimes we dressed alike, though. It was always Caitlyn's idea. Boys, you know? The whole twin thing got their attention. Then Caitlyn culled the herd and picked out the one she liked."

"And you?"

"I was never really into that whole thing, but I didn't see any harm in doing it. It made Caitlyn happy."

"It appears as if Caitlyn spent a lot of time on boys."

Jenny nodded. "I didn't understand it for a long time. I mean, she never seemed to take any of them seriously and was always scheming about how to get one, even if she already had one on tap. But as I got older, I started to realize why."

"Do you mind telling me?"

"It was because of me. I got all the attention, you see.

Not because I wanted it, but because of my health, I always needed more than Caitlyn. I hate to say it, but our parents barely noticed what she was doing half the time because they were too engrossed in whatever malady I'd acquired. That's why I didn't mind doing things like dressing alike. Caitlyn liked the attention and it was the least I could do, really."

Shaye nodded. "I can see why you'd feel that way. For a long time, I felt guilty for being a burden to Corrine, my adoptive mother. Even though she'd chosen to take me on, knowing exactly what she was up against, I know that I altered her life in ways she could never recover from."

"See? That's why, after Marisa told me about you, I wanted you for this. I knew you'd understand in a way that no one else could." Jenny glanced at the house, then looked back at Shaye, a sad expression on her face. "Do you think your mother regrets it?"

"No." Shaye's response was immediate. "And neither does your mother. Your parents tried for years to have children—she told me so herself. They wanted you and did the best they could. That's all any of us can ask."

Jenny nodded. "I know you're right. Momma has always said as much. But I can't help feeling like I weigh her down. Especially since Caitlyn disappeared. I made things harder on everyone, and I regret that."

"Everyone understands how difficult this is for you. I think you underestimate how much they care about you."

Jenny frowned. "No. I don't think I do. I think the

reason I feel guilty is because I know exactly how much they care. Therefore, I know how much I affect their lives. Which leads me to where I am now and why things are going to change."

"Like what things?"

"For starters, I'm going to ask you to stop the investigation. I don't know what happened to that bartender or why, but I don't want it happening to anyone else. He was perfectly fine until I had you poke around in the past. Whatever he did doesn't matter now. Maybe it never did."

Shaye studied the girl for a bit. Her voice was calmer than usual, but Shaye could see the strain on her face when she spoke, and her clenched hands gave away how much tension she felt.

"I will respect whatever you choose," Shaye said, "but Cody Reynolds's death changed everything. Even if I stop asking questions, the police will continue."

Jenny sighed. "So you're saying it's too late—that what I set in motion can't be stopped?"

"I don't know. Maybe. Maybe not. You said something happened to you earlier. What?" Shaye didn't believe for a moment that Jenny had changed her mind just because of Reynolds's death. She'd known about that yesterday and still been adamant. Something else was driving this change of heart, and Shaye wanted to get to the bottom of it.

Jenny stared out into the woods for a long time.

"Someone tried to kill me today," she said finally, her voice barely a whisper.

"What?" Shaye straightened on the bench. "When? How?"

"In the woods. I like to walk on the paths. It's peaceful, and it gets me out of the house. But today, there was something wrong. Something restless and, I don't know, malevolent. I could feel it all around me. When I started back to the house, I heard someone behind me. I tried to see, but the woods are too dense. I started to jog down the path, as fast as I could through the uneven terrain, and when I reached the fields, I ran."

"The shot came past my head," she continued. "It was so loud—like a cannon going off right beside me. I knew he was close, so I just kept running like I've never run before. Momma came off the porch with her rifle, but I ran right past her and into the house."

Jenny looked Shaye straight in the eye. "Don't you see? I could have died. Momma could have died, and I don't know what I'd do without her."

"Did you report it to the police?"

"No. There's deer poachers this time of year. And with nothing to go on but my feelings..."

"I'm sorry," Shaye said. "I know it was horribly frightening. Are you all right? Your mother?"

"Momma tries to never show she's scared, but I know it shook her."

"And how are you doing?"

Jenny gave her a small smile. "I'm drinking and

reading romance novels, which I haven't done since college. A farmer's wife who lives a ways past us stops by to see if we need anything when she's headed into town. She's a nice woman. I think I startled her by asking for romance books and beer, but she delivered it, just like I asked for. Momma took one look at my choices and opted for an early bedtime."

Shaye nodded, struggling to control her disappointment. Not because she was losing the case but because she was losing her ability to protect Jenny. But if Jenny felt more comfortable with the investigation stopped, then that's what she would do.

"I'm really sorry that happened, and I understand your reasons," Shaye said. "I'll type up my notes and deliver them to you. But you still need to be very careful. My involvement, one way or another, might not make a difference now. Is there somewhere you and your mother could go for a while? Even a couple days?"

"Marisa tried to get me to stay with her, but I told her no. I've already put her in harm's way by asking for her help. I can't stay with her. Not with Maya there. And the only way Momma's leaving this house for more than groceries or a doctor visit is if the coroner's carrying her out."

Jenny's eyes widened. "I shouldn't say that. It used to be a joke, you know, about her being such a hermit. But now..."

Shaye rose from the bench and went over to squeeze Jenny's shoulder. "You have my number. If you need something, anything, give me a call. It doesn't matter what time."

Jenny nodded. "Thank you for everything you've done. I know you think you didn't do much, but talking with you really helped. People don't know what it's like to have gaps in their own mind. They think I can just push it away and go on like nothing happened. But it's not that easy."

"No. It's not."

"But you did it. Even before your memory started returning, you got your degree and started your business. And you had it way worse than me. So if you can do it, then so can I. Sitting in this chair is fine for today, but I don't want to become Momma."

"Then you won't. Stay safe, Jenny."

"You too."

Shaye headed around the house and took off in her SUV. When she got to town, she started to veer toward the highway, then changed her mind. Before she left, she wanted to have a chat with Marisa. It wasn't that she didn't believe what Jenny had told her. She thought everything had gone down exactly as the young woman described. But Jenny's comment about the poachers had also gotten her to thinking, and Shaye would feel better if Marisa confirmed that it was most likely a case of a stray bullet from illegal hunting.

She checked the time. Almost 6:00 p.m. Late enough that Marisa should be home from work but not too late. She wouldn't stay long, but she didn't want to leave Ponchatoula without getting Marisa's take on things.

Both cars were in the drive when Shaye pulled up to the curb. She made her way up the sidewalk and rang the bell, hoping Maya wasn't already asleep. Several seconds later, Marisa opened the door, giving her a surprised look. She pushed the door open.

"Please come in," Marisa said. "I was expecting my mom. She's had Maya out all day and I figure bath and bedtime will be in short order after they arrive. What can I do for you? Do you have more questions?"

"A few. Can we sit for a minute?"

Marisa seemed anxious, and her flitting around made it harder to get a read on what she was thinking.

"Sure," Marisa said. "The kitchen is the only place not cluttered with toys. Is that okay?"

Shaye nodded and followed her through the living room and into the kitchen, where they sat at the same breakfast table they had last time they'd talked. "Is Rick here?"

"He's in bed. He wasn't feeling well. Do you need to talk to him too?"

"No. I just came from speaking with Jenny. She wants me to stop the investigation."

"Oh no!" Marisa said. "She's spooked, isn't she? Did she tell you what happened?"

"That's why I'm here. It's not that I don't believe Jenny's account. I just wanted to get a more levelheaded opinion on what it meant."

Marisa nodded. "I have to admit that the first thing I thought of when she called was poachers. The investigation didn't even factor into my thoughts until Jenny brought it up. Granted, that was a couple seconds later, and I probably would have gotten around to that possibility, but still. It wasn't my first thought."

"And now that you've had some time to dwell on it?"

"I still think it was poachers. I do believe someone fired a gun. Jenny was terrified when I spoke to her. I could hear it in her voice, and Virginia heard the shot and reacted, so that much I'm certain of. But if he wanted to kill her, wouldn't he have fired again when she was running in the open field?"

"Maybe. But playing devil's advocate, if we assume he was firing at Jenny, then maybe he retreated because he gave away his position and plan with that first shot that missed. He might have valued getting away before she called the police as more important than setting up for another shot. It's not like he could walk onto the street and fade away in the crowd."

Marisa bit her lower lip. "I told her she could come stay here, but she refused because of Maya. Maybe I should ask again."

"I don't think she'll leave, and honestly, she seemed less frightened when I talked to her and more determined. Almost calm compared to her previous demeanor. She said being shot at had made her realize how much she'd been holding on to the past and she was going to change that."

"Really? That would be great." Marisa's voice sounded resigned, not hopeful.

"But you don't think it will actually happen."

Marisa shrugged. "I don't want to be that way, but I also don't want to get my hopes up, you know? I've done it so many times before. It's been hard to watch Jenny slide downhill a little more every day. I guess I've been praying for a miracle but not really thinking it would happen."

Shaye nodded. "I understand. Well, I can only hope for your sake that she's serious about making changes. I told her I'd type up my notes and get them to her. I'll also be writing a check to refund the balance of my retainer. I can drop it off here if you don't want to wait on mail."

"Yes." Marisa frowned. "No."

"Mail it?"

Marisa looked at her. "I'm sorry, I'm not making sense. Do you think you could just hold off a couple of days? See if she changes her mind?"

"If that's what you'd like. I won't work on the case, though, unless she asks me to start up again."

"That's fine. I just have a hard time believing Jenny is done with this. But maybe it turns out I'm wrong and we'll all be better off."

Shaye rose. "That's what I'm hoping as well. Please call me if you need anything. And just in case this wasn't a random poacher misfire, please be careful."

19

JACKSON SHOVED HIS HANDS IN HIS POCKETS AS Grayson knocked on the door of Garrett Trahan's condo. His unit was located in one of the upscale buildings in the French Quarter complete with a doorman and front desk. The desk clerk had checked their ID, made a log of their names, and then contacted Trahan to let him know they were there. Given Trahan was an attorney and had a reputation for being a jerk, he'd half expected to be told to go away and contact Trahan's attorney if they wanted to speak to him. He was a bit surprised to be standing at the door now.

But that also told him one of two things—either Trahan had nothing to hide or he thought he was smarter than them. Hopefully, they'd be able to figure out which during the interview. The door swung open, and Trahan motioned them inside. Jackson recognized him from his picture on the law firm's page. He'd thought the man in the picture looked egotistical and overly impressed with himself. Seeing him in person hadn't changed that assessment.

"What can I do for you, Officers?" he said, his tone both condescending and amused.

"Detectives," Grayson corrected even though Jackson was sure the use of the wrong title was an intentional slight. "We're investigating a recent murder and have reason to believe you might know the victim."

"I can't imagine that I do," Trahan said. "I don't usually consort with the kind of people who get murdered."

"You're implying that decent people are not subject to the same risks as criminals?"

"Less so for sure," Trahan said. "But if a friend, family member, or someone I worked with had been killed, I think I would have heard about it before now. So who's the victim?"

"A man named Cody Reynolds. Do you recognize the name?"

Trahan shook his head. "It doesn't sound familiar. But the firm I work for represents a lot of people. I suppose it's possible I've seen his name listed as a beneficiary of a trust or maybe a trustee."

Given that the firm Trahan was employed with mostly did the bidding of the wealthier set of the city, Jackson doubted he'd seen Reynolds's name on any paperwork, but he also hadn't shown any signs of recognition when Grayson had stated the name. And he'd been watching closely. Either Trahan didn't know Reynolds, or he was a great actor. At the moment, Jackson could go either way.

"Mr. Reynolds was a bartender at the French Revival," Grayson said, "the bar your girlfriend disappeared from six years ago."

"Caitlyn was just a girl I dated, not my girlfriend. And I've never been in that bar."

"Why not?" Grayson asked.

"What do you mean, why not?" Trahan asked, his perfect veneer showing a tiny crack. "Because I haven't. Is there a law that says if I live here I have to go in every bar in the French Quarter?"

"No," Grayson said. "I just figured a young single guy like yourself would have made the rounds most everywhere, and the French Revival is a fairly popular place."

"Yeah, well, it isn't popular with me," Garrett said.

Grayson nodded. "Maybe that's because you found out Caitlyn had been seeing Reynolds at the same time she was seeing you?"

"What?" Trahan asked. "I don't know...you don't think...?" His face turned red and Jackson could see his jaw clench. "I'm going to ask you to leave."

"Why is that?" Grayson asked. "If you don't have anything to hide, what's the problem?"

"I'm an attorney," Trahan said. "Don't try to bullshit me. If you want to speak to me again, you can talk to *my* attorney." Trahan pulled a card from his wallet and handled it to Grayson. "So unless you have a warrant or you plan to arrest me, I believe this conversation is over."

Grayson stuck the card in his pocket. "Your choice, but lack of cooperation only makes us look harder."

"Look all you want—you and that Archer bitch can look until the cows come home. You won't find anything."

Jackson clenched his hands, fighting the urge to punch the asshole right in the mouth.

"We'll see," Grayson said, casting a glance at Jackson. "Good night, Mr. Trahan."

Jackson followed Grayson into the hall and headed for the elevator.

"Good job not clocking him," Grayson said.

"I'll probably regret it later. We got him rattled, though."

Grayson nodded. "He's a cool customer. Took some poking to do it."

"You insulted his manhood. Good call on that one. We didn't get an alibi for time of death though."

"Wouldn't have mattered. Trahan lives alone. He'll just say he was at home asleep or getting ready for work or having breakfast. Whatever. No one to prove it either way."

"The building has security."

"For strangers coming in, but there's a parking lot. I'm sure residents can come and go using pass codes or key cards or something of the like."

"Then wouldn't we be able to track his movements that way? Or maybe the parking lot has cameras."

"We'd need a subpoena, and we don't have enough for one."

Jackson sighed. "Too bad being an arrogant ass isn't enough."

"Then half of New Orleans would be on the chopping block."

"Sure feels that way some days."

Grayson clapped his hand on Jackson's shoulder. "Don't worry about it. Guys like Trahan always slip up eventually. Too smart for their own good. Let's go see if the computer came up with anything on the images we loaded. I have a feeling it's going to be a long night."

SHAYE SEPARATED the folders she'd gone through by year and then stacked them on her desk. She grabbed another box and headed to her kitchen counter, where she'd already had a pot of coffee and a container of Corrine's sugar cookies. She'd managed to cram ten boxes into the back of her SUV, and she was about to start her review of her fourth box. So far, she'd found a whole lot of nothing. Most of Allard's work centered on child custody cases during divorce. She'd reviewed the files of a couple of them, just to get a feel for his thought process, and decided Mr. Allard worked with a single-minded purpose.

To win at any cost.

Some of the things he'd put forth in court as reasons to deny custody were simply egregious and even worse, they seemed to have worked in some cases. Which was exactly why he used them. Shaye figured if Allard was willing to manufacture evidence for his client's benefit, he didn't have a problem crossing the line. Given that he'd actually kept documentation on his transgressions just reinforced her belief that Allard thought he could get away with anything. The fact that he'd died of natural causes and not in a jail cell backed that up.

She pulled all of the files out of the box and put them in two big piles to her right. Then she grabbed one off the top and opened it to begin reading. Since Jackson was no longer working the kidnapping case, she'd been hoping that he would be able to help her plow through some of these files after he got off work, but he'd called her around six and said he had to work late and had no idea when he'd be done. His voice had sounded strained when he'd called, and that wasn't the norm. Jackson was usually unnervingly calm about most things. Something must have happened at work, but she didn't want to ask him about it then. When he could tell her, he would.

That was probably the hardest thing for her to adjust to in their relationship. The necessary secrets. She understood, of course, that Jackson couldn't tell her certain things, and 99 percent of the time, she was fine with that. But that 1 percent caused her enough anxiety to feel like more. The irrational, distrustful side of her crept in, whispering in her ear that if he could withhold things from her with good reason, then he could withhold things from her for bad reasons as well. In her heart, Shaye knew Jackson wasn't that kind of man, but the demons of her past were never completely at rest. And given that all of the fallout with her grandfather was fairly recent, some demons were a little more active than others.

But all of that was hers to deal with, and she shouldn't subject Jackson to her emotional baggage. He already made enough concessions for her. Not that he ever said anything, but she noticed the deliberate things he said and did and more importantly, the things he didn't say and do. And she appreciated all the adjustments he made to accommodate her and make her feel more comfortable, so she wasn't about to pile on more with her own occasional insecurities. Jackson would tell her what was going on with him when he could. She knew that. She just had to keep reminding herself.

She opened the next file and scanned the documents. Another divorce case. At least it was easy to eliminate those. She sat it in a pile and put a sticky on top with the year of the case on it, as she was attempting to return the files in better order than what they were now. If a former client contacted Brenda, a more organized storage system would help her locate files. She'd claimed she was going to have them scanned, but who knew if that would ever happen. To be honest, Shaye wasn't sure she would bother if she were Brenda either. The likelihood of people coming to ask questions was slim.

She managed another two hours and almost three more boxes before exhaustion started setting in. Her shoulders and neck were stiff from sitting for so long, so she hopped off the stool and stretched, thinking that a long, hot shower and a soft bed might be in order. She glanced back at the counter. Only five more files before she'd finish this box. Might as well clear them out. That would only leave her four more boxes to do tomorrow morning, and then she could go trade that set for another and start all over.

And you can get back on invoices.

Sighing, she climbed back on the stool. Since Jenny had asked her to stop the investigation, it looked as though invoices were her priority again. That was disappointing on several fronts, but mostly because Shaye had a feeling that something was about to break loose on the case. Cody Reynolds's murder indicated she had made someone nervous, and the fact that it happened six years after Caitlyn's disappearance was definitely interesting. She wished Jenny had given her a little longer. Even a couple more days could have made a difference.

The reality was, if she wanted to, she could keep looking. It wasn't as if she had to have a client to poke into things, but having a client gave her weight with people when she interviewed them. "I'm just being nosy" probably wouldn't be taken as well as "my client wants to find her missing twin sister." Maybe she'd get lucky and Jackson and Grayson would find the person who killed Cody and it would all come out. Then everyone would finally have their answers and she wouldn't have an ethical dilemma to consider.

She opened the next file and scanned the top, expecting to see the usual divorce rhetoric that she'd seen over and over again, but this time she stopped. It was an adoption case. She checked the date. The month and date matched the entry in Clancy's journals. She sucked in a breath.

Stay calm. This still might not mean anything.

But she couldn't stop her racing heart as she read the name of the adoptive parents on the legal document. Her hands shook as she pulled her laptop over and did a search for their names. A Facebook profile for the woman came up with a location of Dallas. She clicked on the link and opened the woman's profile. There in the banner was a woman, a man, and a boy and girl.

Her breath came out in a whoosh and her heart clenched as the room began to spin. She made the image larger just to be sure her eyes weren't playing tricks on her, but the longer she looked the more certain she was.

It was like looking in an age-regressed mirror.

She had zero doubt this was her daughter.

20

CAITLYN SAT IN THE TRUCK SHE'D STOLEN AND WAITED. It was 11:00 p.m. The next on her list would come home sooner or later, and she'd be there to greet him. She couldn't wait to see the look on his face. Her fingers brushed against the torn cloth of the truck seat, and she shook her head. How stupid could people get? Just leaving keys in the visor. She'd figured the farmer's truck was old enough that she might be able to boost it the same way she'd learned before. She'd only checked the visor on a lark because she'd seen it in a movie. She was still amazed that people actually did that, even out in the country.

She pressed her fingers to her temples and drew in a long breath. She'd found a bottle of aspirin and some spare change in the glove box and had stopped and bought a bottle of water. But despite taking several of the aspirin, her headache hadn't subsided. It probably didn't help that she couldn't remember the last time she'd eaten. And she was certain that the drugs she'd been given were causing problems as they worked their way out of her system. At least she hoped they were working their way out, because she couldn't live this way. Not for very long. She looked back across the street and blinked twice to clear her vision. It was still going blurry sometimes. She'd had to pull over twice while driving just to give it a chance to refocus.

A car moved down the street and she watched as it passed under the streetlight, trying to make out the man inside. She smiled when she saw him. He had no idea what was coming.

But she'd bet money she'd be smiling when she left him, too.

21

GRAYSON HANDED THE BINOCULARS TO JACKSON. "What do you think?"

Jackson looked down the street into the house at the end. Drapes covered every window, but he could see the faint outline of a person behind the fabric. The image search had been a success, producing two hits—a pair of childhood friends who had apparently carried their juvenile records into adult life—Louie Sutton and Brock Tasker. They had no affiliation with any one particular group or gang or any obvious preference for type of crime. What they appeared to be were opportunists for hire, and the job didn't matter.

Their arrest records contained fraud, drug running, arms dealing, and plenty of theft and bribery charges. The DA had managed to make some of the charges stick, but others had been too flimsy on the evidence end, although Jackson had no doubt they were probably guilty of everything they'd been investigated for. They'd just gotten better as they'd gotten older, and the arrests were further apart. More concerning was that each was a person of interest in three separate homicides, all of which had the markers of being contract hits.

It had taken several hours of digging to run down some known associates who could be persuaded to talk but finally, they had an address where the two were supposed to be staying for the time being. The woman who'd owned the property was the great-aunt of one of the men and had passed away six months ago without children or a will. So currently, it was vacant until the courts decided who inherited it. Well, it was supposed to be vacant.

Louie and Brock had apparently taken advantage of the situation and set up a temporary address for their criminal empire. The question was whether or not they were holding Brianna inside.

Jackson handed the binoculars back to Grayson. "Someone's inside. At least one someone, anyway. Looks tall, so probably Brock. Assuming it's our two guys in there, of course."

Grayson nodded. "There's no alarm system connected on the house. Doesn't mean they don't have their own safeguards, but I'm guessing they didn't bother."

"Probably not."

They hadn't been able to determine where Ian LeBlanc had crossed paths with the two men, but Jackson seriously doubted it was at work or the country club. If Victor LeBlanc hadn't hired a PI to follow his son, it was unlikely anyone would have ever put them together. Which meant Louie and Brock weren't worried about being found. They had the simple part of the equation. All they had to do was keep the girl hidden until they got a payoff, then drop her off on a street corner and leave. It was an easy payday, assuming Ian lived up to his end of the bargain, which unfortunately was the big open-ended question.

"I have a FLIR in the trunk," Jackson said. "I say we walk closer and find out how many heat signatures are inside. If Brianna's in there, she'll register smaller."

Grayson looked over at him. "You keep a FLIR in your car?"

Jackson nodded. "This is my surveillance car. You never know what you might need if you're watching someone, so I picked one up a couple months back."

"Cool. The street is pretty dark and there's that tall hedge between the houses. We could probably head down the sidewalk and then into the hedges. Should be close enough to get a heat signature, and the house being wood helps."

"And if the neighbor sees us and comes out with a gun?" The neighborhood was an old one, so large trees lined both sides of the street, blocking what little light there was from illuminating much of the yards. And few people had on front porch lights, so the whole street was very dim, but the vigilant neighbor was always a concern.

"Then I'll show him a badge and suggest he head

back inside and remain very quiet until I say otherwise," Grayson said.

"You really want to do this? Just the two of us?"

"If that girl is in there, then we'll call for backup, but I'm not waiting around. If we see an opportunity to get her out, we're taking it. And before you say anything, yes, I've been thinking of nothing but the repercussions all night, but it doesn't change the fact that there's a little girl in there who might die because she had the misfortune to be born to a sociopath. If we bring the FBI in, they'll haul in Ian and then the whole thing is blown."

"I agree." Grayson and Jackson both figured either one of the men was keeping watch on Ian to make sure he did what he was supposed to, or they'd drafted a third party to do it for them. If Ian was hauled out of his house by the FBI, no doubt they'd know something had gone wrong. At that point, Brianna was a huge liability and the best thing for them to do would be to get rid of her. If she couldn't identify them, then they might just haul it out of town and leave her there. But if she'd seen their faces, they might not be willing to run that risk.

They climbed out of the car and put on their bulletproof vests, then Jackson grabbed the FLIR from the trunk. It was close to midnight, and the street was quiet. A few houses still had lights on inside, but it looked as though the majority of the block were regular working people or retired and they'd turned in for the night. They crossed the street and headed up the sidewalk. Jackson carried the FLIR in one hand, and his other rested on the gun under his jacket. When they got to the hedges, Grayson gave the neighbors' house a quick once-over, then darted into the bushes.

Jackson stepped in behind him, then turned on the FLIR and directed it at the house. He picked up the person he'd seen in the window immediately. Scanning back through the house, he saw another heat signature in a back room. This one looked as if it was sitting but was definitely also an adult. He directed the FLIR toward the far end of the house but didn't find anything. Disappointment flooded through him and he blew out a breath.

"Let me make another pass," Jackson said.

"Move down a bit farther and try a different angle."

Jackson took several steps farther down and started the scan again. He was almost done when he saw a patch of light that wasn't there before in the far corner in the back of the house. Grayson pointed at the screen and Jackson nodded. The signature was small and appeared to be huddled on the floor.

"That's her," Grayson said. "I'd bet on it."

"You are betting on it," Jackson said, "but I'm with you. So how do you want to do this?"

Grayson pulled out his cell phone and dialed. "This is Detective Grayson. I have a possible hostage situation and need an unmarked backup unit sent to this location. No sirens, please, and have them park down the street." He gave them the address and disconnected.

"Let's see if we can get a look in that room," Grayson said.

They started to move, but then Jackson noticed the front door open and grabbed Grayson's arm. They both ducked back into the foliage and watched as Brock Tasker walked out onto the porch with his cell phone.

"What the hell, Ian. You said this was going down today, and now you're saying we have to wait longer. I don't like it, man. This isn't what we signed up for. Yeah, I hear you. Do you hear me?"

He hung up as Louie Sutton walked outside. "Problems?" Louie asked.

"I think he's flaked on us," Tasker said. "I don't trust him to pay, even if the old fart sends the money. I think we should clear out of the city for a while."

"What about the girl?"

"She's a liability. Handle her and grab the guns and money and we're out of here."

Louie nodded and headed back inside, Tasker close behind.

Jackson's pulse shot up, and he pulled his pistol from the holster. "I'll take the front, you take the back?"

That gave each of them one man to take down in order to get to Brianna. They couldn't afford to wait on backup.

Grayson nodded, his expression grim, and they headed out of the bushes, each taking a different direction around the house. Jackson ducked below the level of the front hedges, then crept onto the porch. He plastered himself flat against the wall just outside the front door and pulled out his cell phone to send Grayson a text.

In place.

Several seconds later, the response came.

Five-second countdown.

Coordinating a takedown from two different entry points without radios wasn't optimum. Even a couple seconds' delay between entries gave one man an opportunity to retaliate or make a break for it. Jackson hoped that this house hadn't gone through a contemporary remodel and still contained the compartmentalized rooms that homes built in this era usually had. If the rooms were separated by walls and hallways, that gave them some leeway to take down both men before they could retreat and converge, assuming they were in different locations in the house.

The second big issue was that they were entering the house blind. They knew where the heat signatures were located before they'd come onto the porch, but had no way of knowing what room the men were in now or how they were armed.

Jackson got in ready position a couple feet from the front door, ready to launch against it as soon as he heard Grayson breach. A couple seconds later, he heard a crash and the sound of glass shattering. He launched at the door, praying that it broke, and he got his wish. The thin old wood cracked away from the hinges and he almost fell into the room.

Brock Tasker had been digging some things out of a

coat closet and he whirled around, then made a break for the hallway. Jackson did a flying leap and tackled him from the back before he could flee the room. They crashed into the floor and slid into the wall. Jackson felt a bolt of pain shoot through his shoulder, which had taken the brunt of the impact, but it didn't even cause him to pause. Tasker struggled to flip over, and Jackson shoved his pistol into the back of his neck.

"Police! Stop or I shoot!"

Jackson had expected a fight but apparently, age had made Tasker a little smarter. With Jackson on top of him, knee in his back and gun pressed into his neck, Tasker's chances of overpowering the detective were slim to none. And if there was one thing Jackson had learned about criminals, they preferred prison to death.

Jackson pulled out his handcuffs and secured Tasker's hands behind his back before running to the kitchen, where Grayson had Sutton cuffed to the refrigerator. Jackson gave his partner a long enough glance to assure himself Grayson had the situation under control before running for the corner room.

"Tasker's cuffed in the hallway!" Jackson yelled as he ran. "Call for an ambulance."

Jackson hoped Brianna wasn't physically injured, but he wanted a professional opinion on that and wanted it as soon as possible. He slid to a stop in front of the door and realized it was padlocked from the outside.

"Brianna LeBlanc," he yelled. "This is Detective Jackson Lamotte with the New Orleans police. I'm about to break down this door. Please stay down and move as far away from the door as possible. Do you understand?"

"Yes." Her choked response made Jackson's heart clench and despite his injured shoulder, he launched at the door and broke it away from the frame.

The girl in the corner jumped up as he entered but stood in the corner shaking. She was either in shock or still not convinced that she'd been rescued. Jackson pulled out his badge and slowly approached the terrified girl.

"Here's my badge. I'm a cop. You're safe now. Are you hurt?"

The girl leaned forward enough to read his badge, then launched at him, wrapping her arms around him and sobbing. Jackson held the girl as she cried, relieved to hear the sound of ambulance sirens in the distance.

"You're going to be okay," he said.

Even as he said the words, he knew that Brianna's nightmare wasn't over. Soon, she'd know that her father was behind all of this horror. Her future depended on how she managed to deal with that. If her mother died, it added another layer of difficulty to all of it.

But she was alive, and that was the most important thing.

Alive meant she had a chance.

SHAYE'S CELL phone went off at 3:00 a.m. and she bolted

up from the bed, grabbing the phone on her way up. Jackson's number flashed on the display, and her heart leaped into her throat as she answered.

"Are you all right? What's happened?"

"I'm fine," he assured her. "Well, a little banged up, and I've taken an ass-chewing to end all ass-chewings, but nothing that I won't get past. I'm leaving the hospital now. I know it's a ridiculous hour, but can I come by and tell you about it?"

"Hospital?" Shaye bolted out of bed. "Let me come get you."

"No. It's okay. One of the patrolmen is going to give me a ride. But if you have something to eat, I'll be forever grateful."

"Corrine dropped off pot roast last night. I'll go heat it up now. Are you sure you're all right?"

"I'm all right. I'll be there soon."

Shaye hurried into the kitchen and pulled the leftover pot roast from the refrigerator. Corrine always overdid it on portions, so there were easily two servings left. But if Jackson was at the hospital but worried about food, he must be starving. She poured the whole thing into a pot and turned on the stove. It would taste better reheated that way than nuked. She grabbed a package of French bread rolls from her pantry and popped three of them into her toaster oven.

Then all she had left to do was wait.

She huffed out a breath. Waiting was the worst. Especially when the man she cared about was getting a ride to her place from the hospital and she wasn't quite clear if he was the patient or someone else was. And did any of what Jackson was coming to tell her have something to do with Jenny Taylor? So many questions and so many minutes to wait until she had answers.

Her feet tingled from the cold kitchen tile, and she headed back to her bedroom to get dressed. By the time Jackson got here, ate, and filled her in on whatever had happened to him tonight, it would probably be close to wake-up time anyway. And that didn't include telling Jackson about her own findings in Allard's files.

She'd spent over an hour lying awake in bed after her discovery. So many questions swarmed through her mind, but the most important was how to proceed. Shaye had no desire to upset a little girl's life, but she couldn't rest until she knew for certain that her baby had the life she deserved. The life all children deserved. The question was how to find that out without alerting others. The press had backed off a lot from their constant hounding, but she still occasionally caught someone following her or saw a television van parked down the street. She couldn't afford for anyone in the media to get wind of this. Not even a tiny whiff. If they did, any chance her child had at a normal life would be gone forever.

She pulled on yoga pants, sweatshirt, and socks and called it done. All she'd need to do was slip on tennis shoes before heading out for the day. Assuming she headed out at all. Her entire schedule was on hold at the moment, depending on what Jackson had to say and what she decided to do about the files. She'd already promised herself that she wouldn't make any decisions on the second item until she had thought through everything at length and let it sit for a while before making a move. Despite her overwhelming anxiety about it, there was no rush. Things would hold just the way they were until she could be certain she was making the best decision for everyone.

She headed back into the kitchen and snagged the forgotten French rolls from the toaster oven just as they started to darken a tiny bit too much around the edges. It was the story of her life. Cooking definitely wasn't her skill set. She was too easily distracted by other things. She lifted the pot and stirred the pot roast, her stomach growling at the savory smell as it wafted up. Her own dinner had been the few bites she'd managed to consume before the butterflies in her stomach prevented her from eating more.

She grabbed two bowls from her cabinet and sat them next to the stove. Maybe she'd join Jackson in his middle-of-the-night dinner. What the heck, right? It wasn't like she kept nine-to-five hours. And being a detective meant Jackson rarely had any schedule resembling regular. He did the job when it needed doing and stopped when he was done.

The sound of a vehicle pulling up in front of her apartment sent her scrambling for the front door. She peered through the blinds and saw Jackson get out of a police cruiser. She sucked in a breath when she saw his right arm in a sling and rushed to turn off the alarm and open the door.

"What happened?" she asked as he walked inside. "Are you hurt? Can I get you something?"

"Just a place to sit and some food so I can take a pain med," he said. "I've been holding off until I could get some food in my stomach. It's been a while since I had anything."

"Middle-of-the-night dinner is ready to serve, and I have a stool with your name on it. Do you want a beer?"

"Better not with the pain meds. Sweet tea would be great, if you have it."

"Corrine would probably cut me out of her will if I didn't have sweet tea on hand."

Jackson gave her a smile that turned into a sort of grimace as he slid onto the stool. "I like a woman who has her priorities straight."

Shaye poured two glasses of tea and served up the pot roast and bread, then sat next to him. He took a bite and sighed.

"This is incredible. Or I'm starving."

"Probably a bit of both. Okay, I'm officially dying here. Talk in between bites. What happened? How did you hurt your shoulder? Was the ass-chewing from the chief?"

Jackson nodded. "Him and the FBI. Grayson and I aren't currently the most or least popular detectives in the department, depending on which side of the political fence you're on. We rescued Brianna LeBlanc tonight."

"What? Holy crap!" Shaye spun around on her stool to face him. "Is she all right? How did you find her? Why is the FBI mad? Who did it?"

Jackson grinned. "You want to write them all down?"

"Stop holding back. Jesus! That is huge. Go. Talk. Eat. Then talk more."

"I know this goes without saying, but you have to keep it all under wraps, especially the stuff about Grayson's and my involvement. That part will never hit the media. The department can't afford the press on it, and the FBI wouldn't take kindly to the embarrassment of having the case solved under their noses."

"Of course."

He started by telling her about their meeting with Victor LeBlanc, which caused her to drop both her jaw and her spoon. "Her father? His own son?" she said. "I can't imagine what it took for him to tell you that."

"If his appearance was any indication, he looked on the verge of a heart attack and about to be violently ill at the same time." He continued with their background check on the image and how they located the house where Sutton and Tasker had Brianna. Shaye was certain she wasn't breathing when he told her about breaking down the door and wrestling with Tasker. When he told her about Brianna, tears rushed into her eyes and spilled over the edges.

When he stopped to take a breath, she leaned over and circled her arms around him, careful not to squeeze his shoulder. She kissed him soundly, then whispered,

"You are a wonderful, awesome man. Thank you for breaking all the rules and rescuing that girl."

"Grayson helped too."

"Yeah, well, I'm not kissing him. Not on the lips anyway, but he might be in danger of a hug. So that's how you injured your shoulder—breaking down two doors."

Jackson nodded. "It's not broken, which is a plus. I just dislocated it and I'm sure it will be bruised all to hell soon, but it doesn't matter. I didn't even feel it until after the paramedics asked why I was holding my arm funny."

"Adrenaline is an amazing thing. So what happened with Ian?"

"Right after Grayson called for an ambulance, he called the chief, who sent two units over to arrest Ian."

"Was he at the hospital?"

Jackson's expression shifted from pleased to angry. "Hell, no. The mother of his child is fighting for her life, and he was at his house in the hot tub with his girlfriend."

"No! That's horrible."

"It was all I could do not to punch him when they brought him into the station."

"I can imagine."

Jackson smiled. "Someone did it for me though. Victor LeBlanc practically ran into the interrogation room. Ian jumped up, thinking his dad was there to bail him out, as usual, but instead Victor punched him so hard in the jaw he broke it."

"No, he did not."

"Yep. Took three officers to get him out of there. He may be older, but he's strong as an ox. Unfortunately, he collapsed completely when we got him into another room. I think it finally all hit him."

Shaye nodded. "Now that Brianna is safe, he has to deal with all the emotions he's been holding in. I feel sorry for him. I know what it's like to be betrayed by those closest to you. But I feel even sorrier for Brianna. I hope her mother makes it."

"Me too."

"So what happened with the chief and the FBI? How much of your butt did they take?"

"Probably enough to leave me a size smaller."

"Do you think your job is in jeopardy?"

"I doubt it. The chief was mad, of course, and the FBI was furious, but Victor told them that we'd acted on his instruction and if anyone had anything to say about it, they could take it up with him and a couple of his friends."

Shaye shook her head. "Victor LeBlanc sure likes playing games with his political connections, but I can't really blame him in this case. If it were my granddaughter, I would have used anything I had to get her back."

She frowned and dropped her gaze down to her bowl.

"What's wrong?" Jackson asked. "Did something happen to Jenny? I've been going on and didn't even ask about your case."

Shaye looked up at him, locking her eyes on his.

"I found her. I found my daughter."

22

Thursday, February 18, 2016
Ponchatoula, Louisiana

RICK GRABBED his briefcase and car keys, prepared to dash out of the house. He was already running late for a meeting at a client's house. If he didn't get there soon, the client was just volatile enough to fire him, which he couldn't afford, either with his bosses or his bonus checks. He threw open the front door and held in a stream of cursing. Not only was Marisa's car parked behind him, but he'd just remembered that he needed gas in the SUV.

"Marisa," he called out. "I'm late. I need to take your car."

Marisa hurried out of the bedroom carrying Maya.

"That's fine. I wasn't going anywhere today anyway." It was her day off.

He dropped a kiss on her forehead and then on his daughter's cheek and practically ran out the door. Since it was warm outside, he decided that meant the engine didn't need to warm up, so he fired up the car, threw it into Reverse and launched backward out of the drive and onto the street. He shifted to Drive and squealed the tires as he pulled away.

Damn it, damn it, damn it.

This kind of mistake was exactly the sort of thing he couldn't afford. Sure, he wasn't planning on making a career out of working at the firm, but he couldn't afford to lose the job either. Everyone knew it was easier to find a job when you already had one. Rick figured part of the reason for that is no one could call your current employer for a reference.

He watched his speed through the downtown area, then pressed the accelerator down hard as soon as he turned onto the long, empty farm road. The client owned several restaurants in New Orleans, but he'd had a fixation on farming since he was a child. At least, that's how he explained to Rick why he lived on two hundred acres in the middle of nowhere. Rick figured it was just a passing fad for a man who had more money than time. As it was, his client probably didn't make it to the farm but a few days a month because most of his time was spent in New Orleans, running his restaurants.

But even with the occasional appearance, he'd

managed to piss off the man who owned the neighboring farm. A big to-do about changing drainage and flooding crops, and the long and short of it was the other farmer sued and Rick's client wanted a local firm defending him because he figured a lawyer from New Orleans might not be looked upon favorably. The two partners at Rick's firm had met with the man and probably decided he was going to be a colossal pain in the ass. But no way were they turning down the money he wanted to hand them. So they did what all partners do—they turned the case over to a staff attorney so they could make the bucks but avoid the aggravation.

Rick had drawn the short stick.

He slowed as the road twisted in a ninety-degree turn to the right and pressed down on the brakes. The wheels locked for a second then broke loose, and the car continued forward. Starting to panic, he lifted his foot and pressed again but the car didn't slow even a bit. He cut the wheel, praying he could slide around the corner and let the car roll to a stop, but the tires had already lost traction in the loose dirt and the car shot off the road and through a fence.

He threw his hands up in front of his face and screamed as it slammed into a combine.

Then everything went black.

JACKSON STEPPED out of the shower and grabbed a towel.

He and Shaye had spent what was left of the night talking and hadn't even noticed the time until sunlight began to peek through the blinds. So much had happened in such a short amount of time. Every time he thought about Brianna's rescue, he was both grateful and relieved at how it had turned out. Everything could have been so much worse. Granted, the family had a lot of healing to do, but at least they were getting the opportunity to do so.

Then just when he thought he'd heard the most amazing thing he could hear in one twenty-four-hour period, Shaye had blown him completely away.

Her daughter.

He still couldn't believe the words, even just repeating them in his own mind. He'd been cautious, of course, wanting to see the evidence before he processed what it might mean. Shaye wasn't a woman given to fancy or one to jump to conclusions, but this was different. This was about as personal as it got, and he wanted to make sure her emotions hadn't clouded her judgment.

But faced with the legal documents, he had to admit that the timing was right. When he saw the picture of the child on Facebook, he was as certain as Shaye. Probably no one would ever make the connection between the pretty little girl and her somewhat famous mother, but if you called someone's attention to it, there was no way they could miss it. There were ways to check, of course, to be sure, and they'd need to figure out how to do just that without upsetting everyone. It was going to require a real delicate touch, and Jackson was already worried about what knowing for certain was going to do to Shaye.

Right now, she claimed that as long as the child was being raised by loving parents, she didn't want to interfere. And no matter what the situation, she never wanted the girl to know the circumstances of her birth, something that Jackson agreed with absolutely. No child should have to carry that burden and no way would Shaye intentionally place it on her own child. Even if it meant never being in the child's life, even peripherally.

But even though Shaye planned to do nothing with regard to the child going forward, this was still huge. Maybe one of the top five huge things that Shaye had dealt with, and that was saying a heck of a lot. Still, Jackson was grateful that Shaye had a strong support system. One of the first things he'd asked her was when she planned to tell Corrine and Eleonore, but she'd been somewhat evasive. He got the impression that she wasn't avoiding answering the question so much as she wasn't yet sure of the answer. Jackson was pleased and honored that he was in a position to be there for Shaye in whatever way she needed him to be in order to deal with this, but he knew that Corrine and Eleonore would be necessary components to helping Shaye figure out how to balance this new revelation from her past into her present.

He pulled on a pair of sweats and T-shirt that he kept at her place and headed into the kitchen. Shaye had promised that coffee would be ready by the time he got done with his shower, and he was happy to see a steaming cup of dark liquid at his usual place at the counter and, even better, a Danish beside it.

"Where did you get Danish?" he asked.

"That new bakery down the street," she said. "You know how I like to support local businesses."

"Uh-huh. How many times have you been to the salad bar next door?"

"Touché." She pulled a plate with another Danish on it from the microwave and sat down next to him. "In my defense, these are raspberry and you know how I feel about raspberries."

"You'd marry them if possible?"

"Not unless it was an open marriage. I still have a thing for strawberries as well."

"Cheater."

"At least it's not with a salad."

Jackson laughed. "So what do you have planned for the day?"

"Invoices, probably. Unless I hear from Jenny that she's changed her mind."

"You think she will?"

She shrugged. "I don't know. If she's really determined to move on then maybe not, but I got the impression from Marisa that this might be a temporary feeling."

"Makes sense. It's hard to just wake up one day and completely change your way of thinking, especially about something so important and when you've been doing it a certain way for so many years."

"True. What about you? Are you still on the Reynolds's case? Or did the chief put you and Grayson on traffic duty?"

"Don't say that too loudly. It might give him ideas. And yeah, as far as I know, Grayson and I are still on Reynolds, but I have a note from the emergency room doctor suggesting I take a day off."

"Are you?"

"Doubt it. But it's nice to have a fallback in case my total lack of sleep catches up with me. Besides, I'm sure we'll be dealing with more fallout from the LeBlanc case as well. We probably won't get much of a chance to dig into Reynolds's murder today."

"Were you getting anywhere?"

"Not really. Other than verifying that Reynolds and Caitlyn were definitely involved, we're no closer to answers than we were before."

"He had something to do with her disappearance," she said. "I'd bet money on it."

Jackson nodded. "Or he knew who did it. Either way, he was culpable enough that someone killed him for it. I think—"

Jackson's cell phone interrupted them, and he grabbed it from the counter, frowning as he checked the display. "It's Grayson. They probably shorted us a couple of ass-chewings yesterday and want to make sure we don't miss out."

He answered the phone.

"You're not going to believe this," Grayson said. "Garrett Trahan was murdered."

"What?" Jackson clenched the phone. "When?"

"Last night in his parking garage. A tenant found him this morning on his way to work. Since I entered his name into our case log yesterday, the chief called me personally to give me the good news."

"Shit."

"Yeah. What the hell is going on, Lamotte? I know we missed something but what?"

"I don't know but we need to figure it out. The bodies are piling up."

"And so is the chief's blood pressure. Are you at home?"

"No. I'm at Shaye's."

"I'll pick you up in ten minutes. We need to get down to the crime scene before the chief blows a gasket."

Jackson disconnected the call and shook his head.

"What's wrong?" Shaye asked.

"Someone killed Garrett Trahan last night."

"What?"

"In his parking garage is all I know. Grayson is on his way to pick me up. We interviewed him yesterday over the Reynolds case, and the chief is fit to be tied that another body turned up on our watch."

"I don't understand..."

"Neither do I, but I'm going to figure it out. Sorry, but I have to run."

"We didn't launder your work clothes."

"I'll get Grayson to stop by my apartment so I can change. I'll just go have a quick shave before I leave here to save the time." He jumped off the stool and headed for the bathroom.

"I'll wrap your Danish and coffee to go."

"Thanks." He hurried to the bathroom and grabbed a spare razor to give his face a quick pass. To quote Shakespeare, "something is rotten in the state of Denmark." They'd missed something. All three of them—him, Grayson, and Shaye—and that was saying a lot as very little got past any of them.

Even though he knew it would piss her off if he admitted it, Jackson couldn't help but be a little happy that Jenny had pulled Shaye off the case. He knew a cleanup when he saw it. And whatever was going on, he didn't want Shaye in the middle of it.

23

MARISA RUSHED INTO THE EMERGENCY ROOM, completely frantic. "Rick Sampson?" she practically yelled at the nurse at the desk.

The nurse nodded and waved her through the doors. "Dr. Potter wants to speak to you. I'll take you back to him."

"My husband?" Marisa asked, choking on the last word as she hurried through the doors.

"He's critical, but I'll let the doctor explain," the nurse said as they hurried down the hall. She tapped twice on a door and poked her head inside. "Dr. Potter— Mrs. Sampson is here."

The nurse opened the door and motioned Marisa inside. An older man with silver hair rose from a desk and extended his hand. "I'm Dr. Potter. Please have a seat."

"Can I see my husband?"

"In a minute, but I wanted to prepare you. Your husband sustained serious injuries in the accident. Several broken ribs and a broken femur and both his wrists. He also has swelling on his brain. His leg needs surgery to be set properly, but unfortunately, his heart is too erratic to risk surgery right now. And the swelling is a concern as well."

"But he'll recover, right?"

"I'm sorry, but I simply don't know. His condition is critical and barely stable. I'm afraid all we can do right now is wait and see how his body reacts."

Marisa's hand flew over her mouth. "Oh my God."

"Are you all right?" Dr. Potter asked. "Can I get you something to drink?"

"No." Marisa rose from the chair. "I'd just like to see my husband."

Dr. Potter nodded, and Marisa could see in his expression how serious the situation was. He didn't think Rick was going to make it. He refused to take away all hope because there was always a chance, but Marisa could tell by the look he gave her that it must be slim.

Dr. Potter guided her down the hall and into a room. Rick was in a bed in the middle of the room, tubes running from his body, most of which was wrapped with bandages. His face was swollen almost beyond recognition, both eyes completely shut and already showing signs of bruising. Small cuts covered his skin.

"The windshield shattered on impact," Dr. Potter said. "The engine broke loose and shoved the dashboard into the driver's area. He was already in cardiac arrest when air transport picked him up. The paramedics worked on him all the way to the hospital."

Marisa crept up to the bed and reached over with her hand to touch one of the few unmarred spots on his arm. He was so still. If not for the machine forcing his chest to rise and fall, she would have thought he was already gone.

"I don't want to leave," she said.

She expected an argument. It was the emergency room and Rick was critical, but Dr. Potter simply gave her a sympathetic nod.

"I'll have the nurse bring you a chair," he said. "Is there anything else I can answer for you?"

"No. Thank you."

"If you need something, call the nurse. I'll be on duty for another six hours. I'll instruct the nurse to provide you with a sedative if you feel you need it."

Marisa nodded but didn't respond. She didn't need a sedative. She was already numb.

She stood there, touching her husband's arm and trying to imagine her life without him. She'd thought about it before, but not in this light. Not with Rick dead. Never that. No matter her issues with her husband, she still cared about him, maybe even still loved him. And there was no argument at all about what a great father he was. Maya adored him.

She choked back a cry. What was she going to tell their daughter? What if he didn't make it?

"Mrs. Sampson?" The nurse who'd helped her earlier entered the room, pulling a chair. "This isn't the most comfortable, but we don't usually have people staying in rooms on this end of the hospital. I've called maintenance to see if they can get you a recliner from the other wing."

"Thank you. This is fine."

"If there's anything I can do, just press that button. I'll be making rounds in about ten minutes. I'll bring you a glass of water then."

Marisa barely heard the woman speaking, she was so wrapped up in her own thoughts. Why was this happening? Ever since she'd taken Jenny to New Orleans to hire Shaye Archer, it seemed as if the dominoes had begun to fall. But she had no idea why. So many odd and horrible things, but none of them appeared to connect to each other aside from the thin thread of Caitlyn's disappearance.

This, of course, had nothing to do with Caitlyn. It was simply a horrible accident with even worse timing, but Marisa couldn't help but feel that everything was piling up in one giant, dreadful mess. She frowned. Maybe this was all related. Rick was normally an excellent driver. Maybe her continued support of Jenny's emotional outbursts had exhausted Rick to the point that he'd made a mistake, or worse, fallen asleep. He had stayed home sick yesterday, and that was unusual. Maybe he'd needed to stay home and rest another day.

She placed her arms on the bed and lowered her head

into them, letting out a deep breath. There was no point in second-guessing everything now. She needed to focus all her energy on what to do moving forward. Her parents could keep Maya so she could stay at the hospital, and once Rick was released, he'd need in-home care. There was no way she could take off from work for weeks without the owner replacing her, so it might be necessary to quit altogether. Without either of them producing income, it made things difficult, but with the small inheritance she'd gotten from her grandmother and maybe a little help from her parents, it wasn't impossible. She could probably cover four months or so of living expenses. The medical costs would be a whole other ball game. Rick had insurance, but she knew they'd still be on the hook for a lot of the costs, especially if he needed medical home care.

Don't panic.

She rose back up and drew in a breath, then slowly let it out. Worst case, they could move in with her parents and let the bank take the SUV. The car was paid for but also totaled. With the insurance money they got for it, she could buy a cheap sedan. Enough to get her back and forth to work until things improved. It wasn't what anyone planned for their life, but with her parents' help, she could make it work.

Unless he dies.

She shook her head. No. That **was** a place she wouldn't go. Not unless she had no other choice. It was going to be hard enough to explain to Maya why Daddy wasn't going to read a story to her tonight at bedtime. She couldn't conceive of explaining to her daughter the alternative. She leaned back in the chair and closed her eyes. Her head pounded, making her eyes hurt. As soon as the nurse came around with that water, she'd take a couple aspirin. In the meantime, she'd just sit quietly with her eyes closed and maybe the feeling of nausea would pass.

A couple minutes went by, and she heard footsteps entering the room. She looked up, expecting to see the nurse, and was surprised to see a police officer standing right inside the doorway.

"Mrs. Sampson?" he asked.

"Yes."

"Can I speak to you for a minute in the hallway?"

Completely confused, she pushed herself up from the chair and headed out of the room. The officer who'd called her had said it was a single-car accident and that no other person had been injured except Rick. She knew a fence and tractor had been damaged, but surely the owner wasn't so crass as to send the cops to hound her for insurance information right now.

"Mrs. Sampson," the officer said, "I need to ask you a few questions about your husband."

"Okay," she said, still confused.

"Did he have any enemies that you're aware of?"

"What? No. I...why would you even ask that?"

"He's an attorney, correct? Sometimes people don't

take kindly to the service they provide, especially when they're the losing party in a lawsuit."

"My husband didn't work with criminals. He mostly dealt with property line disputes and estate planning. I've never heard him mention a problem with a client. Again, why are you asking this? Rick wasn't drunk. He would never drink and drive. And I'm sure he had things on his mind—we all do—but that doesn't mean this accident was due to anything but a horrible mistake."

The officer frowned. "I'm afraid it wasn't an accident."

Marisa felt the blood rush from her face. "What?"

"The brake line on your husband's car was cut. That's why he couldn't stop."

"Cut? You can't be...you're sure?"

"I'm sorry, ma'am, but two mechanics and the owner of the shop where we had it towed all agreed. The line wasn't worn in any way. Just sliced clean through."

Marisa shook her head. It wasn't possible. Someone had made a mistake.

"Maybe it happened during the accident," she said. "Maybe something from the tractor cut it?"

"There was brake oil in your driveway. He probably didn't notice when he left. You mentioned he might be distracted?"

"He was running late," Marisa said, her voice barely a whisper. She couldn't believe what the officer was saying. It couldn't be true, could it? But why would he be here asking her questions if he wasn't sure?

The officer gave her a sympathetic nod. "I'm really sorry to have to tell you this, especially given your husband's condition. But if you think of something, please give me a call. This is my cell phone. Call anytime." He handed her a card. "I'm going to talk to the sheriff about putting an officer on your husband's room. At least until we sort this out."

She took the card but couldn't even form any words. A police guard on Rick's room? What in the world? Nothing he'd said made any sense. She watched as he walked into the waiting room, then the crux of everything he'd just said hit her and she choked back a cry.

Her car.

Rick had taken her car because she was parked behind him. He hadn't been the intended target. She had.

She rushed back into Rick's room as a wave of dizziness passed over her. She barely managed to grab the arms of the chair and sit before she collapsed. The room tilted and began to spin, and she lowered her head to her knees and closed her eyes, trying to stop the whirling room.

It couldn't be. Why would anyone want to kill her?

Caitlyn.

She raised back up and sucked in a breath. Everything that had happened had only one common component. Caitlyn Taylor. But why her? Because she'd provided Jenny with the money to launch an investigation? But Jenny had called it off. Last night, she reminded herself. So whoever was behind this might not have known the investigation had ceased. Maybe he'd figured with Marisa out of the picture, the money to pay for Shaye would go away. The worst part was he would have been right.

Then a second thought charged through her mind like a lightning bolt, and she barely choked back a scream before beginning to sob. What if Maya had been in the car with her? Was someone really so evil that they would risk killing her child? But even before her mind formulated the question, she already knew the answer. Whatever was going on, he'd managed to hide it for six years. Something about the new investigation had him spooked, and he was making sure that no one would be left to talk about things again.

She leaned on the hospital bed, her arms resting on the edge, and closed her eyes again. Her heart beat so loudly in her temples that it sounded like a drum inside her head. What did she do now? Was she still in danger? Or would he stop when he found out the accident had police attention? If he knew Shaye had been dismissed from the case would it be enough to stop him? Or would he figure that as long as she was alive, there was a risk of the same thing happening all over again?

Her head hurt so much she thought she was going to be sick. She desperately needed the aspirin. The waiting room had a ladies room. If she couldn't locate the nurse, she'd grab the aspirin and get some water from the sink. With the rate her stomach was churning, it was probably a good idea to head for the bathroom anyway.

She started to rise, but Rick stirred. His eyes flew

open and he tried to bolt up, then let out an agonizing cry when his battered body stopped him. She jumped up and put her hand on his shoulder.

"Don't move," she said. "You were in a car accident, and you're hurt really bad."

He looked momentarily confused, then his eyes flickered with recognition. "Couldn't stop," he whispered.

Marisa's eyes filled with tears and she began to cry. "I'm so sorry. It's all my fault."

"No. Too fast."

He thought the accident was because he'd been going too fast. "The brake line on the car was cut. Someone was trying to hurt me."

Rick's eyes widened, and she could see the fear in his expression. "How bad?"

Her breath caught in her throat. He was asking how bad his injuries were. What was she supposed to tell him?

"Let me call the doctor," she said and reached for the button.

"No!" He grabbed her wrist with more strength than she would have thought possible given that his own wrist was broken. "Listen to me."

"Okay." The look on his face was so scary, almost deranged.

"The bartender hid her body."

24

MARISA GRIPPED THE RAIL ON THE HOSPITAL BED, unable to breathe. Rick's words had come out chopped, and she could tell he was straining to speak at all. But he wasn't making sense. Maybe it was the injury or the drugs.

"What are you talking about?" she asked.

"He wanted to tell...feeling guilty. Couldn't...I couldn't let him ruin everything. Had to protect you and Maya. Sorry...I'm so sorry."

Horror rushed through Marisa, and she clutched the side of the bed to remain upright. "What are you talking about? What did you do? Did you kill the bartender? Oh my God, Rick!"

"So...very...sorry."

Rick's hand dropped from her wrist, and his head slumped to the side. The heart monitor flatlined and an alarm went off. Medical staff rushed inside the room, and

Marisa felt one of them pull her away from the bed and lead her into the hall. She stood there, listening as the doctor gave orders to the staff, trying to save her husband. The seconds ticked by like hours, and all Marisa could focus on was the straight line on the monitor.

"Call it."

The doctor's words barely registered, then she realized everyone had ceased moving in the room. Two of the nurses turned to look at her, their expressions filled with sympathy.

"No!" She shook her head as the doctor hurried into the hallway, managing to grab her as her knees buckled.

The doctor guided her into the waiting room, and she slid into a seat. Her whole body was numb, and her mind was so foggy she couldn't formulate a thought. What had Rick been trying to tell her? She didn't understand. She'd always known he'd do anything for her and Maya, but had he really killed a man? And why?

"Mrs. Sampson?" The doctor knelt in front of her, looking at her eyes. "Are you all right? Can I call someone for you?"

Marisa nodded. "My mother." She gave him the number and he rose. Marisa needed someone here, and she didn't trust herself to make that call and keep from blurting out everything. But someone needed to be here to handle all the things she probably should be taking care of but couldn't, because her mind was too wrapped up in the cut brake line and the dead bartender and Caitlyn. No matter where you started, everything circled back around to Caitlyn.

"Wait here. I'm going to go to the desk and call. I'll be right over there."

Marisa stared at the dotted floor and tried to focus. She had to pull it together. Rick was gone, and it was partially her fault. She'd been the one to push Jenny to hire Shaye Archer, and if she was being honest, it was for selfish reasons. Marisa never resented Jenny for needing her, but she also needed to know that at some point her life would be her own again. Maya was getting older, and Marisa's obligation needed to be to her daughter first. Jenny needed to learn to live again, and Marisa had hoped that having Shaye go through the motions would help her friend get past everything.

Instead, she'd unintentionally stirred up something dark. Something evil. And now it was focused on her.

Her phone buzzed, and she reached into her purse and pulled it out, frowning when she saw it was Jenny. Not now, she thought. She couldn't handle any of Jenny's drama right now. The call dropped and the phone started to buzz again. She pressed the button, sending the call directly to voice mail. Several seconds later, a text came through. She looked at the phone, and her blood ran cold.

Can't find Momma!

Marissa glanced at the front desk, where the doctor was on the phone, probably explaining the situation to her parents. She clutched her phone and slipped out the door and into the parking lot before dialing.

"Marisa!" Jenny sounded on the verge of complete panic. "Momma's gone."

"Calm down," Marisa said. "Maybe she went to town to buy groceries. Or to a doctor's appointment."

"Her car is in the driveway where it always is. She didn't feel well last night and went to bed early. When I didn't see her this morning, I thought she was still feeling bad. You know how she hates to be bothered when she doesn't feel well, so I figured I'd leave her sleeping. I waited and waited and then finally, I opened her door. She wasn't there! Her bed was made but she was gone."

Marisa searched her mind for any reasonable explanation. "Maybe she left the house before you got up. She might have gone into the barn." Virginia Taylor had never used the barn, but Marisa was looking for any reason to keep from believing the worst.

"I checked the barn," Jenny said. "I checked everywhere...the shed, the walking trail to the pond. I called the neighbors. No one's seen her. And her hiking shoes are on the porch, right where she always leaves them. She wouldn't have gone off far without her hiking shoes. And her coat is hanging next to the back door. You know how cold Momma gets."

Marisa was struggling not to panic, but the situation Jenny described didn't sound good. Virginia had been different lately. She'd always been a silent person, but the last month or so, she'd seemed contemplative. And

Marisa had noticed she'd been losing weight. She'd wondered if the woman was ill but knew that if she was, she'd never tell because she wouldn't want people fussing over her. She came from old stock. The kind that cut off a limb with a thresher, tied it off, and finished up in the fields before going inside to take a better look. But if she was ill, maybe she'd wandered off. Maybe she was off down one of the paths and had gotten lost. That wasn't optimum, especially without her boots or coat, but it wasn't completely dire.

What if it was something else?

But why would Virginia be in danger? She hadn't prompted or endorsed Shaye's hiring. She hadn't protested once she'd found out, but that wouldn't be her way.

"Did you call the police?" Marisa asked.

"The police," Jenny said, clearly disgusted. "Of course I did, but they just said that Momma was an adult and I had to wait twenty-four hours before reporting her missing. It's like Caitlyn all over again. Oh Marisa, what if someone took her? What if I'm next?"

Marisa clenched the phone, Jenny saying the very thing that she'd been thinking. "Can you drive into town? It's not that far. You could go very slow."

"I can't find the keys! Mama always hid them so I wouldn't drive. I've looked everywhere but I can't find them."

"Okay." Marisa put one hand to her forehead, trying to think, but it was so hard to gather a single thought. "I want you to get the rifle and go into the living room. Make sure all the windows and doors are locked. I'm on my way to get you. Do you understand?"

"Please hurry."

Marisa cast one last glance at the hospital before hurrying to her SUV. There was nothing she could do here. Not anything that mattered, anyway. And she needed to get away. Away from whatever Rick had done. She knew she'd have to deal with it eventually, but right now, she couldn't think about it.

There was nothing she could do for Rick, but if Jenny was in danger, she could get her out of there. The police wouldn't do anything, and the only other people who could go get her were her parents, who had Maya and were probably preparing to come to the hospital. She'd call them from the road. They'd understand and would handle things until she could get back. But someone had to get Jenny out of that house before she was in the morgue next to Rick.

She put her vehicle in Drive and squealed out of the parking lot, praying that something hadn't happened to Virginia. And that Jenny would be safe until she got there.

JACKSON LOOKED down at Garrett Trahan's body, then back at the ME. "What can you tell us?"

"He was struck on the back of the head with something fairly thin and hard," the ME said. "Something like a pipe or tire iron."

Jackson stared at the gaping wound in the man's stomach. "Is that what killed him?"

"No. My guess is it incapacitated him. Maybe even rendered him unconscious. I'll have to do an autopsy, but my best guess is that he bled out from the stomach wound."

"Was his wallet on him?" Jackson asked.

"No. The resident who found him provided a positive ID."

"Robbery?"

The ME hesitated, then shook his head. "My gut says no. There are multiple stabs and they're wild. The attack looks personal."

"Any idea on time of death?" Grayson asked.

The ME frowned. "Unfortunately, he was still alive when the resident found him."

"What?" Jackson stared. "How long had he lain there like that?"

"Most likely hours," the ME said, "and in extraordinary pain."

"Where's the resident who found him?" Grayson asked.

The ME pointed to a man wearing a suit and sitting on a curb next to an officer. Grayson and Jackson headed his way. His shoulders slumped and he looked pale. The knees of his suit were stained dark with blood, and more blood trailed down his jacket and shirt. He rose when they approached, and his hand shook when he extended it to shake.

"You found Mr. Trahan?" Grayson asked.

"Yes," the resident said. "My space is near his. We paid extra for the spaces with no direct open air. Keeps the weather off our cars."

And offers a nice dark place to attack someone with no fear of witnesses on the street or in a neighboring building, Jackson thought.

"Did you see anyone else when you entered the parking lot?" Grayson asked.

"Just a couple other people walking to their cars at the far end of the garage, but they live here."

"Walk me through what happened from the time you entered the garage," Grayson said.

"I came through the door over there." The resident pointed to a door nearby. "It's the stairwell. I sit at a desk all day so I take the stairs when I can. My car is the black BMW next to the white SUV. I saw something on the ground when I entered the garage, but the lighting is dim, so I didn't know what it was. When I realized it was Garrett..."

The man took in a deep breath. "I'm sorry. When I saw, I immediately called 911. There was so much blood, but I still checked for a pulse." He looked at them and Jackson could see the haunted look in his eyes.

"I felt a pulse," the resident said. "I thought I'd imagined it but when I pressed his neck again, his eyes opened. Scared the hell out of me. I told him to stay still

—that I'd called for help—but he kept trying to talk." He covered his mouth with his hand and coughed, trying to regain control of his emotions.

"Red bubbles were coming out of his mouth," the resident said, "but I leaned over, trying to hear what he was saying. I could only make out one word."

"What was it?" Grayson asked.

"Caitlyn."

Grayson looked at Jackson, then back at the resident. "Does that mean anything to you?"

The man shook his head.

"Did he say anything else?"

"No. After that, he started choking and blood gushed from his stomach and then he just went limp." The man started to shake, and Jackson put his hand on his shoulder.

"Thank you," Jackson said. "You did everything you could. The officer took your name and number, right? We'll contact you to sign your statement once it's ready. But for now, you should go back home, take a shower and get a change of clothes, and call in sick."

"Yeah." The man nodded. "That sounds like a really good idea."

Grayson handed him a card. "If you think of anything else, or if you need anything from us, please call."

The man took the card and shuffled off like a zombie. Jackson glanced back at Garrett Trahan's body and shook his head. "Full circle right back to Caitlyn Taylor," he said.

"Could Reynolds and Trahan have been in cahoots?" Grayson asked.

"At this point, anything is possible. But if they were, then who killed them?"

"I think if we knew that, all of this would make sense. It feels like there's just that one thing that needs to fall into place, you know? Like it's all right there but we haven't arranged it properly."

Jackson nodded. He'd felt the same way since the beginning. That there was some undercurrent they were missing. But what?

"Did you tell Shaye?" Grayson asked. "This doesn't look good for her clients."

"I told her that Trahan was dead. I guess I should call her and tell her about his last message. She needs to warn the clients even though they're technically not clients anymore."

"What? Why not?"

Jackson told Grayson about Jenny Taylor's change of heart and Shaye's conversation with Marisa.

"Jenny might change her mind after this," Grayson said. "I understand her sentiment, but I'm afraid the horses are out of the barn. I don't think asking Shaye to step off is going to put them back in."

"No. I think this is going to keep going until it's done. I just wish we knew what 'done' looked like."

25

SHAYE PUT DOWN HER CELL PHONE FOR A SECOND TO think. Jackson didn't have much information, but what he did have was frightening. Someone had waited for Garrett Trahan in that parking lot, fully intending to kill him. They'd probably assumed he was dead or near death when they'd left. Based on the injuries Jackson had described, it was shocking that he hadn't, and also horrifying. She definitely hadn't liked Garrett Trahan, but he hadn't deserved to die, especially in such an awful way.

The ME had said the attack looked personal, and Jackson had concurred. Which begged the question, what had Garrett Trahan put out into the universe that had come back on him this way? Had he killed Caitlyn Taylor? What about Cody Reynolds? Shaye had no doubt that both deaths had everything to do with what happened six years ago, but who had killed them? Her investigation must have been the catalyst, but no matter how many times she went through every single second of it, she couldn't figure out what had caused the devastation that had ensued.

She picked up her phone again and called Jenny. She needed to know about Trahan's murder. It might change her mind about keeping Shaye involved. And it might prompt her to get out of that remote house and stay with Marisa until everything was sorted out. Jenny didn't answer, so she left a message to call her and dialed Marisa.

"Shaye, thank God," Marisa answered. "I was just about to call you."

"What's wrong?" She could hear the panic in Marisa's voice.

"Virginia Taylor has disappeared, and Jenny is losing it because, of course, the police won't do anything until twenty-four hours have passed. I'm on my way to pick her up now." Marisa gave her the details of Virginia's disappearance.

"I just called and Jenny didn't answer," Shaye said.

"I told her to get the rifle and wait for me in the living room. There's something else—Rick's dead."

"What?" Shaye bolted off the stool, not believing what she'd just heard. "How?"

"Car wreck. This morning. The police said the brake line was cut. Shaye, he was in my car!"

Shaye clenched the phone, struggling to remain calm. Marisa needed her thinking clearly, but everything she'd just heard had sent her dangerously close to panic mode along with Marisa. She grabbed her keys and purse and ran out of her apartment.

"I'm on my way," she told Marisa, and she pulled away from the curb. "Call me as soon as you have Jenny and we'll figure out where to meet. Do not take any chances. Get Jenny in the car and get away. We'll get a search party together to look for Virginia. Something is very wrong."

"Please hurry."

Shaye disconnected and dialed Jackson's number, but it went straight to voice mail. He'd called her with the information on Garrett Trahan on his way back to the police station. It was highly likely he and Grayson were in with the chief, taking a round of thrashing for Garrett's murder or maybe another round for the Victor LeBlanc situation.

She left an urgent message asking him to call her as soon as possible, and sent a text as soon as she was stopped at a red light. Then she dialed the number for the Ponchatoula police. When the dispatcher answered, she asked to be put through to an officer.

"Officer Dupree," the man answered.

"My name is Shaye Archer, and I'm a private investigator from New Orleans."

"I know who you are, Ms. Archer. What can I do for you?"

"I have a client who might be in danger. Her mother is currently missing."

"You're talking about Jenny Taylor. I told Ms. Taylor

this morning that we can't do anything about her mother just now. She's an adult and has a right to take a stroll if she wants to."

"Without her hiking shoes or a coat?" Shaye asked, growing frustrated. "Look, since Jenny hired me to investigate her sister's disappearance, three people have died, two of them this morning, and all three were murders. Jenny Taylor is in danger, and that means her mother is as well. I'm not asking you to mount a search party, but can you at least send someone to check on Jenny? She has no way to leave her house except on foot, and it's not safe for her to do so."

"Three murders? Are you kidding me?"

"No. Two in New Orleans and Rick Sampson this morning."

The officer was silent for a moment. "Everyone is busy with a fire in one of the buildings downtown. There's people inside, people looting, and traffic is a mess. Even if I thought you were right, I don't have anyone to send."

"No one at all? Not a neighbor or friend who's a good shot? I am on my way now, but I'm coming from New Orleans. I just need someone to make sure Jenny is safe until I can get there."

He sighed. "Okay. I'll go out there myself, but I'm hauling Jenny in when I do because I can't afford any more distraction."

"Perfect."

Shaye disconnected the call and pressed the accelerator down as she entered the highway. She understood the officer's disbelief, as she was having a hard time wrapping her mind around all of it herself. And with the department currently stretched with an emergency situation, it was probably hard to work up the energy to take an emotionally unstable woman's fears seriously. But Shaye knew better. Jenny Taylor might not be emotionally sound, but Shaye was.

And she'd bet everything that Jenny was in danger.

MARISSA TURNED onto the Taylor's drive so quickly that the SUV slid a bit in the dirt. She lifted her foot, reminding herself that she couldn't help anyone if she had a wreck. Virginia's car was still parked up front where it usually was and didn't look as if it had been driven recently. She parked next to it and ran for the house.

"Jenny!" She banged on the front door, surprised her friend hadn't been watching for her. "Jenny, it's Marisa. Come on! Let's get out of here!"

But Jenny didn't answer.

Marisa froze and sucked in a breath. She reached for the doorknob and it turned easily in her hand. She'd managed so far to keep the worst of her panic under control, but now it flew into overdrive. She pushed the door open and peered inside, but the room was empty. She stepped inside the eerily quiet house. The ticking of the old kitchen clock echoed throughout the house like a drum, the stillness seeming to increase its volume.

"Jenny," Marisa called out. "Jenny, it's me. If you're hiding, come out."

She waited, listening, but nothing indicated that Jenny was inside the house.

Get out!

The commonsense answer raced through her mind and she knew it was the right call. Every single time she'd watched a movie where the woman had gone further into a dangerous situation, she'd yelled at the television. But now she could see the dilemma. Jenny wasn't just her friend. She was like a sister to Marisa. No way she could run back to her SUV and leave her here.

Maybe she was having an episode—a psychotic break as she'd had after Caitlyn disappeared. The doctor had said it was possible, and Jenny had suffered from mini-breakdowns over the past few years. Given all the stress of the investigation and now with Virginia missing, Marisa wouldn't find it surprising if Jenny had another breakdown. A large one.

Which meant she could be hiding somewhere inside the house.

Marisa pulled her cell phone from her pocket and pressed in Jenny's number, but the call dropped. She checked her signal strength and cursed. Service had always been sketchy out here, but with a storm moving in, it was bound to be worse. She shoved the phone back in her pocket and headed upstairs, figuring her bedroom was the logical place for Jenny to hole up. But the room was empty. A quick check of the closet and bathroom revealed nothing. Something banged outside, and Marisa froze. It sounded like something hitting wood, like a door slamming, but it hadn't been on the house. It was farther away. Maybe the storage shed or the barn.

Jenny had said she'd checked both, but maybe she'd gone to check again. Or maybe Virginia had returned and was outside in one of them. Marisa hurried downstairs and into the kitchen to peer out the back window. The skies overhead had darkened as the forecast thunderstorm began to move in. The door to the shed was closed, and Marisa could see the latch was in place. She looked over at the old barn but didn't see any sign of movement.

The back door was unlocked, and she stepped out onto the porch to check the ground surrounding it. Maybe Jenny had gone outside and fallen. She scanned the hedges surrounding the porch but saw nothing. She was just about to head back inside to check Virginia's room when something moved in the barn. She jerked her head around, trying to lock in on what she'd seen out of the corner of her eye, and saw the upstairs window move a tiny bit.

Jenny!

She should have remembered. Once, Virginia had called Marisa looking for Jenny, worried because it was past midnight and she couldn't find her. Marisa and Rick had rushed out in the middle of the night to search and after spending hours in the woods, they'd found Jenny hiding in the loft of the old barn. She'd probably gone there to hide now.

Marisa jumped off the porch and ran for the barn, casting an anxious glance at the angry overhead skies. She'd barely made it to the barn when the rain began to fall. The barn door was old and heavy, but she managed to get it opened enough to slip inside, then realized she should have looked for a flashlight before leaving the house. She pulled out her cell phone and accessed the flashlight app, then shone it around.

At one time, the barn had held farming equipment and housed an array of livestock, but now it just held the remnants that the previous owners had left behind. Virginia had never had any use for the structure but hadn't wanted to spend the money to tear it down either. So it had stood, deteriorating, along with its contents.

"Jenny?" Marisa called out. "Are you in here? You're safe now. I'm going to take you home with me. Just come out."

The rain pelted against the tin roof, creating a faint roaring sound inside, and wind whistled through the cracks. Could Jenny hear her upstairs given the noise from the storm? She took a couple of hesitant steps toward the ladder to the loft, then grabbed one of the wooden rungs, pulling on it to test the strength. It felt solid, but Marisa was still carrying around that extra twenty pounds she'd put on after having Maya and Jenny had always been really thin.

"Jenny?" she called up. "Are you there? Please answer me."

Seeing no other option, she put her phone in her mouth and started up the ladder. She was halfway up when she heard movement outside the barn. Then the barn door slammed shut.

She scrambled back down, dropping her phone, and ran for the door, thrusting her body against it, but it held. She peered between the cracks and saw that someone had placed a board across the brackets to hold the door in place.

She was locked inside!

26

THE HEADACHE THAT HAD NEVER REALLY GONE AWAY came back full force and Marisa clutched the side of her head, pressing her temples in an attempt to stop the pain. *Think!* Now was not the time to lose it. She had to stay in control and figure a way out.

The double doors on the back of the barn had been nailed shut since Virginia and Jenny first moved in. They used to come open at night and bang in the wind, so Virginia had nailed planks across them to keep them permanently closed. The windows were all boarded up except for the one in the loft, but that was a two-story drop. Still, a two-story drop was better than whatever the person who'd locked her in had planned. But who was it? It couldn't have been Virginia or Jenny, because they would have opened the door when they heard her pound on it. Besides, neither of them would have bothered locking the barn to begin with. They never had.

And she still hadn't located Jenny. Maybe the person who'd locked her in the barn was doing the same thing. Maybe Jenny had hidden from him and that's why Marisa couldn't find her friend either. She needed to get up to the loft and see if Jenny was there. Surely, somewhere in here was a rope she could use to climb down from the loft.

She grabbed her phone from where it had dropped and was happy to see it was working, even though she still didn't have a signal. No matter, she thought, and accessed her text messages. She sent an emergency group text out to everyone she knew, telling them she was locked in the barn at Jenny's house and to send the police. As soon as her phone got enough signal, the message would go through.

She accessed the flashlight app again and climbed up the ladder and into the loft. It was basically one big open space that used to hold hay. It had been empty since Virginia bought it but Jenny had found a hiding spot between some framing in the far corner. Marisa carefully picked her way across the loft, testing the flooring beneath her with every step before she put her full weight on it. It was rotted in several places, and she couldn't afford to fall through.

When she reached the corner, she peered into the hiding space, but it was empty. Jenny wasn't here, but someone had closed the window. Where were they now? Had they been inside the barn when she'd entered, then slipped out when she'd started climbing the ladder? It was the only thing that made sense, but it also scared the hell out of her. She felt as though someone was playing a game and she'd walked right into their trap.

She headed for the window. Rope be damned. She'd lower herself as far as she could over the edge, then drop. What was the worst that could happen? She broke a leg? Then she'd hop to her vehicle. But she was getting the hell out of here and she was doing it now. She headed over to the window, ready to throw it open and begin her descent, when the light from her phone reflected back at her.

When she saw the shiny new padlock on the window, she started to cry.

Checkmate.

OFFICER DUPREE PARKED his squad car behind the SUV in the driveway and called in to get an ID on the plate. When it came back with Rick Sampson's name, he looked out at the blinding rain and sighed. This whole thing was going to be an exercise in futility. Jenny Taylor was a nice girl and he felt bad for what had happened to her family, but she was also unstable and prone to dramatics. Her mother had probably caught a ride to town with a neighbor and would come walking up any minute, wondering what all the fuss was about.

No doubt, Jenny had contacted her friend Marisa, and now the woman who should be in the hospital mourning the death of her husband was probably in the house trying to talk sense into Jenny. He let out a sigh and threw open the car door. Might as well get inside and get this over with.

The rifle blast rang through his ears a millisecond before he felt the pain in his chest. He looked down and saw blood seeping out of a hole right where his heart was. He slammed the door and reached for the radio, but before he could even press the button, everything faded out.

At some point, he drifted back into consciousness, but only barely. His body jostled around, and he could hear his car engine running. He felt a weight on his back and realized someone had shoved him to the side and was driving away in his police cruiser. He tried to reach for his pistol, but he couldn't lift his hand.

"You should have stayed away," he heard a woman say before he drifted off again.

SHAYE SPOTTED Rick's SUV parked next to Virginia's car. She'd been trying to contact Marisa for the past thirty minutes, but her phone had gone straight to voice mail. She checked her cell phone again, to make sure she hadn't missed an incoming call or text, and saw the problem. The signal strength was nonexistent.

But Marisa had said she was going to get Jenny back

to town. She had to have reached the house over thirty minutes ago. Why was she still here?

Maybe she's looking for Virginia or worse, for Jenny.

Shaye reached into her glove box and pulled out a penlight and her nine-millimeter. She had no idea what she might find inside. The storm had made it fairly dim outside and no lights were on in the house. The power might be out. She watched the storm for a moment, hoping for a break in the blinding rain, but when it was clear that one wasn't coming anytime soon, she flung open the door to her SUV and sprang out, then sprinted for the house.

She paused long enough on the front porch to wipe the rain from her eyes, then immediately checked the front door. It was unlocked. Unsure whether that was a good sign or a bad one, she clutched her pistol in ready position and pushed open the door, peering inside. The room was dark, so she reached around the side of the wall and flipped on the light switch. Nothing happened, so she pulled the penlight from her pocket and shone it into the room, scanning it from left to right.

Nothing looked out of order, so she moved inside and crept through the living room to the kitchen. Again, everything appeared in order. She was just about to check Virginia's room when her phone signaled an incoming text. She pulled it out and saw Marisa's message. She whipped around and hurried to the window, looking into the storm at the barn. She could tell that the doors were closed and could see the big plank across the front of them. Someone must have closed Marisa inside. But was it an accident or intentional?

Clutching her pistol, she crept out the back door and down the porch steps, then ran for the barn. The plank was so heavy and bulky, she had to shove her pistol in her waistband in order to lift it, but she managed to remove it from the brackets and dropped it to the side. She pulled open the door and looked inside.

"Marisa?" she called out.

She heard the footsteps behind her too late. The storm had masked the sound of them approaching. Someone shoved her from behind, pushing her into the barn, where she tripped over something big and heavy and sprawled onto the ground. As she sprang back up, the door slammed shut and she heard the plank drop back into place. She reached for her waistband and cursed. They'd taken her pistol when they shoved her inside.

"Shaye?" Marisa's voice sounded above her. "Is that you?"

Shaye pulled the penlight from her pocket and shone it up at the loft. "Yes. Are you all right? Is Jenny with you?"

Marisa's face appeared over the edge of the loft. "I couldn't find her. I saw something moving in here and came to check, then someone locked me in."

"We're both locked in now."

Marisa climbed down the ladder. "Did you see who it was?"

"No. They shoved me from behind. We have to find another way out of here."

"There's not one. Everything was boarded shut years ago. I went to the loft to check the window up there and it has a new padlock on it."

"New?"

Marisa nodded, and Shaye could tell by her expression that she understood the implication. It was no mistake that they were locked inside.

"The storm is dying down," Shaye said as the noise inside the barn decreased to a light patter of rain on the roof. She checked her phone. "Still no signal but I'm going to send a text for help like you did."

"What's going on?" Marisa asked. "I don't understand any of this."

Shaye shook her head, but the thought that had been lingering in her mind the entire drive was still there. And maybe, just maybe, it was more than a wild thought.

"Is it possible that Caitlyn is still alive?" Shaye asked.

Marisa's eyes widened. "What? No. I mean, I don't think so. You don't think..."

"I think that Caitlyn is the common denominator for everything that has happened. Garrett Trahan and Cody Reynolds both dated her; you were friends with her. You've all been careful with your descriptions of Caitlyn, but I'm good at reading between the lines. I don't think she was a nice person, and I'm going to guess that she resented all of the attention that Jenny got by being ill, which is why she tended to be more outrageous in her behavior and why she was always chasing after some guy."

Marisa opened her mouth to respond, then closed it and dropped her head, averting her eyes from Shaye's. "You're not wrong. Caitlyn was sometimes mean, borderline cruel, especially to Jenny. But why does that matter now?"

"What if all of this is Caitlyn? What if she killed Cody Reynolds and Garrett Trahan? What if she cut your brake line? What if she's the reason Jenny and Virginia are missing, and we're locked in the barn?"

Marisa shook her head. "No. That's not possible. Maybe if you'd asked me yesterday I would have thought...but not now."

"Why is yesterday different from today?"

Marisa looked up at Shaye, tears pooling in her eyes. "Because today is the day my husband apologized to me for killing Cody Reynolds before he went into cardiac arrest and died."

Shaye stared. In a million years, she wouldn't have seen that one coming.

"He was in New Orleans early that morning," Marisa continued. "I found a coffee cup in his SUV and the mileage was all wrong if he'd just gone to work like he claimed. I asked him about it, and he said he had an interview and didn't want to tell me in case it didn't pan out. I knew he was lying about something, but then he got an email last night requesting a second interview. I saw it myself and thought maybe I'd been wrong. That maybe he really had gone into New Orleans for an interview."

"But why would Rick kill Cody Reynolds? You didn't even know him."

"I didn't, but apparently Rick did."

Shaye looked at Marisa and could see how haunted the other woman was. "What did they do?"

"Rick said Cody hid the body," she whispered. "He must have helped."

"Caitlyn's body?"

Marisa nodded, then burst into sobs. She crumpled onto the ground and covered her face with her hands. Shaye knelt in front of her.

"Tell me what happened," Shaye said. If one text had gotten through, then another could. And the storm wouldn't last forever. If Shaye knew who was behind this and why, she knew what warnings to give those who came to help.

"It's important that I know," Shaye said. "Other people could walk into this trap."

Marisa's shoulders shook but she finally looked up at Shaye. "Jenny killed her."

Of all the things Shaye had thought Marisa might say, that one hadn't even entered her mind. "Jenny?"

Marisa nodded, clearly miserable. "Jenny was mad at Caitlyn. She made a pass at Sam even though she knew how Jenny felt about him. Jenny followed her to the bathroom to confront her."

"Then what happened?"

"I don't know exactly. They were gone a while, so I went to look in case I needed to referee. When I didn't find them in the bathroom, one of the servers sent me out the back door and that's when I found Jenny standing there and Caitlyn—"

She choked on the last words.

"Dead?" Shaye asked.

Marisa nodded. "At least, that's what it looked like. She was on the ground and wasn't moving. I tried to find a pulse but couldn't. Jenny was totally freaking out. She said they'd gotten into a fight and Caitlyn had shoved her and then Jenny shoved her back and she fell. There was blood coming out from under her head, so I figured..."

Marisa shook her head. "I knew we needed help, so I managed to get Jenny back inside and I told Rick what had happened. He tried to talk to Jenny, but she just stared at us like we were crazy. She said that she'd never seen Caitlyn and then she started freaking out, asking where we were and where Caitlyn was. It's like she blanked the entire thing."

"It's possible her mind separated because the shock was so severe. She couldn't face what happened so her mind tucked it away somewhere. Why didn't you call for an ambulance?"

"Rick said he would when he got outside. No way they could have heard him in the club. But when he came back in, he said Caitlyn was gone."

Shaye frowned.

"I shouldn't have believed him," Marisa said, "but I

guess I wanted to bad enough that I took his word for it. I figured I was wrong about the pulse. I was drunk so I could have been. I convinced myself that Caitlyn had gotten up and wandered off because of the head injury, and that something else had happened afterward. I kept waiting for the police to call and say they'd found her body somewhere."

"But the call never came."

Marisa shook her head. "I think I always knew that he was lying, but I never understood why he needed to, so I never pressed the point."

"I don't think we'll ever know for sure, but I have a guess. My guess is that when Rick went into the alley to check, Cody Reynolds walked out and saw him standing there over Caitlyn's body and accused him of killing her. Rick probably denied doing it and told Cody the sisters had fought over a guy. But if Cody told the cops what he saw, then Rick could have been arrested."

"I don't understand why he didn't tell. Cody didn't know Rick. Why would he help him?"

"Caitlyn had treated Cody pretty shabby, and he might have seen Caitlyn kiss Sam and figure she'd done it in front of his place of employment just to get to him. If she turned up dead there, he would have been the number one suspect."

"So they hid the body. It seems so foolish."

"Yes, but they were both young and I doubt either was completely sober. Cody was looking at a murder rap once the police went to digging. And Rick was caught standing over the body while Jenny couldn't even remember being in the alley. And then there was you."

"Me? I didn't help. I didn't even know. I swear."

"Rick loved you, and you loved Jenny. You've spent your entire life protecting her, and if she realized that she'd killed her sister, she might not have recovered from that."

"You're saying he did it for me?"

"You and Jenny. And himself."

"Jenny never remembered," Marisa said. "The next morning, she got up asking where Caitlyn was like nothing had ever happened. I thought Caitlyn was gone, just like Rick said." She shook her head. "At least that's what I wanted to believe."

"So you never told Jenny the truth and you called the police and reported Caitlyn missing."

"Yes."

"And either Rick or Cody sent a text from her cell phone and withdrew some money from her account the next day to make it seem like she'd left on her own accord."

Marisa's eyes widened. "I didn't even think about that, but if Caitlyn was really dead in the alley then one of them must have. Rick could have guessed her PIN. She used the same lucky numbers for everything. But why would Rick kill Cody? They were both in on it."

"You said Rick couldn't let Cody ruin everything. My guess is the guilt had continued to build over the years and when I questioned Cody, he decided he wanted to tell the truth. It would have cost Rick everything."

"Oh my God. What have we done? So many lies." Marisa looked Shaye directly in the eyes. "But if Rick and Cody got rid of Caitlyn's body, then she's really dead. So who's doing this?"

Shaye shook her head. "I don't know."

But she had a bad feeling. Everything she'd speculated with Marisa fit with what Marisa had admitted and with Rick's confession, but it wasn't quite right. They were still missing a crucial piece of the puzzle.

The barn door flew open, and Shaye whirled around as Jenny walked inside holding a rifle.

"Jenny, thank God!" Marisa jumped up to run over to her friend, but Jenny leveled the gun at Marisa.

"I'd stay put if I were you. I'm a good shot. Just ask Officer Dupree."

Shaye stared at Jenny, her blond hair and pink dress marred only by the cruel smile she wore, and suddenly that last piece fell into place.

"Jenny? What's wrong with you?" Marisa asked. "It's me. Your friend."

Jenny smiled at Shaye, and she felt a chill run down her neck. "You figured it out. I can tell by the look on your face. Do you want to tell her or shall I?"

"Tell me what?" Marisa asked.

"That's not Jenny," Shaye said. "That's Caitlyn."

27

Marisa's eyes widened in horror. "No. That's not possible. Caitlyn is dead."

"That's what you were supposed to think," Shaye said. "But she fooled everyone. It wasn't Caitlyn who died in that alley. It was Jenny."

Marisa's hand flew up to cover her mouth. "No! It can't be. I know them both. That was Jenny that I pulled out of the alley."

Caitlyn smiled. "I was always a great actress and fooling a couple of drunks wasn't all that hard. Just swap the masks and cell phones and act completely incapable of handling life, and that's all that was required."

"But why?" Marisa asked.

Caitlyn let out a single laugh. "Because if poor, pitiful Jenny claimed I'd tripped and fallen then the police wouldn't have done a thing. But if Jenny had been the one who turned up dead, then everyone would have blamed me. The amnesia act was just a stroke of genius on my part. Imagine my surprise when it turned out to be totally unnecessary because the body had disappeared, but I'd already picked my poison. I just had to ride it out, then graduate, get the hell out of Ponchatoula, and be whoever I wanted to be."

"But you couldn't handle it, could you?" Shaye asked. "Your mind locked away what you'd done and at some point, you started believing you were Jenny as well."

"It must have been when that car hit me," Caitlyn said. "I woke up and everyone was calling me Jenny. It didn't seem quite right, but the truth was gone. It was the weakest moment of my life, really. I still can't fathom it. I mean, for so long, I actually thought I was her...that sniveling deadweight that I was forced to drag around my entire life."

Marisa choked back a cry. "How can you say that?"

"Don't give me your heartfelt crap," Caitlyn said. "Jenny held all of us back. Everything we did had to be modified to accommodate her. Always sucking the life out of a room with her maladies. Always garnering all the attention because she wasn't healthy. I endured watching her play the sickly princess for so long that it must have been easy to become her. But then, how hard could it be to sit around and have people wait on you?"

"When did you start to remember?" Shaye asked.

"I think I had flashes over the years, but then they went away, and everything got foggy again. When the dreams started, I still thought I was Jenny and that my memory was returning, but I think it was my real self trying to push through the facade. Then the day someone shot at me in the woods, it broke something loose. I woke up that evening and it all flooded back to me. Every detail. Every lie."

She glared at Marisa. "Including the fact that my 'friend' covered up my murder to protect my sister."

Marisa gasped. "It was you, wasn't it? You're the one who cut my brake line. You killed Rick."

Caitlyn shrugged. "Even before I heard you tell Shaye about Rick's deathbed confession, I figured he was involved up to his eyeballs. I knew for certain you were lying because you were there and had seen the body. But Rick was always hanging around, taking care of everything you needed. I'm not surprised he tried to fix this too, nor does it surprise me that idiot Cody Reynolds helped. So forgive me if I find it hard to mourn his death or Cody's. Just like I'll find it hard to mourn yours."

"And Garrett Trahan?" Shaye asked. "That was your work as well, wasn't it?"

Caitlyn laughed. "He got exactly what he deserved. He beat me, you know. The day I broke up with him, he raped me afterward, then dared me to call the police. Who were they going to believe, right? The nobody girl from the nowhere town or the privileged son of a connected family? But I still won. It took me six years, but he paid for everything he did to me."

She leveled the rifle at Marisa. "I just have this one last piece of business before I leave this place and become someone else all over again. Someone fabulous. Someone who can accomplish anything she wants."

Her finger moved to the trigger, and Shaye grabbed Marisa's arm and yanked her behind an old engine. The rifle went off, and a bullet ricocheted off the metal and flew right by her head. She dived for the ground, pulling Marisa with her, then looked around, trying to find some sort of weapon, even though nothing in her hand could compete with a rifle. She felt around on the ground and her fingers finally wrapped around a pipe. She pulled it out and motioned to Marisa to stay still and quiet.

The storm had picked up again outside, and the roar of the rain on the metal roof made it hard to hear any movement inside the barn. Another disadvantage. Caitlyn knew exactly where they were, but they couldn't hear where she was moving. Shaye strained to pick up the shuffle of feet or an intake of breath, but it was all drowned out in the storm.

She pulled her cell phone out of her pocket and checked the signal. Still nothing, but she sent another short text to Jackson, telling him that Jenny was Caitlyn and was the murderer. Then she shoved the phone behind a framing stud. Worst case, if they didn't make it out of here, and Caitlyn didn't find the phone and destroy it, someone would know what happened and who to look for.

Something dropped to the right of them and Shaye crawled farther around the other side of the engine, Marisa right behind. She realized her mistake immediately. The light hit her right in the eyes and she put her hand up to block it. Caitlyn was standing about ten feet away. She put the flashlight on a crate beside her and lifted the shotgun. Shaye and Marisa both launched backward, but it was too late.

The shot rang out, echoing through the barn. Shaye dived for the ground, her face slamming into the dirt so hard she inhaled some of it. Fighting off the urge to cough, she twisted her head back expecting to find Marisa dead. Instead, she saw Marisa struggling to get up and Virginia Taylor standing over her dead daughter's body, clutching a pistol.

"And so it is done," Virginia said.

Shaye rose from the ground and looked at Virginia. "You knew."

Virginia looked up at her and nodded. "From the moment I saw her in that hotel in New Orleans."

Marisa stared at Virginia, clearly distraught. "Why didn't you say something?"

"I'd already lost one daughter, and given that the one I had left was claiming to be her sister, I figured I knew the score. Caitlyn always resented Jenny. I thought she was faking for the attention, but after that car accident, I realized she had truly forgotten who she was. Would have been no point in saying something then."

Shaye moved next to Marisa and placed her arm around the distraught woman's shoulders. "But she started to remember," Shaye said.

"From time to time, she did," Virginia said. "The

drugs helped erase most of it. When I saw that look creep back in her eye, I gave her a dose in her soda or her breakfast cereal. Sometimes I'd lock her in her room until I was certain she was Jenny again."

"Did her father know?" Marisa asked.

"He never said, but I figure he knew the score. Put him in an early grave."

"I can't believe she fooled me," Marisa said. "How is that possible?"

"Because you explained away any differences in behavior as shock from Caitlyn's disappearance," Shaye said. "It wasn't an illogical conclusion to make. Caitlyn did such a good job acting like Jenny that she fooled everyone except Virginia."

"She even fooled herself." Marisa sank onto the ground and started to cry. "I'm so sorry, Ms. Taylor. I should have been there. I should have been in that alley and none of this would have happened."

Virginia shook her head. "You were always a good girl, Marisa, but you couldn't have done nothing to prevent this. Caitlyn was on a path to destruction her entire life. Started in the womb and just got worse. And my poor Jenny never really stood a chance. Not from the beginning."

"What happened to you?" Shaye asked. "I figured Caitlyn had killed you."

"She drugged me and stuffed me in my bedroom closet. Took me a long time to wake up and even longer to kick the door down. I'll be paying for it tomorrow. I figure she was going to come back and handle me later. Or maybe she was going to leave me be. After all, I'd kept her secret this long. Guess I'm free from that burden now."

"The New Orleans police are probably going to arrest you," Shaye said.

"Doesn't matter," Virginia said. "They can't do nothing worse to me than what's already coming. Doc gave me six months."

Realization flooded through Shaye. "You stopped drugging her. You let her memory return."

"It was going to happen sooner or later. I figured we was all better off if I was here to try to head off the worst of the fallout when she realized who she was. But I overestimated my own strength. Or underestimated hers. Same result. Either way, it's over."

Marisa turned to Shaye and buried her head in Shaye's shoulder, sobbing. Shaye wrapped her arms around the other woman as Virginia's words echoed through her head.

Either way, it's over.

Except it wasn't. For Marisa, it never would be.

28

ONE WEEK LATER

French Quarter, New Orleans

JACKSON GRABBED two beers from the refrigerator and carried them onto his patio, handing one to Shaye. Then he moved to the grill and checked the steaks he'd thrown on a minute earlier. Shaye sat in one of the bistro chairs and stared over the garden his patio overlooked.

"It's nice outside today," she said. "Maybe we'll have an early summer."

"I don't think one unexpected warm day is indicative of a whole movement of season," Jackson said, "but I wouldn't turn it down."

"Me either. I'm tired of the rain. Tired of the gloom."

He nodded. Shaye had bad memories associated with thunderstorms and although she'd figured out how to deal with them, she still wasn't a big fan. To be honest, he preferred sunnier days himself, but winter in New Orleans often meant rain. At least they weren't shoveling their cars out from under snowdrifts. He wasn't sure how people coped with that every day.

"Did you see Marisa today?" he asked.

She nodded. "We had a long talk and, I'm not ashamed to admit it, a long cry. I feel so bad for her. Her entire life was undone in a matter of days. Her husband and the father of her child is dead, and he'd been lying to her for years."

"Then there was that whole murder thing."

"Yeah. I think that's what bothers her the most. That Maya will eventually find out what her father did. And she's terrified she'll be arrested. Any word on that?"

"Grayson and I talked to the DA today to lay it all out for him. It was a lot to cover, and with crimes happening here and Ponchatoula, we had jurisdiction issues, especially with them losing a cop over this mess. Then there's the fact that the primary guilty parties are all dead. Garrett Trahan's family is screaming for justice, but we don't have anything to give them but a name and a grave site. The crowbar Caitlyn used to kill him was in the truck she stole, and her prints and DNA are all over everything, so there's no doubt as to who did it even without her confession."

"What about Marisa and Virginia?"

"The DA isn't going to pursue anything against Marisa. The only thing she's guilty of is lying to the police about what she saw in the alley when they reported Caitlyn missing. And her defense will be that Rick told her Caitlyn/Jenny was gone when he checked. We have nothing to connect her with Cody Reynolds, but we got Rick on camera at a gas station on the highway to the cemetery just before the scheduled meeting time."

"That will be a huge relief for her that the DA isn't pursuing charges."

Jackson nodded. "He could have gone for obstruction of justice or accessory to murder, but what was the point? It would have been hard to make it stick and in the end, Marisa is also a victim. The DA doesn't want to mar his record with a loss, and a jury would have a hard time orphaning a toddler with only circumstantial evidence."

"And Virginia?"

"That one is a little more difficult. She knew the person living with her was Caitlyn and not Jenny, but that in itself is not a crime. And she could only guess what had happened in New Orleans. She had no proof other than an innate knowledge of her daughters."

"But when Cody Reynolds was killed, she must have known that things were going south. She should have taken her suspicions to the New Orleans police then."

"I agree. But what would have happened if they'd arrested Caitlyn? At that point, she still thought she was Jenny. And once her true identity returned, she would have simply continued to pretend she had no memory of that night and swear she was Jenny, like she believed herself for years. A psychiatrist would have made the argument of a psychological break as a result of the shock. Eleonore's already verified that was probably what happened."

Shaye nodded. Her friend and therapist had been fascinated with Shaye's latest case, particularly Caitlyn's psyche. She had taken copious notes and intended to interview everyone who had come in contact with Caitlyn after that night to try to pin down some indicators that might help doctors identify similar cases in the future. Not that she anticipated it happening often. The circumstances surrounding the entire case were very specific. Shaye figured Eleonore was simply interested in figuring out the why of it for her own knowledge. She was like that—always pushing to understand things about the human mind that defied explanation.

"I guess you're right," Shaye said. "I suppose the most that would have come out of it is that Caitlyn might have been committed. But then she couldn't have killed anyone."

"And that's exactly what Garrett Trahan's father is saying. But the reality is Virginia Taylor won't live long enough to see the inside of a courtroom."

"I went by to see her after I left Marisa's."

Jackson's eyes widened. "Really?"

Shaye nodded. "I know she might have been able to prevent some of this if she'd told the truth long ago, but I feel sorry for her. One daughter murdered by the other.

Her husband's heart attack. Then she had to kill her own child. I can't imagine how that felt."

"How did she seem?"

"As stoic as ever. I'm not sure even Eleonore could crack her. But she seemed pleased to see me and was happy to hear that Marisa was doing all right. I think she regrets not saying something sooner."

Jackson took a seat next to Shaye. "The whole thing is fantastic. Caitlyn kills her sister and decides to pretend she's Jenny—but why?"

"Because no one would believe Jenny had killed her sister on purpose, maybe? Because the death would have been ruled accidental and Jenny's health would have precluded her serving time anyway."

Jackson nodded. "Plus, I guess as Jenny, she got all the attention she thought she'd been cheated out of. But it didn't work out like she'd planned. Why? What did Eleonore say?"

"That Caitlyn was likely a narcissist but not a sociopath and that killing Jenny was so dreadful, she couldn't cope with what she'd done. So her mind splintered. Eleonore thinks she started out pretending to be Jenny and that when she was knocked unconscious by that car, something shifted and she began to believe her lie as well."

"But it didn't stay shifted forever."

"No. The truth was there in her subconscious and starting to reveal itself in her dreams. If Virginia hadn't drugged her, it probably would have happened sooner."

"It's ironic, her hiring you. She must have flipped when her memory returned and she realized she'd brought the house down on herself."

"I'm sure that's why she asked me to stop the investigation. The woman I talked to that evening was all Caitlyn—drinking beer and reading a romance novel—that wasn't something Jenny would have done, according to Marisa. I should have realized it sooner. Even Virginia left hints, making comments like 'I lost my daughter a long time ago' and suggesting that once her daughter made up her mind, it was over. She was talking about Caitlyn, not Jenny."

"So the story about someone shooting at Caitlyn was all made up as well?"

"I don't think so. Virginia saw her run out of the woods and she heard the shot. And she claims that it was Jenny who came out of the woods. Not Caitlyn."

"Poacher?"

"Maybe. Or maybe it was Rick Sampson. He called in sick that day, and Marisa told me today that she'd found mud on his boots when she went home for lunch."

Jackson shook his head. "How could someone get it so wrong? Rick Sampson compounded one horrible decision with another."

"In his mind, he was only protecting himself and his family. But yeah, it's amazing how far off track an otherwise normal person can go."

"And scary. It makes you think, you know? How far would you go to protect someone you loved?"

"I don't know, and that's not a good answer from someone in my profession, but just take this past week into account. Between Caitlyn killing her own twin, then pretending to be her, and Victor LeBlanc having to turn in his son for arranging the kidnapping of his own daughter, it keeps getting harder to place much faith in humans as a species."

"Eleonore says that's because we see the worst of things all the time—me, you, Corrine, her. Our professions constantly expose us to the darker side of human nature."

Jackson reached over and took her hand. "And yet we wouldn't change a thing."

Shaye smiled. "Never even crossed my mind."

29

ONE MONTH LATER
Dallas, Texas

JACKSON KNOCKED on the front door of the modest home in Dallas, Texas. His plane had landed an hour ago and as soon as he finished this conversation, he would be on the next flight back to New Orleans. But first, he had to do the most important thing he'd ever done.

A woman answered the door, and he identified himself. Monica Peterson was in her forties, but still had a youthful appearance. Her Facebook page had been filled with smiling pictures of her, her husband, Stephen, and their children. But now, anxiety tugged at her lips, leaving her smile less than radiant.

"Please come in," Monica said. "My husband is on his way down. The kids are with my parents. We wanted to see what you had to say first before we decided what to share with them."

"Of course," Jackson said, relieved that the children wouldn't hear their conversation.

A trim man with a bit of silver starting to show in his dark brown hair came down the stairs and stopped to introduce himself as Stephen Peterson. "We really appreciate you making the trip here," he said. "Please have a seat. Would you like something to drink?"

"No. Thank you," Jackson said as he sat in a chair. The couple took a seat across from him on the couch, Stephen putting a protective arm around his wife.

"Before I tell you my information," Jackson said, "I'd like to ask you why you put your name on the adoption registry to obtain information about Abbey's biological parents."

They looked at each other, then back at Jackson. "She started to ask questions," Monica said. "We've always told her she was adopted, in an age-appropriate way, of course. Now that she's older and understands better, she grew more curious. She asked us if we could find out something about her parents. We tried to contact the attorney who handled the adoption, but he'd passed and there was no one to assist us with his prior cases."

"We didn't pursue that line of questioning further," Stephen said, "because it was a private adoption and the records were sealed. We had no rights to information that way."

Jackson nodded, relieved. His worst fear was that

there was going to be a medical reason for their inquiry. Basic curiosity he could deal with.

"I'm here because I have information for you," Jackson said. "But I doubt you're going to like what I have to say."

The disappointment was clear.

"The parents don't want to meet us," Stephen said. "We knew that could happen. There are all kinds of reasons someone gives up a child for adoption, and they're entitled to their peace and privacy. It's disappointing, but we respect their wishes."

"I'm sure you do," Jackson said. "You're adults and understand there are reasons for wanting to remain anonymous, but your daughter might not feel the same way. I'm here to give you some information so that you can hopefully prevent her from looking further. For her own good."

Their eyes widened, and the father nervously cleared his throat. "Perhaps you'd better tell us what you came for, Detective."

"Your daughter's conception and adoption are problematic," Jackson said. "And that's rather an understatement."

"We used a family law attorney," Stephen said. "All the correct paperwork was filed."

"You paid extensive fees for the adoption," Jackson said. "That didn't concern you?"

He glanced down, and Jackson knew he'd touched a nerve. They might not have known for certain that they'd bought a baby, but they suspected it at least. But with Allard recording everything as one type of fee or another, the purchase price was buried in the details.

"The attorney said the costs to adopt a healthy American baby were high given medical costs," Stephen said, determined to hold on to his belief that everything was on the up-and-up.

Unfortunately, Jackson was about to blow that out of the water.

Jackson nodded. "I'm sorry to inform you, but the biological mother was told that the child died. It was a home birth, so no medical professionals attended."

Monica's hands flew over her mouth and she cried out. "No! They stole her baby! Oh my God. What are we going to do? She's been with us since she was a month old. She doesn't know anyone else."

"You don't have to do anything," Jackson said. "The biological mother is not interested in pursuing custody. In fact, she thinks it best if she has no connection with your daughter at all."

"And the father?" Stephen asked.

"The biological father is dead, and the biological mother prefers that Abbey never learn the details of her conception."

Monica sucked in a breath and glanced over at her husband. Based on the looks on their faces, Jackson figured they both knew the score.

"I understand," Stephen said, his face grim.

Jackson pulled out an envelope and handed it to

Monica. "This is the medical history of the mother. As much as she knows, anyway. She wants you to know that she's thrilled that her child has a great home and although she loves her and would love nothing more than to meet her, it's more important to her to protect Abbey. And the only way she can do that is to remain unknown."

Monica began to quietly cry. "I can't imagine what she must feel. Being told her baby died, then finding out it's not true but choosing to stay away for the child's sake. She must be an incredible person."

"She's extraordinary," Jackson said.

Monica jumped up. "Give me a minute."

She hurried out of the room and came back a minute later with a school photo of Abbey. "Do you think she'd want this?"

Jackson took the picture and looked down at the smiling face that looked so much like Shaye, and his voice caught in his throat. "I think she'll love it. Thank you."

"Thank you," Stephen said. "We'll figure out something to tell Abbey. If necessary, we'll lie. But the mother's secret is safe with us."

Jackson rose from the couch. "If you ever need anything, please give me a call. My card is in that envelope."

He headed out of the house, managing to hold back the tears until he climbed into his rental car. He lifted the picture and looked at it once more before slipping it into his laptop bag. In approximately four hours, he'd be back home. That gave him about 240 minutes to pull himself together.

He hoped it was enough.

SHAYE LOOKED up from her desk and out the window of her office for the millionth time in the past hour. Jackson would be here any minute. His plane had landed thirty minutes ago, and he'd promised to come straight to her place from the airport. He'd called her after he'd talked to the parents, but she hadn't wanted the details. Not over the phone. This was one of those discussions that needed to happen in person. And probably sitting with a tumbler of whiskey.

She heard his truck before she saw it, then a couple seconds later, she saw it pull up to the curb in front of her apartment. She jumped out of her chair and rushed to the door, throwing it open before he'd even climbed out of his truck. He smiled as he made his way over to her, but he looked tired.

Guilt coursed through her because she knew what she'd asked him to do would be hard, but she didn't trust anyone else to handle it. Corrine would have been too emotional and would have had trouble letting it go afterward. And both she and Eleonore were too close to Shaye. She didn't want any chance of the parents figuring out who she was.

So Jackson had been the best option. He'd presented

his request for hair for DNA testing because of information he'd acquired during an investigation. That way, the adoptive parents wouldn't suspect for a moment that his interest was also personal. When the test had returned the positive result they'd anticipated, he'd asked for a meeting.

He gathered her in his arms and hugged her long and hard.

"Come tell me," Shaye said.

"Are you sure you want to do it right now?"

"I've been waiting for long enough. I need to close this chapter in my life. It's been hanging over my head too long."

He nodded and they headed into the living room, where they both sat on the couch. Jackson took her hand in his and relayed to her every word, every gesture, every nuance of his conversation with the parents. The tears welled up in her eyes when he described Monica's reaction to the news, and enormous relief swept through her when he said they promised to make sure no one pursued this any further.

When he was completely done, she drew in a breath and slowly blew it out. "That went as good as it possibly could."

"Yes. There's one last thing." Jackson reached into his laptop bag and pulled out a photo. He handed it to her and slipped his arm around her, drawing her close.

Shaye looked at the photo, and the tears that had been threatening to spill over fell with abandon. She choked back a cry and leaned into Jackson's chest, letting him cradle her against him. Of all the things she'd endured, this one hurt the worst.

But her daughter would be all right.

And that was all that mattered.

FOR NEW RELEASE NOTICE, please sign up for Jana's <u>newsletter</u>.

ABOUT THE AUTHOR

Jana DeLeon is a New York Times and USA Today best-selling author of mystery and thriller series. To get release notices, please sign up for Jana's newsletter on her website.

janadeleon.com

Jana also has a reader group on Facebook where she hosts weekly Q&A sessions. If you're on Facebook and would like to join in the fun, please check out the InstaGators on Facebook.

87371789R00216